# The Mule Shoe

# THE MULE SHOE

Perry Trouche

*The Mule Shoe*

cover photo — Matthew B. Brady, photograph of
Confederate soldiers after the battle of Gettysburg.

cover design by Trisha Hadley

Published by

~Star Cloud Press®~
6137 East Mescal Street
Scottsdale, Arizona 85254-5418

StarCloudPress.com

ISBN:
Cloth edition — 978-1-932842-33-3 — $ 29.95

Paperback edition — 978-1-932842-34-0 — $ 18.95

Library of Congress Control Number: 2009925313

Printed in the United States of America

This novel is dedicated
to my wonderful, loving wife, ALICE
for all her encouragement and support,
and to my two marvelous children,
EMORY and PERRY,
for their help and understanding—
and in memory of my father,
P. EDWIN TROUCHE
and my brother,
TIMOTHY JOSEPH TROUCHE
and my father in law,
DR. JOHN E. HOLLER

and for all those who have suffered
during times of war, past and present.

Thanks also to
Nicole Beaulieu and Dodie Altman,
for typing my barely legible longhand.

Thanks also to my niece Caroline
for her helpful computer skills.

# FOREWORD

IN HIS NOVEL, *The Mule Shoe*, Dr. Perry Trouche assumes the burden of Southern literature in a very ambitious manner. He is a trained psychiatrist with a keen sense of history (his own and that of his native South), and displays an entertaining way with words. He undertakes to explore the personal torments of a young Confederate soldier who confronts the tumult of one of the most tragic campaigns in the latter part of the American Civil War.

Mule Shoe is described as a military formation often used by an inferior force in a desperate attempt to fend off a much larger attacking army. The specific confrontation of this novel refers to the battles in the neighborhood of Spotsylvania Courthouse, Virginia in early May of 1864. The Confederate Army of Northern Virginia led by Gen. R.E. Lee was being relentlessly pursued by Gen. U. S. Grant's Army of the Potomac. For three days the Union forces assaulted and fractured the fortified line that Lee's army had dug in at the Mule Shoe. Close to 30,000 men were lost on both sides and Conner's friends were virtually extinguished or wounded beyond functionality and recognition. Trouche's battlefield descriptions seem very consistent with the histories of Bruce Caton and James McPherson.

In the tradition of Faulkner, Trouche presents a psychological struggle laced with racial guilt, family psychosis, and such other mental baggage that habitually finds its way into the Southern literature. We follow the internal convulsions of his protagonist, Conner Dumont, in a stream-of-consciousness full of hallucinations, ghosts, conversations with dead family and friends. He is haunted by demons, guilt, temptations—real and imagined. He is haunted by Grandma Mamere the "bitch-witch of Meggett" whose constant refrain reminds Conner of his cowardice. He is haunted by his drunken Irish father who fell off of the Stone Ferry and washed up dead on John's Island. He is counseled by Uncle Paul who after being blinded by a mule-kick to the head, can "steer dreams" and read the future. And his entire existence as a slave-holding white Southerner is condemned by Ezekiel his boyhood slave companion and lifelong antagonist. In the critical climax of hallucinatory delusion they fight to the death while surrounded by Yankee cavalry in Central Virginia, and his love interest, Helen, a woman whose favors had been known by seemingly hundreds of men, fades into distant memory as Conner returns to what might be deemed a more normal state of mind in the end.

In the tradition of Flannery O'Connor his protagonist wrestles with the multitude of problems that accompany Catholics in the 19th century South. Father Reilly constantly reminds Conner of the duties of his faith. Spiritual shortcomings are pointed out to him by his priest, his mother, grandmother, and childhood friends. Comrades in the army ridicule his religion for perceived hypocrisy and corruption. Conner struggles to reconcile his beliefs with his often sinful and sometimes horrific actions. His Mother constantly recites decades of the rosary as he evades enemy shelling and impending death.

In the tradition of wartime novels such as *Slaughterhouse Five* and *Catch-22,* Trouche depicts the life and tragedies of the foot soldier. Vulgar slang and colloquialisms spice up their conversations as they attempt to divert attention from their horrendous surroundings and mission. Graphic descriptions of battlefield slaughter and mayhem are found throughout this novel. Acceptance, rationalizations, recriminations, guilt, absolution, glorification, and surrender to the horrors of warfare permeate this novel. Vivid accounts of hand-to-hand combat and explicit scenes of blood and gore bring the military conflict into focus with a painful reality.

There are wonderful scenes of prewar life in the Carolina Lowcountry, on the streets of Charleston, on the farms and creeks of Younges Island and other barrier islands from McClellanville down to Edisto. The characters are easily identifiable with their familiar names taken from Charleston families. He meets Ravenel Meggett as they board the military train at the John Street Depot. He and his Grandma Marguerite, who lives on Longitude Lane, attend Mass conducted by Father Reilly at St. Mary's Church. Early in war-torn Charleston he failed to save the life of friend Elliott Tradd who suffered fatal wounds in an explosion while trying to re-supply Fort Sumter.

There is much in this novel for all readers—physical combat, romance, military tactics & strategy, grim day-to-day routines, psychological profiles, fantastic imagery, delightful visions of life in the Low Country, descriptions of wonderful landscape throughout Central & Piedmont Virginia. *The Mule Shoe* employs a specific historical event to frame a more universal story, and it acts as a metaphor for many aspects of that story as well. As I stated at the beginning of this Foreword, this is an ambitious undertaking by Dr. Trouche. Yet it is a too-modest dose of his talents. If I have any complaint, it is that I wanted more of everything that he offers his readers.

Stephen J. White, Sr., *Director*
Charleston Historical Society
17 Smith Street
Charleston, SC 29401

The Mule Shoe salient and fortifications
of the battle of Spotsylvania May 12, 1864.
Map courtesy of Mr. William Prouty.

# I

The asylum gate clanged shut behind me. Ornate twirls of wrought iron hummed as I climbed aboard the visitors' wagon and helped my mother and grandmother to a seat. The mute driver sighed and rolled his eyes. He flicked the reins and two mules hauled us up a little grassy hill to a red brick building overgrown with ivy. A grizzled old keeper stood frowning in the doorway with his arms crossed.

"Wait here," he said gruffly.

The source of his irritation stood inside on the white columned balconies overhanging a dirt bare courtyard. Dandies from town and their ladies leaned over the railing giggling and drinking. A young man in a blue coat yelled out to no one in particular, "We demand to be entertained! Bring out the lunatics! Do you hear me? Bring them out!"

The rest of them had a good laugh, chanting, "Bring them out! Bring them out!"

As if by command an ivy covered door set low in the wall swung open. Disheveled inmates swarmed into the light. The dandies tossed down tidbits of food inciting bedlam in the courtyard and more raucous laughter above. Grandmother Marguerite laughed with them for a while until she'd emptied her first flask. She always laughed when she drank. She sucked down another half then pushed past the keeper into the courtyard calling to grandfather and the other blank faced, babbling inmates.

"Quiet please. Quiet everyone." A big smile erupted on her red face. "You-hoo. You up there. Yes you young man. In the blue coat. Please look at me young man." Her voice became honey sweet. She pointed a tremulous finger at the balcony youth all dressed up in silk and ruffles. The courtyard and balcony went silent and still. "You will soon go mad with the syphilis. Show the young lady your red sore."

His face turned white and the ladies were stunned dumb. A young superintendent appeared and quickly hustled us out as if Marguerite were contagious herself. She laughed whiskey breath in his face until the shivering man threw up his hands, retreated behind the thick oak door of his private office and let her take Grandfather O'Conner away. He never said a word about the dandies.

Just out of sight of the asylum walls grandfather dumped a jar of molasses on his head and started chanting, "Black Irish have their needs. Get on your knees with the Rosary beads."

Marguerite told him to be quiet but couldn't stop laughing. He calmed down only after he rubbed more molasses into his scalp. Mother blessed herself and made me say the Rosary with her all the way back to the station. I finished the last decade just as I woke up.

~VIRGINIA, MAY 1864~

First light found me curled up against a chestnut log. A cool breeze stirred the shade of the forest floor. It caressed my face and rustled the mattress of leaves just enough to rouse me. I resisted as long as I could, but teasing patches of sunlight wouldn't let me sleep. They danced through the highest branches and poked at my eyes until I warded them off with my hat. The little bastards wouldn't give up though, darting back stronger and dragging me along against my will. I grabbed hold of a tree root and propped myself up. Rows of stout oak trunks surrounded me like pillars of a great cathedral. A raggy congregation appeared out of nowhere. Thousands of men milled about the hazy forest floor. Their clothes a riot of colors, shapes and sizes. Mostly brown and gray but accented here and there with red stripes, black checkerboard and different hues of green, yellow and blue. Patched jackets dangled like oversized croaker sacks. Shreds of cotton or canvas draped over torn trousers tied together with pins and twine. Except for a few slaves following their officers, all the men were white and as restless as the tree tops. They surged through choke points between the huge oaks like Easter Sunday mass had just ended.

The breeze stirred me completely awake from what seemed like an entire life of sleep. I rubbed my eyes open. Men all around me stumbled down freshly slashed stump aisles, through dense stands of dogwood, chestnut, hickory, and oak. Three columns stretched out in both directions as far as I could see, emerging from the smoky woods at one end, disappearing at the other, each moving steadily with a rhythmic tin-clinking through the trees. Men of all ages hurried past as if I were invisible. All haggard, hollow-cheeked and filthy. I couldn't help but feel ashamed, but the ground kept a firm hold until a dusty mirage appeared above me.

His bloodshot eyes glared at me. Sweat drenched his jacket. He poked me hard with a rusty scabbard. "Get up, keep movin'. No stragglin'." His voice just a hoarse whisper. I stood up fumbling for words, but he quickly moved on, picking his way through freshly cut stumps prodding and herding grumbling sleepers who staggered up like drunks.

I looked around for Mr. Clement, Macfadden and others from my group from Charleston, but they were nowhere to be seen. Just the endless streams of scarecrow soldiers, shuffling along exhausted and numb in the morning light, and lines of wagons, full of wounded, bumping painfully along the rut.

I felt sore all over and my stomach growled, but I knew I'd been lucky to come up late. Thousands dead, just in the past few days, or so the rumor went. I thanked God I'd missed it. But I admitted my cowardice only to myself.

"Bullshit! Everybody knows! You've always been a Goddamned coward!" My grandmother Mamere screamed in the distance. It was definitely Mamere. I could have sworn it. As mean as Marguerite was jovial. I knew her raspy voice and got a whiff of the sickly-sweet stench that always warned of her approach. I cringed. Mamere always surprised attacked out of the smoke. It was my earliest recollection of her. A hazy room, a sudden shriek then a screaming mouth of gold teeth coming at me out of a dense mist. I may have been four. A bamboo cane dressed in rattlesnake skin, rattles and all, lashing at me like it was alive. Then full flight in terror with the snake etching whelps and pain across my back. It all came back in an instant. I knew she was long dead but I still cringed.

"Poisonous snakes can kill after they're dead!" She shrieked again from out in the smoky woods. "Cowards deserve to die!"

"Go to hell, Mamere." I remembered her funeral mass and decent burial. The whole time knowing justice would have been better served with her collapsing in the swamp and being eaten alive by feral pigs.

"I won't forget that Conner. Cower and die." Mamere snickered in the haze then hushed.

Maybe I was a coward, but I'm sure I wasn't the only one. I'd heard the rumors. More deserters than ever before. Men who just disappeared, some cowards like me, some just sick of it all, never to be seen or heard from again. It was said to be happening more and more. What struck me odd was how easy it would be to just wander off in the night forest and vanish. Some had, but thousands still shuffled past in the long lines through the trees. Maybe it wasn't such an easy thing, in some other way. Or maybe they thought it could still end well. No one talked much of victory anymore. Men at home spoke openly now of the armistice and negotiated peace, but home seemed father way than the moon, and I knew I had to forget about it.

Daylight brightened the forest floor, and I finally gathered my wits. I tightened my blanket roll, shouldered my rifle and joined the throng for a long walk, telling myself I'd find my group shortly.

But damn! To fall asleep and get left behind the very first day. I couldn't have felt more worthless or a bigger fool. Two angry redwing blackbirds humiliated me further, picking me out from the multitude, taking turns diving at my head from their nest in a honeysuckle tangle. Soldiers laughed, but I took my punishment silently. I was a "newboy," valued just above an earthworm. I didn't have a right to complain. There were many others worse off than me. Men adorned with red bandages were more common than not. A few half naked men tried to keep pace, chest or abdomen totally wrapped in bloodstained lint and gauze. Many stumbled along dragging their rifles in total exhaustion.

No two were outfitted the same. A jumbled mix of wooden canteens, clay jugs, tin cups, canvas slings, rope belts, bowie knives, bayonets, tomahawks, stone war clubs, blanket and gum cloth rolls strapped across shoulders, and haversacks flapping as empty as my stomach. A phalanx of rifles twitched above the long columns like the twills of a hundred giant porcupines. Officers and sergeants methodically kicked at stragglers. Some like me had slept in the leaves oblivious to it all. It helped a little. At least I wasn't the only one.

# II

I trudged a miserable two or three miles before I spotted them resting with their column in the woods. Other columns moved down the stump road.

Macfadden sat on a freshly cut pine sipping his canteen. He gave me a bit of hell. "You stragglin' already boy? Hell, you ain't even fought yet. Ain't got the trots or nothin'? Just you wait." His breath grew shorter in the smoky air. I took his teasing. There wasn't much else I could do. They'd been chopping trees all night while I'd slept, and him with the pleurisy and all. Anyhow, he'd been decent to me on the train north and seemed to have a good heart. He worried about his sister Helen in Fredericksburg and wasn't sure if she'd made it out before the yanks came. She may have refugeed south to Richmond but he hadn't heard from her in weeks. "Nursed me back from death's door last winter. Swear to God. Trots had me close to the grave. Stayed with me in that shithole 12th regiment's camp. Night and day. Boiled up sweet potato broth with brandy. Brought me back to life." He caught his breath and smiled. "They sent me home to Charleston to recuperate. In the salt air."

"Needed all spring, did ya?" Snake spat tobacco juice at my feet. "Anyhow, pretty boy got too smooth a face to fight. Got to be ugly like me 'fore ya git good at killin' a man." His fingers clawed at the red scars and black greasy pits that covered his cheeks. "That or skinnin' gators alive."

I believed about every word. He was a true denizen of the swamp. A trapper of mink and otter who hadn't set foot out of the Santee delta his whole life until the war came. He was half Catawba Indian too, and

6

touchy about it. On the train, I'd asked about his raccoon moccasins and he'd backhanded me hard enough to rattle my teeth. "Somethin' wrong w'that?"

The others calmed him down before he pulled his bowie knife and I'd learned my lesson. Black hair, black eyes, black clothes, black water-moccasin belt. His dress matched his sudden foul moods.

"Boys I'll say this." He held up his sun brown, thickly muscled forearm with a row of red pits like smallpox scars. "If there's a man alive that's caught more water-moccasins and copper-heads with his bare hands, I'll eat a rattlesnake raw." He rolled up his sleeve to show them off. "Been bit seventeen times. Most on the arm, four on the face. Just don't bother me much like it does most people. Ain't never really swole up bad. Not ever as big as Lady's dick."

"Go to hell." Lady sprawled out half asleep, gray jacket open, butternut trousers rolled up to mid calf. With long yellow hair and bushy red beard, he could have been a Viking. Well over six feet tall, solid muscle, with the reputation of being one of the strongest men in the army. Some said *the* strongest. He cut trees in St. George Parish outside Charleston. Rumor had him cutting a five mile line through pine forest in one day. Lady never denied it. On the train north men sought him out at each stop to pick a fight and make him prove it. Lady just laughed them off. He submitted to arm wrestling, though, joking away as he slammed arms down one after another. Once he answered a dare and tore the stock off a Springfield rifle like kindling. Just showing off, but he was good-natured about it. Everything was a bit of a joke to him. Maybe living on higher ground than Snake helped. Nothing could startle him in the least. He joked about his prowess with women too.

Macfadden vouched for him. "Yep, that fat Charleston whore made helluva screech!" Snake snorted in agreement, and they had a good laugh as a young officer pushed his horse through the columns.

"Make way! Make way! Let 'em through." One trouser leg cut off at the hip, a red stained bandage tied in a big bow around his bare thigh. "Make way!"

He led a line of Yank prisoners through the trees under watchful eye of a bearded sergeant with a double-barreled shotgun. His hair, a mat of tangles and grease. His face scorched black on one side, his eyebrow burned off. Blood stained his filthy gray jacket and one hand bandaged in a dirty rag. The columns made room to let them pass. Thirty or so white yanks in new blue uniforms looking tired but at ease, talking casually like they knew they were safe.

Macfadden nudged Lady, "Bet they ain't heard of Andersonville." He lapsed into a spasm of coughing as three blacks stripped to the waist followed along, hands tied behind their backs, heads bowed in submission. Two lanky, barefoot privates prodded them along with their rifles.

Snake arched a wad of spit in their direction and laughed. "Them's won't live to see dinner. Coloreds ought to know better'n put on the blue." He called out to the young guards, "Them colored's fetchin'a good price down Charleston way. Might better hold on to 'em fo' a while."

They ignored him but Macfadden shook his head. "Ain't right shootin' prisoners. Thought we was ordered not to."

"Them's ain't prisoners." Snake snorted back. "Them's coloreds."

Lady wiped his face with his sleeve. "One thing's sure. Colored troops won't be surrenderin' much once they know they'll be shot. Never understood it nohow. They hep us an' they win either way. We lose, they're free. We win, we hep 'em back."

"Hep 'em back to what? The cotton fields?" Snake laughed.

"They ain't been shot fo' more then a year. Orders from high,'member?" Macfadden coughed as he spoke. "Got t'treat 'em like prisoners...prisoners of the war."

"My ass." Snaked laughed. "Ain't been shot? Shit. Where you been?" He rolled his eyes.

"I tell you they ain't." Macfadden cleared his throated and sucked in a great gulp of air. "Jus' rumor is all."

"Bullshit. Two thousand shot after Gettysburg. Ever'body knows."

"Nope. Campfire talk don't make it so."

The column disappeared into the smoky woods followed by a line of wagons jolting over stumps and felled branches. Brown canvas tops ripped into flapping triangles. Each wagon packed tightly with wounded begging for water. I gave my canteen to an older man whose shoulder bandage glistened with fresh blood. His skinny arm lay limp in a twine sling. Sweat dribbled down his sunburned face through cakes of black powder that left streaks on his gray beard. He sucked the canteen down in one long gulp, head bobbing with the wagon jolts. I followed alongside.

"Thank you son. I was pure parched. Damn if they ain't ruined my arm!" His breath, short, and his once white shirt, tattered, filthy, and soggy wet. He wore remnants of brown socks, toes and bare blistered heals protruding. He coughed out a wad of greenish phlegm panting for breath. "You with Kershaw?" His stretched out his hand.

"No sir. Goin' up to McGowan. Been workin' on the road last night." The wagons paused while men pushed an oak limb aside.

"Lots of trees to cut. Takin' a breather eh?" he wheezed. "Could use some m'sef." He sucked at the air, curling his toes in rhythm. "Been a helluva couple of days back yonder. Been in it? Back yonder?"

"No sir. Just got here, late yesterday from Guiney Station." Crows called out above the trees, and I waited to be punished.

"Good plannin'." He coughed up another green wad. "Don't hurt to be too late to a fight. Yanks whipped worse than us though. Maybe they'll skedaddle." He gulped down another mouthful. "It'll end some day. It will y'know. Hard to believe, ain't it. Take some gettin' use to." He puffed for breath and struggled to reach inside his shirt. "Take this here. Made a promise I'd give it to a new boy." He pulled a loop of sweat-soaked leather cord from around his neck. Tied to it hung a tarnished brass medal. "Saint Sebastian. Got shot full of arrows. Didn't bother him one bit." He stopped to catch his breath. "This'll give ya four lives. I done used mine up. Guess I better git home quick eh? Take ya hat off."

I did as he said and helped him put the cord over my head. It didn't even seem strange.

"Tie an extra knot to keep it tight. Give it to a new boy when yours is used up." He panted harder. "Don't worry none neither. It really works. Like the medal says 'protects in dire straights'."

"I guess so." I rubbed the thick tarnished brass. A smoothly worn Caesar-like face smiled over the word 'protect'. The rest was worn off.

He reached for me and squeezed my shoulder hard. "The name's Abrams. Ham Abrams. Be careful boy. It's bad as hell up there. Take care y'sef."

The wagon bumped slowly down the rut through the trees until the groaning of the wounded faded away. I half expected the medal to vanish too, but I tucked it in my shirt before it had the chance.

Three quick revolver shots rang out from the woods, followed by a fourth. Snake was right after all.

"One was still wigglin." Shiner laughed. "Don't shoot! Don't shoot! I'm a soldier not a colored." He convulsed on the ground laughing. "Jus we heard a rumor?" The dark circles under his eyes glared blue.

"Shut up new boy. You don't know shit," Lady mumbled, half asleep.

Shiner was just as green as me but you'd never know it by his mouth. Always loud and bragging. Equal amounts of confidence and ignorance. "They ain't fightin' animals like us, eh Snake?" He swatted Snake's shoulder and a black sleeve darted to his throat. Shiner's eyes bulged in the vice grip.

"Let him loose, Snake." Lady yawned.

Snakes fist snapped open and Shiner gasped for air. "Horse shit. Cow shit. Mule shit." He laughed as if rewarded, rubbing his throat. "I been in a fight fo' real. Got Nellie Barkin in the reeds behind the rice mill down yonder at Middleton." He coughed and caught his breath. "Daddy's been overseer fo' ten years."

"White trash," Macfadden snorted, but it just egged him on.

"She was on her back and me on top and her clawin' and me pokin' then ole man Barkin runs up with a goddamn shotgun."

"Sowboy pokes sowgirl," Lady laughed.

Shiner waved him off. "Got off both barrels 'fore I had my pants up. Missed both times. Went back a week later and finished her good. Boys, Nellie got a sweet ass and Barkin cain't hit shit."

None paid him any mind except Lucas and Gordon, the simple-minded twins from Pocataligo Swamp who nodded in awe. They had no idea what was happening. They couldn't even say for sure how old they were.

"Maybe seventeen." Lucas whispered into Gordon's ear. Both with a Mohawk of thick blonde hair, long curls dangling down front and back. Bushy blonde eyebrows, sunburned necks, heads shaved smooth on both sides. They groomed each other with their knives and smiled all the time with beaver buck teeth. Both nearly mute except for mostly unintelligible mumbling to each other and constant whistling like dueling mocking birds.

Snake whistled back at them "Them boys ain't got all their dogs in the pen." He was right, but I guess God knew what He was doing, sending simpletons to fight.

Macfadden stood up, swiped off his hat and bowed before me. "You be wantin' a litter fo' y'sef Master Conner? Want us to carry ya? Bein' such a tender newboy an' all."

I managed a smile and luckily the others were focused on a young officer riding up fast through the trees on a strong black mare.

"Damn! It's startin' early." Macfadden nodded towards the rider. The officer's floppy gray hat hung down his back, tied around his neck with a string. Two shiny pistols bulged from his belt and a huge saber dangled nearly to the ground. He saluted to a balding colonel trotting past us on a scraggly mule with three fresh-faced Lieutenants in tow, one with a bloody arm in a sling. All eyes went quickly on him. Snake and Lady jumped up and loaded their rifles as the colonel listened to the breathless officer, all the while wiping his beard with a greasy rag. He conferred with his entourage pointing up and down the road and looking at his gold watch. Then all hell broke loose. They exploded off down the road like a startled covey of quail, crying the alarm as they went.

"Get movin! The yanks are comin'! The yanks are comin'!" The same thing over and over, their yells rippling like waves through the columns.

My heart leapt to my mouth. Mr. Clement ordered the rest of us to load up. His face, taut cracked leather. Blue eyes over high clean-shaven cheekbones. Yellow teeth worn to nubs. Jaw clenching as he smiled. As tall as Lady but thin with wiry muscles under his torn sleeves. Sweat dripped profusely from sun-bleached hair straggling beneath a wide brimmed straw hat bound with a leather thong dangling under his chin. Everyone followed his lead.

Anthony, another new boy like me trembled so badly, he dropped three percussions caps into a clump of poison ivy, his cowardice visible on his sleeve. His face was pockmarked with pustules, his eyes blinking continuously and watering up like he was about to cry. Any loud noise made him jump. He couldn't hide it and didn't try to. He couldn't hide his mountain accent either. He'd come to Charleston from Tennessee two years ago when the yanks had come south. Said his home was a place called Cowan on the Cumberland plateau just west of Chattanooga. His mother brought him to Charleston to stay with relatives and be safe. Snake and Lady called him "Squirrel, the coward from Cowan."

Snake slapped him on the head and growled. "They'll be comin' right at the Squirrel. Comin' for all you new boys. Best skedaddle while you can."

Anthony took it like he always did, silently looking away and furrowing his brow, never defending himself even if he could.

Sir William pulled him along and told the rest of us to stay close and save the last of our water. He was the oldest and frailest, with long gray beard and thinning hair wrapped in a red-checkered bandana with a crow feather stuck above his ear.

"Fightin' in the sun can parch a man quick." He winked at me and tapped his full canteen. Mine was bone dry and the gunfire was louder by the minute. I knew I was a damn fool for sure. A mocking bird flew past me whistling like he knew it too.

We hurried along with the column another mile or so until the woods thinned at the edge of a trampled cornfield overgrown with wild flowers. Men at the head of the column fanned out across the field trotting over a cushion of blossoms. Each regiment roared as they broke out of the trees into the open.

Snake poked at trembling Anthony and yelled in his face, "Wolves smellin' blood!" Anthony winced and fell to his knees. Sir William helped him up and laughed.

"Look here. Red Clover. See? Queen Anne's Lace and snakeroot. See the yella cones?" He stooped to grab a handful of flowers and sprinkled them on his bandana. "These'll bring good luck. Yanks won't shoot a decorated man."

He threw some on me, the twins, and Anthony as an officer galloped past.

"Get to that fence boys! The yanks are comin' for it. Get to it first and hold 'em."

Rifle fire and smoke rose from a split rail fence that curved through a stand of dogwoods and tall pines half a mile across the field. We ran forward up a gradual rise behind the others as Mr. Clement yelled to us new boys above the roar.

"Fire before you reload! Fire before you reload!"

I'd heard it happened. Hundreds of rifles at Gettysburg stuffed with three or four charges. Men so terrified they couldn't remember to pull the trigger.

Smoke rose along the fence as we ran towards a line of dismounted troopers kneeling and firing. Two twelve-pounders fired from the rear over our heads into a pine thicket about five hundred yards ahead where men in dark uniforms crouched in the trees. A man to my left dropped dead on his face, blood boiling from his neck.

Bees buzzed past my head and my ear stung like hell. Blood dropped down my collar. Men fell steadily as we reached the fence. Hundreds were spread out on both sides of us, some standing to fire, others crouched behind the flimsy rails. Over the fence not fifty yards in front came a thick line of blue infantry. I dropped down and hugged the ground as a dirt clod blew up in my face. A red bearded man a few paces to the right dropped with me. His forehead oozed brain and blood, but his eyes still watched in disbelief. He rolled over, his mouth coming to rest on a pine sapling as if trying to suck life from the earth. Mr. Clement yelled at me but he seemed far away. A closer voice mocked me, "He's dead but you're a coward." It may have been Uncle Paul but he didn't repeat himself and Sir William pulled me up by the back of my shirt freeing me from paralysis. That was all I needed. I knelt, leveled my rifle at the line of blue and fired. The butt smashed my shoulder and for a second pushed away the fear.

Everyone fired and reloaded as fast as they could, the twins taking turns like it was play. A stranger with a bright yellow shirt and bandaged forehead knelt next to me, fired over the rails then stood straight up to reload as if his shirt didn't scream for the yanks attention.

He pointed his ramrod casually at one of our dead along the fence. "First dead cav'ry man I ever seen."

We fired together over the rails then he was on his back with a red hole in the yellow. He looked up and tried say something, coughed blood, and grew still. Blood rose in a bubble from his mouth. His eyes still open and staring. Organ music drifted through the trees but vanished before I recognized the hymn. A rail splintered by my face and I dropped down. The yanks just thirty yards away. Their whole blue line tipped with bayonets, but they moved slowly like they were stuck in the mud. I aimed low and pulled the trigger. I couldn't remember if I'd reloaded, but my rifle fired and joined the roar. Men screamed and several close by went down.

Wounded all down the line crawled to the rear with all sorts of bullet wounds. Each of them suddenly isolated from the rest of us. No longer part of a regiment. No longer aware of anything except their wounds. Some collapsing to die just behind the line as their blood poured out on the field. The rest crawling away as if the rest of us didn't exist.

Artillery exploded in the Yank line. Hundreds more of our boys came running, fanning out left and right. The yanks staggered backwards.

"They're runnin!" Shiner yelled and started out over the fence. "Sweet Jesus be praised!"

A wiry cavalryman jerked him back. "Not yet boy. They'll be back di'rekly. Hold yo' britches."

Mr. Clement nodded and Shiner obeyed frowning. But surely we'd won. The yanks slowly pulled back to the far woods, and the firing died out after a while.

"You a soldier now, boy?" Lady laughed. "Shit, I seen more fightin' then that there in a whorehouse."

Shiner propped himself against a fence post, chin jutted out. He slid out his knife and kissed the blade. "Don't y'all worry none. I'll kill my share of yanks."

Snake laughed and blew a kiss but Sir William lost his patience. His breath was short as he reloaded on his back.

"You're a damn fool, ain't ya? Think y'know a good bit? A man who wants to fight is less than a fool. He ain't no man at all." He pulled at his beard for a minute or two.

"Them yanks come to take my farm well then…", He shook his head and fiddled with his crow feather. "That deserves a fight." Yank artillery opened up across the field. Shells clipped the treetops and ploughed the empty field behind us. "Got thirty-seven acres near Columbia for raisin' quail and growin' tobacco. Bout the strongest tobacco in the state I been told, and best eatin' bird there is." Leaves fluttered down on his hat. "Feed 'em cornmeal an' maggots. They love them wigglers." He rolled a leaf up in his fingers. "Got three special birds. Swamp fox, Gamecock, an' Cornwallis. Smart as all git out. Stick together like brothers." He thumped the silvery silk patch on his checkerboard shirt. "Miss 'em more than my wife." A small branch fell next to him. "But I miss her too," He laughed in between puffs. "Did this here for her." He rubbed the smooth patch. "Got this shirt off Bob Malcolm. Got tore through right 'cher…Canister load at Sharpsburg. Took this here silk patch an' had it prayed on by my cousin Lemual. He's a Presbyterian minister y'see. So he says." He pulled the shirt out for all the newboys to see. "Got it blessed by a Catholic priest, and long bearded Rabbi too. Then sewed it on. Cain't be too careful…Ain't no yank bullet come close yet. Cain't git through the silver now. Not when it's blessed all round an all." More yank guns opened up farther down the line. "Best git all y'all's shirts blessed," He nodded. "And git y'sef a crow feather. Crows got powers too."

The twins whistled their approval and Macfadden saluted him. "Yes Sir! Sir William!"

They'd been calling him 'sir' for two years since a courier rode up and saluted him in front of the whole regiment at Second Manassas.

"Don't look the least like Maxcy Gregg, God-bless the gen'rals soul. Nor Sam McGowan even 'fore he got shot the first time. Rider did have a head wound though. Mighta' been feelin' faint in the heat," he laughed while Snake poked me with a stick.

"Hey Conner? You faint last night? Got King's cow shit or somethin'? How 'bout Cornwall this up yo'ass."
I bit my tongue and ignored him the best I could but everyone was entertained. I felt like a fool.

Macfadden nudged at me. "Get some sleep when you can. You won't be alone. Fell asleep at Gettysburg! Middle of the damn biggest artill'ry duel in the whole damn war. Shells landin' all over and me

17

sound asleep. Might never moved hadn't Clement kicked my rear. Only so far a man can go with no sleep. Hell, Stonewall hisself fell asleep a time or two. Back in '62."

He meant well, but I didn't want to hear anything bad about Stonewall Jackson or anything at all about Gettysburg even if true.

Everyone stayed down low behind the rails, rifles ready. Shiner shook his head and shrugged. "I signed on to fight yanks and that's what I plan to do. Daddy said we got to stand our ground."

Snake threw dirt at him. "We don't rightly give a shit what yo' daddy says!"

More artillery opened up to our left and the yanks across the field caught more hell. Shiner didn't seem to notice.

"He's a fighter, he is. Done killed nine men. Daddy could name every one." He laughed, "Couldn't, every whore he done. Too many y'see."

Snake kicked at him. "I said we don't give a shit."

Shiner kept right on, talking loud and fast and trembling like he'd downed a pot of strong coffee. "I swear if she was truly a whore, he'd done her."

"Shut up." Macfadden reloaded on his elbow laughing punch drunk.

Shiner nodded, "Yep, we was down on Edisto havin' a picnic and swimmin' when this here fat woman come down the river on a flat boat with three blacks tendin' to the poles. She takes off her shirt and lets them titties just dangle and wiggle. Each as big as a watermelon."

Three shells burst in the field in front, but Shiner was a deaf man. His voice rose to nearly a shout. "Daddy grabbed a wisteria vine and swung out. Dropped in right next to 'em! Pulled hissef up while she dangled her titties closer." He laughed. "It sure was tormentin' him bad!"

Wounded men cried out for water, ours and yanks, but Shiner just babbled on. "He grabbed one of them melons but she shoved him under and floated off fore he got a second chance. All in front of Momma. She never minded much. Not a damn thing to do 'cept shoot 'im. And she'd done that already. Last year. Point blank in the head with the old flintlock. Cut a line of scalp off and knocked him out cold!"

"For God's sake shut up!" Sir William hissed at him. More shells crashed into the yanks woods across the field and rifle fire erupted down the line to the right. Shiner was oblivious.

"He's a tough son of a bitch. Bled on the porch for two days then got up and butchered a steer"

"Why ain't he in the army, then?" Lady grabbed his crotch and shook it at him.

"Got his legs shot off at Malvern Hill", Shiner snapped back.

Snake laughed, "No legs but a workin' dick."

Shiner smiled back, "Yep, must be."

I glanced back at the red bearded man. He still sucked the sapling. The man with the red stained yellow shirt had stopped blowing blood bubbles. Wounded yanks crawled across the field back to their trees. Noone helped them. I believe we'd shot anyone who tried. There were plenty enough dead along our line to give a man reason.

Shiner waved his knife above his head. "I'll tell ya somethin' else. I'm man enough to stick this blade through a yank's heart."

"Show us please. Show us how to do it right now." Lady unbuttoned his shirt. "Put it through my heart. Let me have the cold steel," he laughed, hobbling toward Shiner on his knees like an amputee. Then a roar of rifle fire came down the line us a Yank volley tore over us. More men were hit. One man to the left got it in the head, killed instantly. Everyone dropped quickly down flat. My heart crept back in my mouth.

"What the shit?" Macfadden glanced up over the bottom rail. "Here they come!"

The rails twanged and splintered as the dark, snaking line came across the field half obscured by smoke.

I fired at least two dozen times until my rifle barrel sizzled and my shoulder screamed. The yanks didn't make it halfway. Scores of blue clumps dropped in their wake as they pulled back to regroup. It didn't seem to bother the bastards for too long though. They came at us four or five times from the woods across the field and caught hell every trip. We piled fence rails and dirt up front like a little fort, loading prone and firing low. Each line broke and ran more quickly than the last until they'd finally had enough.

# III

A bluish-gray fog of smoke covered the whole line, clumping thicker around the trees and swirling about the brims of men's hats like breath on a cold morning. Then a calm, dreary quiet that made it harder to think. The unbearable heat parched my throat drier than a cornhusk. The sun blazed down through powder smoke which made the silence even more foreign, like the quiet didn't belong in the smoke.

Macfadden gave me a sip of water but I could have sucked down a creek full. We rested a short while then the calm exploded again. A phalanx of rifles erupted into flame and smoke, barrels moving up and down like some terrible harvester machine as men fired and reloaded. The fence rails popped and cracked some more. Shiner yelled out and fell to his side. He clutched his arms across his stomach then fell over on his face. He never moved again. It took me a few minutes to believe he was dead, but I didn't have time to linger. The yanks came again and again. My rifle sizzled so hot, I worried a round might cook off in my face reloading.

"I hope it blows your face off you worthless bastard." Mamere shrieked.

"Go to Hell Mamere!" I yelled over the rails. Only the twins glanced at me smiling. No one else noticed. Smoke covered us. Mamere was truly dead. I reassured myself by firing again and again. She'd dropped dead in the parlor while screeching at Uncle Paul. Nearly eighty and still venomous as ever.

"More than any number of live rattlesnakes!" she yelled from farther off. I had to remind myself she was really dead and thanked God for it.

I fired again into the field and wondered how anything could stay alive out there. Mamere was already dead so it wouldn't bother her. But, surely not a stalk of grass or single cricket could escape. Yet yanks still milled about untouched, ironclad in the swirling smoke. The rails splintered in my face and my rifle fired high. Anthony fired into the clouds above then aimed at the yanks and winced. I watched him do it over and over. Only Snake, Lady and Mr. Clement aimed carefully, ignoring the buzzing close to the ears. I reloaded on my back and watched Mr. Clement carefully adjust his rear sight then snuggle his chin on the stock. He fired and some poor bastard met his maker.

Wounded and dead dropped silently to the ground like mutes. The wounded crawling or crouching away, the dead frozen. It struck me odd that a man blasted by metal wouldn't make much of a sound, but I didn't hear too many loud cries. Maybe the rifle fire carried away most of their screams. Or maybe they were just too stunned. A volley raked our section and eight or ten men went down. Sir William was hit in the hand. He rolled over on his side howling like a coondog. It was reassuring in a way; I thought a man *should* scream when he'd been shot. The blue line came diagonally across the field through the smoke cloud taking every bit of punishment our line could dish out. They closed on us just as another brown and gray regiment came running up from behind and volleyed over our heads. It stopped the yanks cold.

"But what if they hadn't come up?" Mamere squeaked in the distance.

Our whole line fired again and again into the blue tide as it ebbed again to the tree line leaving behind a coat of dark flotsam. My rifle tore my shoulder nearly out of its socket and the pain helped. Smoke thickened enough to make it hard to breath. Then consecration quiet as if the bells had rung. Macfadden shared his canteen with me then we lay back and relished a tiny breeze.

22

Snake wiped his sweat-oiled hair. "Them yanks'll blister up black in the sun. Bigger than cows."

For an instant, the black clumps in the field expanded like they were full of air. Lady nodded, "Yep, Our boys'll be thinner 'n sticks an' pale white, maybe yella. Yanks'll be puffed up oozy black.

"Nope", Sir William lay on his side and lit his pipe with his good hand. "Nope. Yall got it all wrong agin." His teeth chattered on the pipe stem and he winced with pain. "Remember Manassas. Our boys were big an' black too. Gots t'do with summertime. Hot air bloats a body. Yank or ours."

"Not our boys," Lady winked at Snake who glared at Sir William.

His bleeding hand trembled. "When its cold, like at Fred'riksburg, our boys were thin as sticks, an' yella. But so were the damn yanks. Remember? A dead man's a dead man. Don't matter where he come from. Gonna rot in the summer sun, same for both."

"No sir." Lady sat and drank some water. "It's that tinned food. All that good eatin' makes yanks rot quicker. Our boy is all cornbread, some bacon. Maybe some onions. Heard an onion helps a man from rottin' quick. Look there. Them yanks is blowin' up big right now."

"Serves 'em right." Snake blew his nose in the dirt. "They'll be stinkin' up yonder for weeks."

Sir William ignored them. "Yep, it's the law of temp'ture. More heat gives a bigger bloat and a good black'nin'. Winter cold keeps a body thin an' white."

"Shit!" Snake lay down and covered his face. "Ain't never seen a thin yank."

Sir William laughed then tried scooping dirt with his cup. He groaned with pain and gave it up. All afternoon the rest of us dug. Scooping dirt with hands and cups and piling every bit in front. It became just a matter of waiting for the yanks. My clothes were totally drenched in sweat, and I ached all over like I'd been beaten. Maybe I'd just dreamed the whole thing. Where had they gone? The low moans of wounded came towards us through the remnant haze of powder smoke. The fighting shifted blessedly far off to our right. We waited, rested and watched a farmhouse burn in a little clearing in the trees about a half-mile down the line. Flames licked out the windows enveloping the roof in a huge pillar of fire. I couldn't tell if it was in our lines or theirs.

"I doubt the farmer gives a damn! You idiot," Mamere shrieked farther off like a rusty hinge. She made me smile. God knew, better even than her family, how truly a miserable human being He'd created. No wonder Mother had taken to church so well. At least there she could find some peace and quiet.

All the while Shiner lay still in the sun and Sir William tended to his hand with a piece of bloody shirt. Lady shared part of Shiner's canteen with me, and the twins went back to whistling and tapping their rifles. I lay back and the daydreams took control. I remembered the newboy who died on the train north. Ravenel Meggett. Perhaps he'd never existed, but I knew better. He'd made vows before he'd joined up to protect him and keep him alive.

"No women. No unnatural acts..."

I remembered how he'd blushed when Snake and Lady teased him. "Tell us what's unnatural. Tell us! We got a right to know."

"...Prayer on the Sabbath, no cursin' or blasphemy, no alcohol or card playin'."

He'd run away from his home on Wadmalaw Island. He said his grandfather beat him daily with a notched bamboo cane. Why big and strong Ravenel would put up with it, he wouldn't explain. He tied Lady in arm wrestling. The only one to do it. Lady liked him right off. His grandfather ran up as we pulled out the station in Charleston and tried to yank him off the freight car roof. Lady put a boot on his shriveled face and shoved him flat on his back down the siding. The old coot got up and chased us, screaming, cursing and whacking at the train car. Everyone enjoyed it immensely.

I could feel the train rumble. We were back in North Carolina racing up through scrub pine thickets, cornfields, and stands of oak. It came back vividly and I welcomed it. Maybe Shriner would come back too. The tracks cut through a bog of gum trees and water oaks. I glimpsed down an overgrown wagon rut to men and horses a quarter mile away. A peaceful scene with just the monotonous rumble of the engine and the clatter of the iron wheels on the tracks. Then the bastards opened up. The slats exploded and everyone fell face down on the floorboards. The brakes screeched and the car shuddered.

"There'll be some ball cuttin' fo' sure!" Lady yelled, first out the door, the train still rolling. Everyone piled out after. I fell into a ditch with rifle fire all around. Blue jackets crouched behind the stumps shooting at us. A cloud of smoke erupted as our boys opened up. Anthony cringed behind a log like a whimpering puppy.

"What is it? What is it?" He stayed hidden, but the rest of us followed Mr. Clement. We chased Yank cavalry through the bog for about half a mile. They didn't put up much of a fight though. Just harassing us from their base at New Bern, the bastards. We'd have chased them all day if they'd let us, but the wailing train whistle pulled us back. It triggered a lot of cursing too. Leaving yanks to roam about North Carolina like they owned the place. It wasn't right at all.

A dead soldier lay face down behind a water oak stump, his head covered in blood and the back of his skull blown off. Sir William turned him over. Ravenel Meggett with a big hole in his forehead. His spectacles shattered, his mouth wide open like he was trying to yell. Like he realized he was about to die in North Carolina. That his vows hadn't worked. That he should have listened to his grandfather. Sir William covered his face with his straw hat.

"New boy's dead before we rightly knew him."

That was all. No one ever said another word about him. We buried him and three others in a shallow grave beside the tracks in the midst of a vast emptiness of scrub pines. He'd disappeared so quickly he may have never existed at all, but I reminded myself he surely had. Now it was Shiner's turn.

The sun baked his still body. It didn't seem right him not moving at all. I half expected him to start babbling again. That felt the strangest. Him just lying there, totally quiet. Not even a peep. Anthony knelt beside him and bent low. He whispered something in Shiner's ear.

Snake poked Anthony with his rifle barrel. "He's dead you dumb shit. But least the boy had balls." Anthony glanced up at me, and I looked away. Macfadden helped him up. "Leave him be Snake. Let's git this newboy in the ground." Snake just shrugged.

We buried him right there. We all helped dig with what we had. Cups, knives, bare hands. Lots of others did the same up and down the line. We dug a decent enough grave just behind where he fell and laid him in it gently.

Sir William took Shiners raggy hat and covered his powder-smeared face. He said a quick prayer before we covered him up with dirt. My breath went short as the earth rose over his head. I couldn't watch. The others had to finish it. Shiner disappeared under the dark Virginia soil like fertilizer. He was dead and we were alive and that was all there was to it. I couldn't begin to fathom it being too exhausted to feel much of anything except a tired numbness. But I felt no fear for the first time in days, and Mamere had disappeared to boot. I listened for a while to make sure, but not a peep out of her. I thought perhaps it was a small miracle.

# IV

Officers began yelling and we were quickly up and off across more fields and down through the woods again, walking for miles through dense forest along the stump road. It felt good to be moving. It helped settle my heart down. The woods thinned to a muddy clearing of stumps and cooking fires. Each of us got a piece of boiled pork and some cornbread.

Mr. Clement nodded like he knew something. "There'll be some hell of ditches dug. Mark my words." He sucked on his canteen. "I mean some hell of 'em."

The wind picked up and pinecones fell all around. The clouds rolled by overhead and the trees rustled and swayed. The breeze brought crisp air to thin the smoke, but we didn't get to enjoy it too long. Our column soon stirred again with blanket rolls and rifles rising from the haze of the forest floor. We quick marched another mile or two before we bunched up and stopped.

More prisoners came through under guard. Six more shirtless blacks. They disappeared slowly into the woods and it didn't take long. Six revolver shots rang out. Snake chuckled but said nothing. Everyone else grew silent. Mr. Clement stared hard at the ground. Sir William and Macfadden shook their heads. Lady could have been asleep. I glanced at the twins and they smiled back like they hadn't seen me for a long time. Anthony frowned and fidgeted with his cartridge box. I knew evil things existed, but I told myself we were at war and evil things had to be tolerated. Anyway, Shiner was dead. Others had to die too. I clenched my teeth hard against the doubts and said a few Hail Mary's to make it better. They didn't help too much. The hickory tree above me waved gently like it understood. Watching the branches move ever so much with breeze became a tonic of sorts. Chattering squirrels scolded us loudly, venturing down closer round and round the trunk of a chestnut tree that dropped nuts on us from its waving branches above.

"Squirrel artillery is the best kind." Sir William whispered tending to his shivering hand. "The only kind I don't mind."

Snake grinned as another squirrel's tail popped into view over the branch above his head. His hand darted and the squirrel exploded up the trunk minus a bit of fur. Snake flicked it at Anthony.

"See here squirrel. Got to be quick to git away." Anthony said nothing but re-furrowed his brow into a deeper crease. I thanked God he'd come with us. Better they torment him than me.

A noise like sticks tapping on tin grew louder in the distance, then a sound like tearing canvas followed a steadier crackle mixed with deep growls and grumbles. It distracted everyone and I was thankful for it. It came and went, sometimes closer and louder. Sir William pulled his hat down over his eyes.

"Fightin' east of Fred'ricksburg. Like I done tole y'all." He wasn't bragging. Just letting us know he was right, as he'd expected. "Got t'be brigade strength easy. Some powerful rifle fire, ain't it?"

"Ours or theirs?" I asked, listening to the canvas-tearing echo through the trees, still as ignorant of what it meant as only a newboy could be.

"Who the hell knows?" Snake growled, rolling his eyes. "New boys' dumb as shit, ain't they."

Macfadden smiled, "No way to know from here, Conner. Yanks' sounds jus' like ours."

Snake shook his head and laughed. "Dumb ass."

Another canvas tear lasted a full minute. Mr. Clement lit his pipe and blew smoke rings while everyone listened.

"Ain't heard it that bad since Gettysburg." The smoke rings dissipated but the terrible word lingered on. He couldn't have said anything worse. Anthony bit his lip and tried not to cry while Snake poked his neck with a stick.

"Deli-kate, ain't ya boy. Deli-kate. Deli-kate."

"Sir William cleared his throat loudly. "We ain't fightin the newboys just yet Snake. Leave him be."

Snake dropped to a squat and bounced on his toes. "Squirrel's a mean one. Don't y'all worry none. Big mean Squirrel." He laughed, crossed his eyes and squatted hunched over dragging his arms like a gorilla. "Gonna eat a squirrel." He kept it up until our column moved on.

We walked in a blessed quiet for miles stumbling through a chaos of troops and camps until we found McGowan's Brigade well after dark. Men spread out around the dozens of cooking fires in a trampled hay field. Snake followed his nose to frying bacon and by chance found his cousin Chandler from back home on Waxhaw Creek. He hollered like a scalded hog and did his Catawba war dance. Chandler's copper skin glowed in the firelight, his shoulder wrapped in a cut off bloody trouser leg held tight with cord, but he could move his arm. He made sure we all had hard tack, water, and a piece of fatty bacon. I gulped mine down too quick to taste.

"Doctor's sendin me back t'Richmond tomorrow. Chimboroza hospital. Says I git t'stay till the shoulder heals up." He squinted his nose up in a smile like he was embarrassed a bit. "Ya'll got t'do without me." Snake squeezed him hard and for a second. He may have had a tear in eye, but Chandler pushed him away and shook his head.

"But there's a bad thing… happened yestiday." He looked away and groaned. "Cousin Reeves…" He took a while to catch his breath and tell

29

Snake the worst of it. "Got a bay'net through the guts. Side to side! Bastard yank bay'net! "

Reeves lay crying in pain by the fire twenty yards away across a log footbridge over a dry gully. A group of men knelt silently around the small boy. He couldn't have been more than twelve. His face, tender smooth as a baby's. Snake fell all fours beside him, groaning and gagging until he threw up. No one paid him any mind. A man with a long black beard held Reeve's head in his lap, dabbing his forehead with a wet cloth. Six others knelt around him watching closely in the flickering light. Seven canteens encircled the boy. Blood glistened through this gray tunic. He groaned loudly and clutched his stomach. I sat down and watched like it was a play at the Dock Street Theater back home. A doctor came and dropped to one knee. His sleeves were bloody to his elbows. He wavered with exhaustion. His head bobbed as he fought off sleep. The dark bottle from his leather kit gave off a purple glint in the firelight. He wet a cotton wad then placed it gently but firmly to the wound. He put the boys hand on top.

"Hold it snug young man. It'll help the pain." His voice was a hoarse whisper. With another bottle, he soaked a piece of clean bandage and gave it to the bearded man.

"Hold it over his face when the pain comes. I'll come back if I can."

"Will he be alright?" Snake wiped his eyes. The doctor stood up behind the boy and shook his head pronouncing his fate.

The boy groaned and the bandage was held to his nose. He coughed and kicked then was quiet. The cycle repeated itself over and over. Groaning and kicking, then medicine and calm. It worked for a while until he started yelling, out of his head.

"Where's the boat? Patrick, get the oars! Patrick hold on! Don't cut the trot line." Most of it mumbled and unintelligible as he drifted off weaker and weaker. A young private with close-cropped hair, scraggly whiskers and bright red pants squatted at the boy's feet. He jumped up trembling.

"That was murder! The boy weren't fightin'! That Yank bastard knew it." He tore off the remnants of his sleeve and held them across his eyes like a blindfold.

"Easy there Peter." The old man shook his head slowly. "You ain't doin' him no good gettin' all riled. Let 'im pass in peace."

Peter couldn't listen. "Had that bastard dead to rights. Dead as Hell. Cain't believe I missed. Just cain't." He held the torn sleeves tightly across his eyes.

"We know. You done tole us a hundred times. We been there too, 'member? Red beard and spectacles. Got a good look. Maybe we'll see his dead ass yet."

"But I shoulda killt him right off."

Peter sat down with his chin on his knees, his eyes still covered up. He let loose a long eerie wail. No doubt what they'd do if they caught the bastard. I lay back and sipped my canteen and listened to the rest of them softly whisper 'Amazing Grace' while Reeves groaned, Peter wailed, and Snake sat like a statue. Sir William's hand still bled badly but he could move all his fingers. He rewrapped it quickly in a cleaner rag, hissing with pain.

"Don't want no surgeon tempted to cut it off. Don't be gettin' pus in y'ear either. Surgeons like cuttin' them off too."

My ear was caked with clot, and the tiptop stung like hell. Macfadden made me wash it in the creek at the edge at the field where we refilled a couple dozen canteens.

I did as he said, taking time to drink as much as I could before filling the others. Muddy water never tasted so good. It might have been sweet tea. I thought of home and felt worse.

"It's all gone my boy," Uncle Paul called to me from the darkness. "Never to return." It was good to hear his voice.

"Of course it's gone." Mamere laughed in my ear. "Christ Conner, what y'think the yanks gonna do when they come? Give it back? Let Charleston stay crazy?"

Tears welled up but Macfadden slapped my back in time. "Don't git so worried up. You done alright. I seen plenty do worse the first time. Jus' you wait an' see. Next time you'll be laughin' at 'em."

I didn't let on. I knew I had to get straight.

"That'll be the day." Mamere snickered in the dark. "Ain't got but that tiny little brain. Only so much a straightenin' can do."

"Go to hell."

"That's the spirit." Macfadden pulled me along "Yanks can *all* go to hell."

We passed around the canteens and listened to the veterans talk.

Mr.Clement's friends didn't say much about the last few days. Just whispers that it had been bad as hell and some men had run. It was a sore point, but not the worst.

"Where's Thomas?" Mr. Clement asked a toothless old man squatting by the fire, sucking an unlit pipe.

"Dead. Back yonder. Got it right here." He put a finger matter of factly to his Adam's apple that seemed to jump in the flickering light.

"Did he suffer much?"

The man hesitated, "Not much."

Two other looked away but Mr. Clement knew the truth.

"Clinton?"

"Gone too. Quick like. In the head." It rang true and Mr. Clement nodded with a deeply furrowed brow.

"George Myers?"

"Hell no. Gone south. Little splinter in the leg." The old man flicked the pipe with his gums.

"John, that splinter was a foot long," added a thin youth with greasy blonde hair, green shirt, and a scraggle of beard. His chin rested against his rifle barrel. "Right through his thigh. Damn lucky if they don't cut the leg off."

I stared at his rifle. I'd never seen a new repeater up close, but no one else seemed impressed. Mr. Clement didn't look up.

"I shoulda been there Benjamin. Never shoulda left." He put his head between his knees.

"Allston and Zachariah too," jabbed the old man. "But we rested today. There'll be plenty more soon enough."

"It ain't fair me on furlough and them dead. It ain't right." Mr. Clement's voice cracked.

"Hell you say. Quit whippin' ya damn sef. None a them would an' you know it." The old man's red gums glowed with the firelight as he spoke.

Mr. Clement shook his head. "You're always right ain't you? You old polecat. It's good to be blessed." There was a glimmer in his eyes. He poked the ashes with a stick.

"I is blessed. Yall just jealous is all." He beamed a red toothless smile. He had the stench of a dead animal and wasn't a hollow cheeked scarecrow. In fact, he was downright plump. He winked at me, turned over a log and popped a wiggling slug, raw and whole, right in his mouth.

"They ain't as tasty as they look. Got to be particular."

He shoved two of the slimy creatures into a clay jug wrapped in cord netting. The others laughed and tossed him some more. He swallowed them whole for our amusement.

Mr. Clement raised his hand for quiet and I heard it too. Horses galloping across the field. The rumble, louder and louder until they were on us. Hundreds of horsemen followed by guns and caissons pulled by horses in pure terror, chain traces whipping their flanks. Men jumped clear just in time leaving blanket rolls to be trampled.

"Nothin lovelier than a twelve pounder cuttin' down a yank line. But nothin' uglier than a wild team whippin' up behind you in the dark." He sighed deeply. "Ya'll 'member them yanks getting their ass chopped comin' cross that field at Manassas. Twelve pounders tore 'em up. What a damn mornin'!" He chuckled to himself, "Mule-headed Longstreet took all day to figure a fight was goin' on." He stared up at the stars for a while. "Lady, 'member crawlin' out fo cartridges off them dead yanks?'

Lady nodded matter of factly. "Yep. Scott Taylor got shot in the head crawlin' back." He tapped the back of his head with his fingers.

"I remember every damn second." Sir Williams waved both arms above him like the spirit had him. "No day's ever been longer. Tom Dukes got his arm blown off right next to me. Tried to hold his rifle up for one last shot. Got it square in the face." He pulled off his bandana and lowered his head, "See this Conner? Got this here. A solid shot near scalped me." He was bald on the right side. His scalp purplish and knotted with scars. He rubbed a prominent ridge and Mr. Clement winked at Lady as if there'd been a joke. I found out later that when he touched a certain spot he'd be quiet for hours like he'd been given ether. He didn't open his mouth again for most of the evening.

# V

Macfadden nudged my elbow again and whispered, "Clement saved my life at Sharpsburg. Pushed me down just as a canister load went over. Killed six men right behind. Clement's like that. Can tell when thing's are comin'. A good man to stick close to. Remember that."

I couldn't help but remember. I'd met him long ago, before father died. He'd danced on my mother's piano on my fifth birthday after he drank my father to sleep. It was a bit vague but Uncle Paul said it actually happened. They'd been friends long before my father's liver went bad, and he'd promised Uncle he'd look out for me.

"As best I can, Paul. Never know what the summer brings. Jus' tell 'im to stay close."

Uncle seemed to hear that one thing. He even smiled. "Conner? You hear that? Mr. Clement gonna look out for ya. So listen to the man. Remember what he did for Mose." How could I forget. He'd retold the story a thousand times like I hadn't seen the whole thing myself.

"Stood down the lynch mob at the lumber yard single handed!" Uncle beamed. I remembered it like it was yesterday. The memory so vivid it caused the ground to shimmer like wind on a still pond. I could see Mose, Uncle Paul's slight, free-black foreman, come diving over a stack of 6 by 12 beams to get behind Mr. Clement, knocking over a fire bucket, ripping his trousers and leaving a bloody patch on a jagged board edge. The mob pushed right behind, down the aisles between stacks of fresh cut pine. Mose stood there in the flesh, terrified. I'd never seen him scared before.

"Honest as a Nun, works like a bitch in heat!" Uncle Paul yelled out, standing there slashing at the mob with his cane like a Samurai, guided by bat-like ears. "Clement trusts him with just 'bout everything and everyone! Runs the flat boat crew at Parker's Ferry! Keeps cash for me weeks at a time! Runs the sawmill for Christ sake! When Clement's gone!"

He even faked a stumble to draw them in then bloodied a man's head. They grabbed him from behind and held him down, but not before he broke another man's finger with his vice grip.

Mose stood shivering behind Mr. Clement who stared down thirty or so white men out to lynch the wrong man. Stared them down without so much as an oak club. The big man up front holding a bullwhip with a bowie knife in his belt was one Mahoney Duncan. Loud and bossy, with a reputation of killing two men in a bar fight. His puffed face overgrown with thick black whiskers making it fatter. I remembered thinking he could have been a bear.

"They broke in on Johnny Marion's wife. Tried to have her. We done hung the other," all cocky and sneering as he stepped forward. "You gonna stop us Clement?"

Mr. Clement squatted down, drew a line in the dirt and spoke gently. "Mahoney, I done known Mose for thirty years. He ain't never done nothin' to nobody. Ya'll come for the wrong man. Anybody want to hang him got to get through me first. Plain and simple."

"Goddamnit, alright then." He dropped the whip, flashed his knife and dove at Clement in a second. Clement sprang forward like a giant frog and stuck a knife blade straight through Mahoney's throat before he could suck air. Where the knife came from I never saw. The big man sprawled dead on the ground with his eyes bugged out and his teeth clamped down on his protruding tongue. He never twitched. The mob went stunned silent.

"Now see what y'all done? Git on home. Mose ain't yo' man."

The mob picked up Mahoney's body and retreated quickly, like they'd expected exactly that. Mr. Clement wiped his blade with a turpentine rag and went back to work like nothing had happened. Nobody messed with Mose again.

The ground shimmered again and I watched Mr. Clement stretch and yawn. He winked at me like he'd read my thoughts.

"Don't y'all worry none. We'll whip the bastards an' git home yet. It'll happen. It'll damn well happen."

"Damn right," Lady whispered half asleep, his hat over his face. I figured they knew. They had to know. Maybe everything really would be all right. Back to the way it was. I lay back and sunk into the ground like I'd always been a part of the earth.

Clement sat quietly next to the fire for a long time, grimacing in some sort of trance. His jaw muscles ground his stubby teeth smoothly and firmly top against bottom like mortar on a pestle. My jaw ached just listening to it. The night grew quiet as more and more exhausted men sank into sleep. A crescent moon shone above the tree line through thin hazy clouds that rolled by silhouetted against its yellowish light. The ground pulled me down and sleep crept closer. My eyes wouldn't stay open. Mr. Clement slowly lit his pipe like his arms were lead ballast.

I thought of how we'd come north just a few days before. It seemed like forever ago. Three raggedy trains out of the Charleston's John Street Station, loaded with recovered wounded, veterans off furlough and new replacements like me and Anthony. Decrepit locomotives pulled a dozen ramshackle cars brimming with men. Flat cars, cattle cars, and freight cars. Anything that rolled would do. Two other trains loaded up beside ours. One with horses for Hampton's cavalry, the other with more troops and provisions.

We'd left the station as Union shells from batteries on Morris Island fell a few blocks away. No one seemed to mind one bit. The cars just screeched louder and the throng milled about busier than ever, as if celebrating still being out of range. Hundreds of people bustled about to see us off, jostling to say goodbye to a loved one or just trying not to get run over. Wagons, carts, hand trucks, and horses pushed through in all directions, competing for space in the tight canyons between row after row of huge cotton bales marooned in the station by the blockade. Loose cotton waved from every car and every warehouse beam. It coated the ties and tracks and peeped out of the burlap seams of countless bales to see what all the fuss was about. A hot metallic wind of engine steam and pine soot whipped some up to follow us for a while as we rolled north through the Santee Swamp where clouds of mosquitoes consumed us. We rolled up in blankets and covered our heads cursing until we came out to higher ground at the railhead for the run to Wilmington. Then we ferried across the Cape Fear River on flatboats, one car load at a time by the light of a roaring fire on a runaway barge in mid river. The flames sprouted up one hundred feet high like a warning from the black river.

"The Point of No Return." Someone had whispered in the darkness. "Who's afraid of the Cape Fear?"

I stepped off that boat and felt like I'd crossed a line from the past to the present. From the everyday routine to make believe. The north bank seemed totally different. Like colors should have had different names but I couldn't quite put my finger on it.

I tried to think it out on the next train north, but it all evaporated with daylight. We made a long, pull through endless North Carolina in a freight car filthier and shabbier than the others, and we broke down a dozen times. Even Sir William flared. "Goddamn shithole engines! How we gonna win w'this shit?" Then he rattled off a long list of what

38

we needed, but I stopped listening after a while. It just made it worse. When we'd finally built up some speed, the yanks surprised us with their cavalry raid in the middle of nowhere. A quick lurching stop, cars shot up, and poor Ravenel dead before we ran them off. All in a great noise of rifles and yelling, clouds of powder smoke, then a row of freshly turned mounds of dirt for those who had disappeared. We'd resumed our ride north up as if nothing had happened. I kept a handful of Ravenel's grave dirt in my pocket. It didn't seem right leaving without something. That night we slept beside the tracks with hot food and clean blankets, courtesy of some Petersburg ladies, but not another spoken word about him. I'd thanked God He hadn't seen fit to leave me covered with dirt in North Carolina, but my heart still raced in the dark. Cowardice had found me again. It had followed me north after all, pricking at me all the next day on the miserable run to Richmond. Troop trains in front and back nearly hit us several times. Engines and brakes screamed all day. We'd inched along for hours then waited on a siding just to watch long trains of wounded roll south.

We crawled across a rail bridge over the James just after dark watching flames belch out of tall brick stacks at the Tredegar Ironworks. Streetlights glowed up the hillside like strings of pearls and thousands of troops milled about the glowing beehive changing trains and marching up sidings. The only greetings this time were cries from sergeants and officers herding men in the lamplight. No ladies brought us food or blankets. We bedded down beside the tracks in the dark. Hungry soldiers griped.

"Mighta given us somethin t'et. We come all this way to' save yo' ass. Now maybe we ain't."

At dawn another train of foul cattle cars took us north to Guiney Station, the place where Stonewall Jackson died just last year. Shot by his own men and still a nightmare. Men doffed their hats and the talk became brave.

"He come outta that house alive an' we long since been home!" a voice called out. "Wouldn't been no third day at Gettysburg. Ole blue light woulda whipped their ass."

"Damn right!" was the chorus, but doubts were freshly stirred, the pain worse with the reminder of what might have been. We wandered through a maze of back roads and forest tracks until we'd come to Lee's army stretched out through the trees. Officers explained that we'd won a battle but Grant was still south of the Rapidan where he shouldn't be so the army was on the move. It didn't quite add up. Doubt crept along with every regiment, half hidden in the shadows but popping out just enough to make its presence known. Maybe it latched on to newboys mostly because I still felt it clinging to me even as sleep descended and I sure didn't want it to show.

I tried to think of something pleasant, so I thought of Uncle Paul. I pictured him telling me about how he could pilot dreams. It felt good to hear it all again.

"I can conjure up a tiller to beat high into the future or bear off into the distant past." He laughed. I knew he was close by and wanted him to stay. "The reward for losing my eyesight at age twenty-nine!"

I'd heard the story many times, but it got better with retelling. The mule that cracked his head open had died the next day just after Uncle came to, blind.

"I'm not sure if it was the blindness, the cracked skull, the mule dyin' or all three. But if it was just the mule dyin' I do wish it'd happened first." He laughed right in my ear. "But it's a gift to be able to see tomorrow. You should practice, Conner."

My first recollection was him standing barefoot over a wash bucket, white sleeves rolled up. Tan canvas suspenders inked up and down with his blackbird-foot's scribble. "It's the secret to the dreams. To life itself, y'see." He thumbed the brass suspender buttons. "The magic word that tames 'em can't be taught or shared. Got to read for yourself."

He washed his face and hands in the bucket and winked at me. His opaque blue-gray eyes swirled in milky layers.

"Feel this water. Feel it." He made me put my hand in the bucket. "It's not just a metaphor. Dreams are like a boat on water. Steerin' a dream's like sailin'. Got to slide with the wind and waves. Especially on the starboard reach." He laughed for a long time.

I wasn't sure what to make of it. Mother and Mamere said he'd never actually stepped foot on a boat except the Stono River ferry, but that fact didn't seem to matter too much. I wanted to believe. I wanted the little bird's feet to mean something. Maybe I could learn to pilot dreams too. At the time it seemed like the only secret to life worth knowing. I'd tried many times, but it was no use. Dreams came and went but if there was any steering, it was the dream steering me . . .

# VI

South Carolina. On a salt marsh creek behind Younges Island.

Ezekiel stood in the stern pushing us along with an oak pole. He was the eldest son of my father's slaves, Luke and Helen, now owned by my Uncle Paul. His younger brother Jacob and his older sister Rosealee sat in the bow. A bilge of creek shrimp, minnows, and pluff mud sloshed over my bare feet with each pull of the oars. The flood tide pushed us through a maze of shell banks along a salt marsh creek alive with swarms of fiddler crabs and rippling with boils of finger mullet. The marsh stretched for miles across the Stono River to the thick canopy of Wadmalaw Island. White dots of houses on the far bluff look like magnolia blossoms against the green tree line.

Ezekiel yelled out. "By God Conner. I am a year older then you, a foot taller , and smarter than you'll ever be. Just cause my daddy's yo daddy's slave don't make me yo's. I'll damn well leave this island anytime I want." He kicked bilge slime at me and laughed loudly. "By God I'm a free man! I'll walk up to Ohio if I like."

I splashed salt water on my face from over the side watching the fiddler crabs scurry in waves across the mud bank. Granddaddy blue crabs marched in perfect columns flanking our skiff, red barnacle-encrusted claws held up as if saluting, hissing in our cadence, mocking the sound of crabs boiling in the pot. They may even have been laughing. It seemed reasonable.

"Ezekiel, hate to give you pause, but you don't have the slightest idea where Ohio is."

Rosealee and Jacob chuckled from the bow seat.

"Give-he paws. Ezekiel be a cat." Rosealee clawed at the humid air.

"He sho' is." Jacob bent over double stomping the floor boards. "Jus' a big kitty."

"Y'all shut up." Ezekiel flicked the pole and splashed them hard with creek water.

"Hey brother, it rainin'?" Jacob brushed a clump of seaweed off his palsied arm and faked like he was crying.

"Ohio's somewhere up nawth. Don't matter no how. I won't be no slave forever, Conner. Gonna get my own land. Git me some women. Ain't talkin black ones neither. White women! My own horse too. Might you be workin' for me." He knocked the oars and pinned my arms until I fought him off.

"But you'll never beat me in arm wrestlin', Ezekiel, will ya? Never could, never will." I smiled at him and he showered me with a handful of shrimp heads.

Rosealee brushed them off, picking the sunburn peal from my red shoulders and threw the skin to the fiddler crabs.

"Come on mister crab. Come eat da white boy."

I stared at her and she stared back.

"Dat right, I be as white as you Conner. Maybe whiter. God made me white so He can watch me cross the cornfield in pitch dark." She smiled and blew me a kiss.

Ezekiel cursed. "You is too strange to be my sister, Rosealee. Nobody else got a white sista'. You ain't right."

"Leave her be Ezekiel." My voice came from across the marsh like the shriek of a gull.

"Leave her be. Leave her be." Ezekiel taunted.

Jacob smiled at me and rolled his eyes. "Conner, why don't y'daddy leave her be?"

43

Rosealee stared at her albino feet and Ezekiel made a sound like a toad fish. I ignored Jacob and focused on Ezekiel's grunts and croaks. He knew just how to do it. He irritated everyone, even good-natured Uncle Paul who waited for us on the oak bluff just beyond the edge of the marsh.

Herons, egrets, and ibises flocked around him swooping up and around the wind, landing with wings spread and long legs penetrating the shallows, with an air of total disregard. Above them, the sky thickened into descending orange clouds like a collapsing tent.

Ezekiel sang "Glory Halleluiah" just loud enough for Uncle's bat ears. He waved his oak cane in our general direction yelling at us.

"God damnit Ezekiel, I hear you! I swear to God I'll stuff lye in your mouth if I hear another word of that Yankee shit!"

Ezekiel laughed and hummed a verse loudly. Uncle exploded with profanity. Rosealee covered her younger brother's ears since Jacob's palsied arm hung thin and limp from his damaged shoulder.

"String arm. String arm." Ezekiel laughed, "Can't cover both ears hisse'f."

Doc Sarah, the ponderously huge black midwife, surfaced in midstream then waded through the marsh, half submerged like a hippopotamus. Her stiff, greased hair unperturbed.

"Leave him be, Ezekiel." She belched creek water, then picked up a mud covered palmetto log and hurled it to the oyster bank like I might throw a bamboo stick. "Jacob!" She yelled, "You didn't get stuck but a second! I swear, I ain't the one that done it. Musta been that way all along inside y'mamma's womb. Coulda been yo' daddy's fault. And you Rosealee. Always sweet natured and simple. Why? Cause you got that 'bill-call' cord wrapped 'round y' neck. Made you red then pearly white. Had to cut it with the straight razor. Hissed at me like a chicken snake."

Jacob swung his arm back and forth like a pendulum. "Watch out it's a chicken snake! Gonna git you Rosealee!"

We all laughed as Doc Sarah grunted disapprovingly then submerged.

"Why she like it so much down there?" Rosealee giggled.

"More freedom of movement, I suppose." I watched Doc Sarah's bulbous shape glide beneath the skiff.

"Freedom? Bullshit. Ain't none underwater neither. Not on this island." Ezekiel lifted his pole until she passed.

Jacob dragged his string arm in the creek. "You's wrong Ezekiel. I can feel it down there right now. Feels kinda soft and slippery like a mullet."

Rosealee giggled louder. "I like 'em fried."

Jacob twirled his string arm, slapping his shriveled hand against the surface to splash her. "See? See there, Lot's of 'em jus' waitin' on the bottom." Ezekiel threw the cast net one last time and caught a thick writhing eel and let it flap and twist on the floorboard on top of the squished stew. It bothered Jacob.

"I hate eels, worse than chicken snakes. They twist up your arm and won't let go."

He swung down hard with a hatchet using his good arm, thick with rippling muscles. He hacked the eel in half but his one chop split the old hull lengthwise nearly in two.

Even Ezekiel was impressed. "That one arm ain't bad."

Jacob was unperturbed. Water poured in and he sighed. "Water ain't exactly evil, but it ain't yo friend, neither."

The boat sank quickly. Rosealee screamed, "Why y'all never taught me to swim?" She slapped and grabbed at me as I went under holding my breath and trying to push her off. She went limp just as an oyster bank sliced my bare feet. I surfaced and dragged her up into the soft black pluff mud leaving bloody footprints up the bank. We stared at her, waiting for her to breath. Her yellowish eyes were open and unblinking in the noon sun.

Mother appeared on the shell bank veiled for Mass and levitating with energy as if she were still alive. I wasn't the least bit embarrassed, and it surprised me.

"She's an albino. You must go to confession as soon as you get ashore. Father Reilly will be furious."

Then father appeared, shimmering like a mirage in the August heat. He pulled up his pants and coughed up a mouthful of hock. "You could say I'm a drinkin' man, but Rosealee's got the vitiligo. Doc Sarah says so. It's just her skin."

Rosealee didn't move. Jacob and Ezekiel pushed on her bare stomach and water flushed out her nose.

"Damn it, breathe for her Conner!" Ezekiel slapped me.

"But, she's not my sister."

"Do it Conner!" Jacob pleaded. "Pretend she's is. She might be."

I held her nose, pressed my mouth down firmly over her lips and breathed hard. Her chest rose. She arched her back, coughed up a quart of salt water then vomited all over Jacob's pants.

"You done made her sick." Ezekiel laughed, tears running down his face. "Lord, she's so sick."

Old rattlesnake Mamere, with her shriveled leather face and powdered gray hair, darted out of the perpetual fog that draped over her. She waved her snakeskin cane and shrieked at us as usual from the tomato field at the edge of the marsh.

"What the hell y'all doin' out there? Damn it Conner! Don't you know when you breathe life into somebody the first thing they want is to be free! I swear to God, I'll whip your backside with thorn bush and douse it with turpentine. You hear me!" The fury of her voice rippled

46

the creek water and even the bravest fiddler crabs retreated to their holes in the mud.

"Why she so mean, Conner ?" Rosealee coughed up more creek water.

"Cause she's a witch." Ezekiel rattled a tin can full of oyster shells. "Hear me, Mamere?" He yelled.

"I hear ya." She called back. "I'll git my hands on ya soon enough."

"But why, Conner? Why?" Rosealee started crying.

"It goes back to her son, Rosealee." Uncle Paul shouted from the bluff. "He was as Irish as the next, but couldn't hold the liquor well. Fell off the Stono Ferry. Drunk, y' see. Washed up on John's Island a week later. Black, bloated, and half eaten by crabs."

"That's enough." Rosealee held her ears.

"Mamere demanded to see the body. She opened his eyes so she could curse him to his face. The constable was stupefied."

"Stupefied!" Jacob laughed. "I like dat word."

"Been a witch ever since." Uncle tapped his cane on a shell mound. "Wasn't exactly sweet to start with. Went from mean as a snake to bitch-witch."

"That's it. That's a fact." Ezekiel laughed. "A bitch-witch all right." Mamere's voice cut razor thin across the creek. "I'll make time for you too Paul. Don't you worry."

Uncle Paul just laughed. "She's been bitch-witch of Meggett for all these years now. Had it in for Conner's mother. Blamed her y'see. Like she made Perry drink." He caught his breath, laughing. "I can assure you. Perry Dumont never needed an excuse!"

Mother whispered to me, "Don't worry. She can't get you. She's landlocked. Mamere's sphere of influence is more like a trapezoid. The creek to the cornfield. The inlet to the woods. See." Mother rose to full levitation and point out the irregular corners. "Just stay out of her territory. The creek is all right as long as you're out of range. Remember, she can throw the tomahawk better than your father ever did."

Mamere screamed all the while, cowering even the always-shrieking seagulls into total quiet.

"I'll send Jacob across first." I whispered. "Mamere never whipped Jacob."

Jacob shook his head, "Not me Conner. Mamere got some kinda taint. She ain't right. She's touched in the head."

Ezekiel laughed and nodded. "Mamere ain't never been right. Runs in the family."

Mother smiled then levitated herself across the creek. "Coming Mamere."

The breeze rippled the marsh grass and I caught a big blast of Mamere's foul urine smell. A full ammonia nose burn.

"And don't y'all bring me no more mullet! I ain't eatin no more mud fish! Mullet and sweet potatoes! You'd think that was all God gave us." She caught her breath, picked up a rotten tomato and screamed. "I ate better in the damn Revolution!"

I covered my mouth and whispered. "You want a white woman Ezekiel? You can have Mamere."

She glared at me and threw the tomato into the creek then hobbled off towards the barn. We waited until she'd disappeared then waded up through the marsh to Ezekiel's one room plank shack, insulated with about a decade's worth of Charleston Mercury newspapers, body odor so strong it gagged me. The stiff swollen corpse of a black man lay on planks across two sawhorses on the porch. No one knew the man but it didn't matter. Rosealee ran up from the marsh still covered in pluff mud and wailed until she fell out in the grass next to the road. Plump Father Reilly rode up with a red face, stiff white collar, and flowing black robe.

"Got to get back to St. Mary's for Mass but this tendin-to won't take long." He dismounted awkwardly produced a tiny bottle, then he dabbed Rosealee and the corpse with holy oil. He sprinkled the rest of us with holy water from a silver flask, then chanted while he sifted the sandy white dirt from the road through his fingers.

He winked at me. "This powder road transects the known world like an axis. Bless this dirt, ground fine and white by wagon wheel and hoof. Lord give us a miracle." He threw a handful into the air and Mother reappeared wearing a Nun's black habit and an enormous starched white hat that looked liked ibis wings. She sprinkled peach scented powder from her copper tin onto Rosealee's bare breasts.

"See, it's encrusted with sea shells and inlaid with a gold crucifix." She whispered in her ear. "Conner's father bought it in Savannah before he sinned. Bought it just for me! Now be gone you plateye devil." Then she chanted out Hail Mary's to the tune of Yankee Doodle.

Father ran up shirtless and then threw a blanket over her winged hat, nodding at the corpse. "That there's ripe. Close to goin' bad." He laughed so hard his belt buckle jumped up and down over his protruding abdomen. He patted his stomach. "They say it's the liver, but I could be expectin'." He laughed until he choked and had to kneel down. "Your Momma's penance is to live with an Irishman with no shame." He jumped up and dragged her into the shack and closed the door.

Father Reilly took his time to carefully wash the peach powder off of Rosealee's breasts using the last of the holy water. She lay still, tolerating him, eyelids fluttering, then sprung up, pushed me down, and kissed me full on the lips.

49

# VII

At daybreak they were all gone. I said a quick prayer that they'd find the yank with the red beard and blow his head off then I tried to put it out of my mind. Reeves was not my concern and the thought of a bayonet in the guts gave me chills. Best leave it be. My ear throbbed and it helped me focus.

An overcast sky smelled of rain. A breeze blew steadily from the east and the lowest darkest clouds raced each other past the treetops. Men were up and about all over camp as if they'd never slept. Others emerged slowly from clumps of soggy blanket rolls like ants from a wet mound gulping a breakfast of water and cornbread then on the move again.

Benjamin offered me chewing tobacco while we marched down a muddy road past fields of red clover and purple thistles. His cap sported two cock spurs.

"Yanks won't shoot a cock spur." He nodded towards the distant rifle fire. "That or a crows head." He reached into his pocket and produced a little green lizard, jaw wide open and ready to fight or flee. "Yank's is scared a lizards too. And the man who wears 'em. Latch 'em on y'ear. See? See here?"

The lizard obliged, chomping down on his ear lobe and dangling as if suddenly asleep.

"Best git ya one." His shiny repeater rifle was slung with rope across his back. "Lizards' better. Even than this here. Seven shooter. Got it off a dead yank back yonder. Got a tube inside here too." He flipped the metal hinge on the stock to show me. "Called a Spencer. See this here. Tubes go all the way up. Seven bullets inside em. Jus' cock an' shoot.

Got the three tubes. I'll muzzle load the minie's when theys' gone." He rubbed the curved trigger guard and tickled the lizard's stomach.

"Will that work?"

He shrugged. "Guess so. Why not? Less I git shot first. But that there's what mister lizard's fo'."

Peter walked by, red eyed and silent, his torn sleeve still tied over his forehead. A lizard hung from his ear, too. I couldn't tell if they were serious, but it seemed to make sense. All I had was St. Sebastian.

Ezekiel yelled from far away. "Two lizards and a Spencer. That does it alright. Gonna make them saints too?"

I scanned the far trees but couldn't spot him. I knew my mind played tricks. I told myself it was just a matter of being hungry and tired, but during the long walk I heard Ezekiel several times. We finally came to a cross roads called Spotsylvania Courthouse, overrun with dirty, worn out troops. The din was terrific. It smelled of dysentery and decomposing bodies.

"Ragamuffins." Sir William whispered in my ear. "Always ragamuffins in Virginia. Worse in the winter though. Jus' you wait n'see. When it gits cold." He laughed, "Men just ever'where. Stooped under blankets like old women with their shawls. See that there courthouse. If it was cold enough, we'd be packed inside like cobs in a bin. Wouldn't budge 'till they dragged us out."

The stately red brick courthouse with white washed columns front and side stood across the street from the newer hotel sporting square wooden pillars scarred with bullet holes. Windows of both were broken out and the front doors ripped off their hinges. Word spread that yank cavalry raided through just yesterday. Shot up the place and killed some of our boys who'd bedded down on the porch. All the yanks had repeaters or so rumor went. Took our boys a long while to run them off. The hundreds of bullet holes looked like proof enough.

A bright new 'stars and bars' hung lazily from a pole jutting out a second floor window claiming the hotel for our side. Broken boards from the window frame dangled underneath like rotten teeth. Two fresh mounds of dirt, shaped like giant loaves of bread and iced with a coating of burlap sacks, guarded one entrance.

"I stayed there once!" Macfadden beamed, pointing to the hotel. "Got up with the McCoull family from north of here. Had a big weddin' party right in there. Fried liver, roast goose, red rice, turnip greens. You couldn't eat it all. Sweets too. Peach cobbler, cinnamon twists…"

"That's enough!" Mr. Clement bowed his head. "We all ate well sometime or 'nother."

Macfadden smiled and obeyed. No one's stomach wanted to know more. Mine felt like a tight fist grinding knuckles against my rib cage. I could smell Uncle Paul's molasses sweetened collard greens simmering in a pot with pork fat and ham bones and it made things worse. The clouds cleared and the sun burned steamy hot.

We rested in the shade beside a whitewashed fence while canteens were refilled from a well behind the courthouse. Columns moved in all directions. Cavalry with nervous horses pushed their way through mobs of infantry while officers and dispatch riders trotted back and forth with endless orders. A curtain of dust and smoke rose thick enough to dull the morning sun into an orange ball that burned partially through the thinning cloud cover and hovered just above the wall of chestnut and hickory trees at the far edge of a devastated cornfield. A few crows flew overhead cawing at us, letting us know they'd seen worse. Coughing men throughout the columns covered their faces with rags. Snake passed around a brown bottle. It tasted like scorched okra laced with pepper.

"Got it back yonder. Artil'ry boys. It ain't is'ackly wine."

My eyes watered and my throat burned but I drank my share and the mood improved quickly. We sat just off the road waiting to be told what to do. The whole brigade stretched out all across the field and way down the road past the courthouse. Caravans of refugees streamed past headed south in creaking wagons and carts pulled by cows, mules, and a few sickly horses. All loaded to the brim with belongings. Tables, chairs, beds, trunks, canvas bags and sheets stuffed with clothes or bedding, sacks of corn meal, kegs of water and molasses, pots, pans, bundles of fat lighter kindling. Children of all ages piled high on top or holding tight to mother's lap. Most of the drivers were women or old men, but a few boys cracked whips and steadied reins looking determined not to mess up.

"Fugees," Mr. Clement waved his hand up and down the road. "Fugees everywhere nowadays. Goin' to Richmond. Maybe Danville. Heard they just 'bout emptied out the whole state. Gotta be a hundred thousand just in Richmond alone. Mostly all white too. The blacks done run off to the yanks."

"Not no hundred thousand. You think?" Lady shook his head. "What they gonna eat? Flours up $200 a barrel. That's what's bein' said."

"Gov'ment helps em." Mr. Clement laughed.

"My ass." Snake lay on his back with his feet propped up on a fence post. "Gov'ment cain't hep shit, much less fugees. What? They gonna stop the yanks?" He jerked his thumb at the wagons, but no one answered.

Two boys with dark mops of hair that could have been birds nests, dangled their back sides off a high, two wheeled cart and let loose the squirts in unison, laughing the whole time. The twins jumped up in a second without a spoken word, darting forward to kick dirt over the brown stains then plopping down facing each other as the cart rolled off.

They promptly launched into the best whistling I'd ever heard. It didn't sound even human. One like a flute. The other maybe a cello. Two intricate interwoven melodies, then a third and fourth, with ups and downs like they each had two throats. We gathered around. A crowd of soldiers stopped and listened, blocking the road and forcing wagons and riders to go around. Sir William danced in a circle.

"That's it. I done heard the fiddle boys in Charleston playin' it. They called it the Bait-hoofin."

The twins stopped as suddenly as they started. Soldiers applauded and whistled while officers pushed through to reopen the road. The twins just sat and stared at each other like they hadn't noticed a thing until Peter herded them to the fence and stood their guard.

Ezekiel spoke in my ear. "Y'cousin Elliott's dead. Git yo dandy ass home. We got crabbin' t'do. I'll whip yo ass one mo'time fo' I go fight for the yanks. Dangle yo' balls for the blue crabs. Yeowee!" His laugh gradually faded into the wagon creaks and scuffling feet. I looked around for him but he was gone. I knew he was free in my mind and might really be free if the yanks came. Anyway Ezekiel could take good care of himself. The best I could come up with was to stay put and ride it out. It didn't make much sense, but I convinced myself all I had to do was follow along. I took a good look around. If thousands of others could do it, so could I.

"Brave talk!" Someone cried from the mass on the road. I knew it was a sign that God was listening. Time to be careful.

Our brigade moved to a hay field on a little rise over looking a pine woods interspersed with dogwoods about a half-mile away, the gentle rise and fall of the land still new to me. Each foot of elevation a small mountain compared to the pancake flatness of Younges Island. The vista of a second tree line past the edge of the field seemed like a mountain range in the distance. Sitting on the ridge of a field that curved gently downwards from me in all directions felt like sitting on top of the world. For a while I stared up at the clouds and enjoyed a dizziness like I'd climbed to a great height, but the gray overcast rolled in to cover the blue sky and pushed me back down to a lower place.

Rumor had us fighting on this spot. Mr. Clement didn't waste any time. He had us tear down a nearby split rail fence and grab pine logs left to rot in the field. We piled them in front and dug with everything we had. Belt buckles, tin cups, knives. There still weren't but a handful of spades or big axes in the whole regiment. But no matter. The holes widened and deepened in the soft dirt and pretty soon we had a decent line.

"It sure beats grave diggin, Conner." Rosealee's voice was right behind me, "It ain't a grave is it?"

"It might be soon." Mamere laughed. "Ya'll ain't shit to the yanks."

"Leave Conner be." Uncle Paul's voice was soft but firm. "He's got enough to worry about with out you vexin' im. If you got to talk to the boy, jus' don't interrupt him when he's working."

It seemed like good advice and I figured Mamere for all her sourness would still mind him. I realized it was strange that I could hear them all but it didn't bother me. It was actually a comfort of sorts, especially since Mamere couldn't whack me anymore.

We fetched a head log from the woods behind us. No one wanted to stick his head up into a yank minie-ball. Every other group was doing the same, and a breast work quickly stretched across the entire field.

"We're diggin' in here to protect the bulge in the line up yonder." Sir William waved his bandaged hand. "This here's to keep 'em from comin' round back. They're callin' the bulge the 'muleshoe.' Heard it was a mile square." He pointed in several directions but spoke with authority.

"Muleshoe my ass. Lee's the damn mule. He's mule headed and y'all know it." Snake spat more defiantly than usual.

"The old man does alright. He knows what he's doin'." Mr. Clement wiped his rifle with his sleeve.

"Hell you say. Tell that to Pickett's boys, what's left of em."

"Shush up!" Mr. Clement spun around. "He done his best. Longstreet shoulda…" he cursed to himself. "Hell with you Snake."

"Call it a muleshoe if you like." Sir William lectured on, oblivious of them, drawing an arc on the dirt. "A big bulge a mile wide. Our boys facin' out in all directions. Yank'll be tempted fo' sure."

Snake glared at Mr. Clement. "A damn muleshoe for Lee's mules. Somebody'll git there ass kicked."

Lady chuckled and stretched, "When you started gettin' all soft 'bout a fight Snake?"

Snake started for him then thought better of it. "Shit on ya."

Lady laughed and blew him a kiss. Mr. Clement stretched out against the logs. "Y'see boys. Snake here's right. Lee's a mule alright, and we're his pride and joy muleshoes. The lowest damn part of the mule. He'll let 'em git close then we'll kick 'em to hell and back."

Snake shook his head, "Ain't no reason to pick this here. Better to keep movin'. Keep 'em on the run. The old man's lost his nerve."

"We'll stop 'em here and swing 'round west like." Sir William kept on pointing, quite satisfied with his lines in the dirt. "They ain't seen Marse Robert do this-here before."

"Shit on your muleshoe." Snake trotted back to the woods to relieve himself, and Lady whistled and laughed.

"The boy can turn a phrase, cain't he."

Macfadden poked my shoulder and shrugged. "No use worryin'. It'll turn out alright. Clement always knows. You just watch. He'll tell us when its time to run."

I believed him and it seemed like we stayed in that one spot for days but I can't be sure. Time seemed different in Virginia. It didn't obey the same rules as home. Maybe tidal forces didn't work there but the ebb and flow could have affected the sun because it went clear around the tree line then back again. I tried to keep track but gave up after a while. I can't say I really cared. Except for the stomach gnawing, it felt good just to sit back against the gnarl of logs and listen to the twins whistling. It sounded like organ music. Ave Maria, Agnus Dei, Kyrie Eleison, Gloria in Excelsis Deo. How could they do it with out moving their lips? I stared at them in awe and they smiled back while the organ blared. No one else seemed to care the first bit or even notice. For a few minutes I could have sworn I heard a choir in the background, as my eyelids grew heavy.

# VIII

Mother, adorned in her ibis wing hat and black habit, levitated up Charleston's Legare Street, a canyon of four story planter's mansions, reciting Hail Mary's and blessing herself repeatedly.

"Mass is about to start Conner. Don't be late." She ignored Dr. Tradd and my cousin Elliott who sat on the columned porch of a towering brick home set back from the street inside a yard full of bright red azaleas. We were shaded by two huge magnolia trees enclosed behind a black wrought-iron fence with a gold inlaid gate.

I stood behind Elliott and read over his shoulder. Dr. Tradd glanced back at me over his spectacles, his sagging face covered with gray brown splotches mirrored in the French doors, his eyes twinkling and a smile barely noticeable.

"The *New York Times*, smuggled in by a blockade runner. Just two weeks old. Perhaps miracle enough even for your mother." He chuckled then coughed in spasm. The *Times* headlines screamed at me. *Devilish atrocities of the insatiate fiends. White and black indiscriminately butchered. Horrible massacre by the rebels.*

Elliott knelt and mocked a Gregorian chant as mother drifted up the street out of our sight. "Forrest killed the whole bunch. He's our savior. He's our savior. Blessed be our savior"

Dr. Tradd nodded in agreement, "He's nothing but an uncivilized slave trader. I don't care what you're Uncle Paul says, Conner. General Forrest is beyond all decency!"

The Times kept stabbing. *Dead bodies horribly mutilated. Negro woman and children killed in cold blood.*

The red bricks of the street seemed to ripple like harbor chop. Then a huge man rode up on a mule, screaming like an engine whistle. The bulky mansions and their towering oaks and magnolias magnified the din painfully. His face was sharp, angular, and dark bearded. His eyes piercing black. His gray general's uniform, caked in dried mud. His saber whipped about like it was alive.

"By God take that back! If you were any part of a man I'd slap your jaws and force you to resent it. By God I'm Nathan Bedford Forrest and I'll damn well have my way!" He bellowed out to a roaring herd of shotgun toting horsemen galloping up Legare Street after my mother. "Git thar first boys! Git thar first and git all the good pews." He spat at Doctor Tradd's feet. "I'd rather the yanks infest Tennessee than live with blue-blooded, plantation princes like you old man. Come on out from y'jasmine wrought iron, you high browed puffball. I'll cut yar head off like I done the others. The boy's too if they's agin' us. That or saddle up and ride. Bring y' shotguns too. Better fo' gittin in close. Yanks cain't stand the double barrels."

He yelled loud enough to rattle the windowpanes. "The papist boy can bring the Holy Water and incense. Needin' all the hep we can git." He took a long swing, slicing off a large, fruit laden limb from a loquat tree.

Doctor Tradd never budged. He smiled and chuckled to himself as the General trotted off, sparks flying from the mules shoes.
"That, my boys, is why we reserve the pews at St. Michaels. It's reason enough to be Episcopalian."

Rosealee giggled from inside the house. "That's right. Ain't nobody gettin' into St. Michael's that ain't invited."

Jacob laughed with her until Ezekiel shouted them down. "Shut up damn it! We ain't been invited neither. Never will."

"That ain't true." Jacob whispered cautiously. "They been lettin' us sit up in the balcony."

Ezekiel snorted with contempt. "Slaves in the gallery, that's just fine."

Mother called me again. She was losing her patience so I hurried along after the horsemen and sat beside her in the hard pew at St. Mary's. The afternoon sun glowed through the ornate stained glass in a rainbow of lustrous blue, purple, green, and gold. The Rosary blended with soothing Latin that fell easily off the tongue. There was a funeral mass. My father's funeral. People I'd never seen patted my head and said, "Be brave young man, for your mother."

I could see the casket dropping into the freshly dug grave just out the window.

Ezekiel knelt beside me. "A big 'old boil 'a blood comin' right out his mouth 'till it filled up the horse trough. Purple stomach went thin an' white the day before he fell off the ferry." He repeated what he'd seen over and over until I could see it too, plain as day. Father with blood boiling out his mouth, skin mottled purple, eyes open and canary yellow. It wasn't the only reason I didn't like thinking of him. There was something about father and Rosealee.

She called to me. "It doesn't matter now. I seen the truth of it. I ain't mad no mo'." She giggled in my ear. "Fustest mostest."

Mother clung tightly to her rosary and my mind wandered. It was the best way to survive funerals, Stations of the Cross, and High Mass. Grandmother Marguerite helped too.

A pistol fired in the distance, and mother hurried me along. "Time to visit your grandmother. She's at it again. I wish Uncle Paul had never given her that gun."

All I knew was that she'd come back to life as the counterweight to old urine witch, Mamere. Like a Papal dispensation. We went to her tenement house on Longitude lane with the smell of rotten vegetables, dead shrimp, and sewage. Joseph Carr, the free black who lived on the first floor, sat on a crate and tied straw brooms. His hollow scarred eye sockets stared at me.

"Eyes poked out with a red hot awl. Street mob caught him looking wrong at a white girl." Mother had caught up with me and always said the same thing. "Sometimes just looking is a crime."

His eyes watered as he nodded. He didn't say a word. The alley was narrow and dark but Marguerite lived in light on the third floor above Mr. Carr and the deaf seamstress, Miss Lelly. The stairs creaked loudly and Marguerite yelled out. "Who's there?"

"Just us dear." Mother answered quickly, knowing Marguerite kept the revolver loaded by her bed and knowing she just might shoot through the door again.

"Sometimes she shoots randomly but mostly at the moon." Mother smiled. "It's her defiance you see. Marguerite believes in whiskey and pistol shooting. It's her way of laughing at God."

A loud shot rang out, then two more. Mother blessed herself, said an Our Father, and whispered. "With what she went through with father and all. Him taking ill after the hurricane of '36. You remember the story. It took the roof off and it did something to his mind. Went around with his head painted yellow for weeks then chased people down the alley with an axe." Mother always laughed telling it, but it seemed a bit forced. I'd heard the story a hundred times. "Made the Constable laugh too. Then they took him off to the insane asylum." She laughed for just a second then Marguerite fired through the door. We retreated down the stairs.

"Alright momma, alright momma," Mother chanted. "We'll just come back another time."

# IX

A cold shiver roused me. The breeze had picked up and the twins knelt beside me, staring and smiling. Mr. Clement whispered to Sir William but I heard every word.

"Rumor is the yanks got seven shooters for the whole army. New ones too. Even better than the Spencers."

"Doubtful." Sir William sighed.

"Called Henry's."

Sir William chuckled softly. "Henry and Spencer. Sounds like a couple of dandies."

A cloud line built up to the north thickening into a black mass that swirled within itself launching wispy tendrils and a thin rain. A crackling rifle fire started slowly but escalated into a steady roar that ebbed and flowed into the distance.

"Must got notion yonder", Sir William nodded picking at his remaining teeth with a straw.

Lady stretched and yawned, "Long as it's yonder."

"That's the problem alright", Mr. Clement laughed. "Never can tell when yonder comes a knockin'

"Nope. It's a fact. Cain't never." Sir William agreed.

The pent up clouds let loose, surging towards us as men emerged from the far woods. Yelling erupted down the line. "Watch your front!"

Mr. Clement stood up and yelled, "Don't shoot! Don't shoot! They're our pickets. They're fallin' back!"

Shells burst in the field in front bracketing the men. Our gunners answered with twelve pounders and I balled up against the logs as our picket line dropped to cover.

"That there's a waste a shells." Mr. Clement nodded toward the gunners, calm as ever. He lit his pipe and returned my stare. "Cause it ain't producin'. Never has. Gunners waste shells ever'day. Hoist a flag over yonder an' they'll blast away. Yanks'll do the same. Never hits shit. Maybe, ever' once in a while somebody gits his head blown off."

Both of us glanced at Anthony as his eyes darted up.

"Yep, ever' once in a while."

Our pickets pulled back across our line, and men from up and down the trench went forward to take their place. Mr. Clement picked up his rifle. "Snake, Lady, Conner . Our turn boys."

Snake bolted up. "Hell yes!"

Lady yawned and stretched. "Don't forgit the barter."

Macfadden dug in his blanket roll and tossed him a canvas pouch. Then aside to me, "Yanks'll trade food for tobacca'. All kinds of good eatin."

"Load your gun boy." Snake elbowed me.

Mr. Clement nodded, "But no caps just yet."

Snake rolled his eyes. "I forgit. New boy don't know shit."

Lady quickly laced his pants legs tight with twine, eye on me chuckling. "Don't let Snake git ya boy. Hey, Clement, let him come with me. I'll look out for Master Conner."

"How 'bout Master my ass." Snake bumped past me holding his rifle barrel under my nose.

Macfadden whispered something to Mr. Clement. He was still too weak, Sir William too old and slow, Peter was half-cocked and the twins might start whistling any second. Anthony was Anthony. No one wanted him to come. They didn't explain but it was understood.

Ezekiel sang out in the distance. "He ain't much but he's the best they got. If that ain't pitiful! Might as well open the latch an' let the

63

yanks come south. Ya'll really think y' gonna win with the likes a' Conner boy? His grand momma's right, he's wuthless as donkey shit."

He made me smile and it helped, sort of. I followed them over the logs and out across the field through trampled half grown corn. Dozens of men moved forward in a line spread out on both sides.

I looked back at the logs and the rifle barrels sticking up all which way. Bare heads, hats, feet propped up. It didn't look like much. Smoke drifted up from dozens of small fires up and down the line. Officers on horseback clustered at a point of small pines jutting out from the woods to the rear. Dispatch riders raced along the edge of the field disappearing into the far trees. The farther out in the field we went, the better the view. The works extended a half mile or so to the west into a clump of willow trees. To the southeast it crept through a stand of oaks and chestnuts and vanished over a rise. Far to the south a gun battery stood alone in a recess of pines and dogwoods with horses and caissons half hidden. Dust rose behind the far woods and slowly moved to the east. Smoke from cook fires filtered through the trees and formed little hazy layers over the field.

"Watch your front, Conner! Remember, Yank's ain't behind us." Mr. Clement spoke gently, but Snake laughed and walked backwards for a ways, making faces at me.

"I wouldn't take that off a' nobody," Ezekiel whispered.

"Neither would I," Mamere hissed. "I'd wait till he's asleep then stick a hot poker up his ass."

Ezekiel laughed, "That'll git 'im Mamere. You is some mean bitch."

Mamere whacked him with her snake stick. "Shut your mouth you black bastard."

I stared Snake down, but halfway across the field I suddenly felt naked. It must have shown.

"Pretty damn open out here ain't it Conner." Lady chuckled "Yanks might have a bead on your head."

"Quiet." Mr. Clement snapped. Snake and Lady whispered to each other and laughed. Ezekiel whispered in my ear. "Why you take that shit off 'em? Shouldn't be fightin fo' 'em no how."

I didn't say a word but Mamere laughed, "Cause you're a goddamn coward."

The last fifty yards seemed like a mile. My heart pounded when I crouched down in the trees beside the others. Mr. Clement told me to half cock and put on a percussion cap.

"Stay behind Lady." He whispered. "Just keep him in sight. Don't git lost." He poked me in the chest and winked. Snake and Mr. Clement spread out with the others and Lady and I pushed up through the woods. The oak, maple and hickory trees filtered out most of the sun. Creeper vines and saplings pulled at my legs. Lady made no noise at all above the faint rustling of the breeze. I made sure to follow just as quietly. He had to look around to make sure I was there. He smiled and I felt just a hint of pride.

Ezekiel just laughed louder. "You might be quiet but ya ain't invisible."

A gray soldier appeared about twenty yards off and my heart jumped. He nodded, crouched back towards us, then knelt down.

His gray eyes squinted into the shadows. "Nothin' movin'. Yanks 'bout seventy-five yards up. See the tall pine?"

Lady nodded. A chestnut branch stuck out of the soldier's brown, mud streaked shirt and another stuck out of his belt in back. He pulled them out and gave them to Lady. All the time ignoring me.

Lady stuck them in his shirt and belt and I broke two pine boughs for myself. The soldier vanished quickly, without a sound.

Lady whispered, "Don't talk. Don't say nothin'. Don't move unless I signal. Watch my hand."

He moved quickly forward through a thicket of oak saplings. I followed three steps behind, ducking my head as the saplings sprang back at my face. He signaled stop and I froze. He pointed to a clump of gum trees and I strained my eyes seeing nothing at first. Then a sudden movement focused my eyes squarely on a yank fifty yards away, his red face sandwiched between dark hat and beard. He turned his head back and forth looking off to our right. He hadn't seen us moving up and now we stood frozen in the thick woods. A breeze rustled through the leaves and a distant bugle sounded faint and tinny.

Lady shouted out, "Hey yank!"

My heart leapt to my throat like someone had yelled during mass. The yank dove for cover.

"Hey reb. What you want?" The yank's head rose up and looked around. Lady hadn't moved an inch and he still hadn't spotted us.

"We want somethin' to eat. What you got?"

"Got some cherry tins. Ham. Oysters. What you got?"

The yank pointed to our right and two more faces appeared next to him. One bald and hatless, easy to spot, the other bearded, head covered with a dark cloth.

"Tobacca. Fresh Carolina tobacca," Lady called back, "Best ever."

They kept looking to the right, still not seeing us.

"All right. We'll trade. Don't be shootin' at us. We got rifles ready."

Lady raised his hand. All three faces snapped towards us.

"Don't y'all be shootin' at us." Lady had his rifle pointed at them beneath the branches.

The bald yank stood up and held his rifle across his chest. "Come on out Reb. We ain't in a fightin' mood. Show yourself."

Lady stood up and I followed, rising up to full view and ready to duck at first flash. The three yanks come forward slowly into a little clearing around a fallen pine scorched by a lightning strike.

"Watchout Conner," Ezekiel laughed. "Sometimes lightnin' *do* strike twice."

My heart already raced and a burst of rifle fire in the distance didn't help. An old bald yank held a burlap sack. The other two looked much younger. One had a large piece of black felt over his head tied tightly with a piece of string. All three wore brand new blue uniforms and bayonets in shiny black leather scabbards. Lady pulled out the tobacco and knelt as they bartered a while, the yank using the pine to display his wares. I stared at the other two yanks' hands the whole time, expecting a fight any second. Lady opened his shirt for all to see.

"Don't want y'all thinkin' I'm holdin' out on ya." He stuffed tins of ham, cherries and oysters inside and buttoned up as the rifle fire crept closer and closer.

The bald man smiled. "Like I said, we ain't in a fightin' mood today, Reb."

Just as he said it, I saw movement in the woods and two more yanks stood up thirty yards to our right. Both carried rifles with bayonets.

Lady stood up smiling, stretched and yawned. "You boys gonna share that tobacca?"

He held his rifle out full length in one hand, arm muscles bulging for their benefit.

The other two came forward, both clean-shaven and sharply dressed in their new uniforms. One with bright blue eyes nervously darting back and forth, the other calm, staring straight at me. He grinned, raised his rifle barrel up just an inch or two, touched his bayonet, and then whispered something to the nervous one. I stared back, winked and tapped my hunting knife. Just pure bluff, but it might have bothered him a bit. My heart stayed put in my mouth as the rifle fire closed in.

"Watch out Conner, that boy is bad." Rosealee pleaded from up above us in the trees.

Lady stepped forward and called out loudly, "Gimme a look see at that there blade."

Blue eyes jumped backwards, tripped over a rotten log and fell down on his rear.

"Hold on there boy. I ain't gonna kiss ya. Don't git all riled." Lady stood in a patch of sunlight that filtered through the trees, "Jus' tryin' to be friendly an all." The shadows danced over his smiling face.

The bald yank smiled back and threw the burlap sack over his shoulder. "You boys best git before we change our minds. Officers might say we're fraternizin'."

Lady nodded. "Yep. Don't wanna hafta shoot y'all, bein' we're friends 'n all." He backed off, rifle ready, and I did the same.

The yanks stood their ground and the one with the felt cloth whispered something. We made it about twenty yards into the oak saplings when a rifle shot exploded close by and Lady snatched me down. The yanks volleyed and tree bark splintered above my head. Lady fired back through the creeper vines and hit bald head square in the chest. He fell straight back like a cut tree. I fired high then we ran for it. Another volley chased us behind a thick oak and Mr. Clement and Snake came up fast.

"Yanks might be comin'." Lady caught his breath and reloaded. "Killt the one tried to shoot Conner here. Four of 'em left and they ain't happy." He opened his shirt to show the tins.

Snake stood up and yelled. "C'mon over Billy. Still the four of ya. Ain't so bad."

He crouched down and grabbed at the tins. His rifle butt rested on a skeleton half hidden in the leaves, all mummified in rotten brown cloth with a tarnished brass CSA buckle. Snaked brushed away the leaves. A skull stared up at me with empty eye sockets, a hole in the forehead, and two rows of bare teeth. "Last year's unburied dead."

I smelled incense and heard Father Reilly chanting. "May his soul rest in peace and may Conner's bones not rot in the leaves."

The congregation murmured in response. "Ora Pro Nobis."

Mr. Clement covered him up with a pine bough as a yank yelled in the distance.

"...Rebel bastards...carve your balls..." The rest was muffled by rifle fire.

More of our pickets came up dropping into a fighting line, but the yanks never came.

"They's jus funnin'," Snake laughed, "Yank pickets ain't never been much fo' fightin'."

Jacob laughed from behind the thicket, "Like Mr. Conner has. I could wup im with my string arm." He hummed the Halleluiah song in my ear all the way back to the line where I wedged myself gladly behind dirt packed logs while Mr. Clement cut open the tins. Lady embellished the story while everyone ate.

"Conner insulted them boys. Riled 'em good. Tole 'em he ain't never met a yank wasn't ugly as a dead lizard. Tole 'em he'd whip their ass they so much as grinned. Had 'em shittin!"

No one paid him any mind except the twins who sat beside me one on each side as usual. They patted my back like I'd done something special. Everyone else focused on the tins. They were all empty in a minute or two. Macfadden lit his pipe and shared it with me. The bald yank's face gradually disappeared and I sunk into the ground.

"One yank worth a treats." Snaked sucked down the last of the oyster juice. "We got to trade reg'lar. A man can git used to a tin ever' day. 'Member that tin a' lamb we got after Fred'ricksburg?" No one answered but Snake lay back content and smiling "Y'all said it tasted like shit. Ain't con'sors like me."

"Conn-a-sore," Sir William added. "Like dinosaur."

The breeze died with the last of the sun then crickets began to roar. Lightning bugs celebrated with a silent barrage over the field. They swarmed everywhere. Landing on Mr. Clement's hat, on Anthony's shoes, Peter's head-sleeve, and Sir William's crow feather. Polecat caught one after another entombing them in his clay jug. Lucas caught dozens in his cup, playing with them in the dirt. Gordon let them climb slowly up his thumb, gently launching them light blinking into the twilight. Snake grabbed and ate as many as he could, crunching them live and wiggling between his teeth then sucking them down until the twins jumped up and boxed him in. Mr. Clement kept Snake in line and the twins sat back down and played. Everyone else had a good laugh.

I closed my eyes and the ground rolled like I was at sea.

# X

Charleston harbor.

Taut halyards tapped against the sloop *Aleta's* mast. The breeze was rising, the clouds rolling in low over the James Island shore. The sun darted in and out, quickly mirrored a thousand times across the harbor chop. We plowed by the anchored *Chicora*, a giant gray and black armadillo of railroad iron and oak timbers. Heavy guns loomed out of open ports. The crew grappled crates, boxes and iron-ringed barrels from two work-sloops and two skiffs to port.

Off to starboard squat *Palmetto State* billowed smoke, water lapping right up to the thick iron gun ports. Behind her, long and sleek, *Charleston* did the same, her gray and black funnel flying the red battle flag, gun ports open and rifled cannon run out and ready.

A shell hit the water between them followed by another to port. Geysers of spray towered above them, motionless for a second or two. The skiffs pulled away quickly as another shell landed astern. Elliott stood behind me at the tiller and unlimbered his privates as the rumble of guns echoed across the harbor. "A canister of cow shit!" He waved himself at the yanks. "Twelve pounds in your face!"

The rising wind tangled his black hair into knots as he pranced about the stern thrusting and howling like a total fool. It picked up until the main sail strained hard against the boom, and the jib snapped full against the sheets. Elliott braced against the tiller holding us fast and steady through plunging spray towards Fort Sumter where he came about in the lee shallows. I jumped over and stood hip deep in a rising tide on the mud flat, luffed gray canvas sails flapping noisily above my head. My eyes squinted into slits from the noon sun burning through the thinning clouds. Heat radiated off the red brick walls of the fort rising high above the waterline to a halo of blue sky above. The *Aleta* lay low and heavy, anchor line straining against the incoming tide pouring into Charleston harbor through the narrow mouth between Sumter and Sullivan's Island. The cargo quickly disappeared into the fort on the backs of sweat-drenched soldiers who emerged from crevices in the rubble like ants carrying food to the mound. Fresh water barrels, black powder kegs, boxes of rifle cartridges and percussion caps, crates of dried peas, sweat potatoes, salt port, and hardened corn bread. Carried across the mud flat studded with oyster beds and strewn with bricks and burned timbers, past old pilings eaten down to thin sticks by sea worms, into the shattered ruins and brick piles of the fort, all topped with layers of sandbags like sugar topping on a cake and wrapped with telegraph wire and rows of sharpened stakes.

Twice everyone flattened in the mud as volleys of shells rained brick fragments like a hailstorm. A chunk big enough to take off a man's head, flew right over Elliott. He didn't so much as flinch. Still sprawled against the transom, arm draped over the tiller, feet propped over the bulkhead. Nothing much bothered him, and he had no intention of helping with cargo. He prided himself in dodging yank shells and coming about just right, into the only protected spot in the lee of the fort. He'd done his job. The rest was menial work, clearly beneath the great Captain Elliott Tradd.

He laughed at me, "As they say on the CSS ALABAMA, 'Captain Raphael Semmes never sweats cargo.' Well neither do I."

I ignored him, grabbed the rope handle of a forty-pound cartridge box and pulled it over the side onto my shoulder. More explosions hit the fort. Chunks of brick wall flew past. The mast exploded backwards like a spear, throwing me under water quick as a mullet. Then stillness.

The mast and sails had disappeared. Half the boom stuck through the solid oak transom dangling remnants of shredded canvas. Blood splattered everywhere. A crimson geyser shot up from Elliott's elbow over the boom. His fore-arm was gone. The elbow was just a white bone jutting out from red torn muscle.

"Jesus Elliot! What the...?" I coughed up seawater watching the crimson splatter everywhere. Elliot picked up what looked like a blood covered crab and stared at me.

"Some fool might even blame some one." Then he jumped over the side, waded ashore, and trotted up the brick pile like nothing had happened.

I followed as quickly as I could through the rubble, the climb hard enough even with two hands. We found Uncle Paul inside the fort. It didn't even surprise me. He sat in the door of a sandbagged bombproof, behind a wheelbarrow loaded with a cigar shaped torpedo-mine covered with tarred canvas. His long gray coat covered with mud, his head freshly shaved bald.

"You boys been there ain't ya'? Y'all seen what they done."

"The boy sees what he wants!" Mamere yelled from outside the fort. Shells drowned her out. They landed in the shallows and sprayed the fort with salt water.

Uncle stared past Elliott who dropped his bloody severed hand on the dirt floor. Uncle's eyes quivered sideways.

"You're a Tradd ain't ya." He wagged his finger forcefully like he'd caught him red handed

"Uncle Paul! For God's sake! Elliott's hurt bad! His arm is..."

Uncle Paul waved me off. "Quiet Conner! Let the boy talk. You a Tradd ?"

Elliott leaned away and groaned. "Yes, sir."

"You Doc Tradd's boy?" Uncle frowned.

"Yes, sir." Elliott grit his teeth and squirmed.

"Of course he is! Uncle Paul, you know Elliott! But he's hurt bad…"

"Shut up Conner. The boy sounds jus' like his dad. Been tole' that?"

"Yes, sir." His eyes welled up.

"Don't worry son. I got nothing but respect for your father. Worked miracles on Conner's daddy back in '54. Seen the whole thing."

"Bullshit!" Mamere screamed like a gull. "Dreamin' ain't the same as seein', you lyin' ass."

"Alright Mamere." He laughed. "Y'see boys, Conner's daddy got drunk. Fell an' hit his head on the cistern. Went paralyzed on one side. Damn if Doc Tradd don't drill a hole on the good side. Used a carpenter's drill. Got the tip red hot over the fire then burred it right through, sizzlin' all the way. Not somethin' I'm likely to forgit, for damn sure."

"Uncle Paul, please! Elliott's…"

"Not another word!" He growled back.

Elliot floated into the air dripping blood into the wheelbarrow, but Uncle ignored him. "Tell ya the truth, thought yo' father was crazy. Thought he'd lost his mind fo' sure, that drill stickin' outta Perry's head an all. But damn if it didn't work." He slapped his thigh and laughed. "That limp side started movin' and Perry walked… walked outta that damn hospital a week later. Mind you, he weren't ever exactly right. But hell, he never was." Uncle laughed. "Your father gave Perry his life back. For one last year." He pointed up towards Elliott who hovered higher and higher like a pelican about to dive. "You see, I'd already known y'father before…"

"You've known him all your life, Uncle Paul! Elliott needs…"

"Goddamit shut up Conner!" He threw a brick fragment just past my head. "Next time I won't miss." He picked up another brick and played with it while he talked, "My baby girl had the scarlet fever." He winced like he'd had a boil lanced. "Stayed up with her all night but she died right before dawn."

"We *all* stayed up that night." Mamere coughed and spat, invisible in a dark corner.

Uncle paused and wiped his mustache. "Lord wouldn't save her. Don't know why."

Elliott soared like a kite, his bloody shirt billowing in the breeze.

"My wife couldn't take it. Only child. Shot herself with my pistol. Right here." He put his finger into his mouth and Elliott blessed himself in midair. "Your father tried…but I knew right off… the back of her head…"

He rubbed his head and sighed. "Got to admit I'd rather the Lord seen fit to save Helen and Sarah 'stead of my brother, Perry, damn his hide. Tole' him to 'is face. Hell he agreed right off. Perry never gave a shit."

He threw an empty bottle in the air and it exploded. Shards of glass embedded in the exposed bone of Elliott's forearm.

I bolted awake. Fort Sumter, Elliott and Uncle Paul disappeared. Explosions echoed across the dark Virginia field. Our guns had opened up, four hundred yards or so behind us at the edge of some dogwoods. The gunners barely visible in the twilight even in their bright red shirts. I followed the shells over the far woods, and they must have hit a hornet's nest. A dozen yank shells came back at us, landing harmlessly in the field and one skipping over trench fifty yards to the right. Mr. Clement pulled at my elbow.

"Sit down Conner."

I realized I was standing straight up on the logs exposed to the world.

"Daydreamin' can git a man killed."

I hopped to cover and everyone had a good laugh. The twins whistled and hummed and patted my back. Lucas carved his name in the head log.

"Lucas." He spoke out loud and everyone looked up. "It's the truth," he whispered.

His brother agreed whispering back. "That's your name alright."

He carved his too then they both stared at me. Peter carved his name next to theirs then my knife came out by its own will and carved mine.

"It's the damn truth," I put my knife away and the twins whistled their approval. I lay back against the logs and wanted very badly to see the stars but there was just the darkness and a thin, prickly drizzle.

Jacob whispered to me, "Carve my name Conner. I ain't got no knife."

I did as he said and the twins hummed for a long time. I don't know how long they let me sleep.

# XI

Snake nudged me. "Wake up. Come with me. We got picket agin. Don't ask why."

His hand grabbed my mouth.

"Just come on," he whispered harshly. Bring yo' rifle."

Everyone else was asleep except Polecat, busy relieving himself behind the trench. I followed Snake over the logs and back across the dark wet field to the same patch of woods. Snake was an old hand, so I told myself he must know what he was doing.

"Christ almighty, you're dumb as shit." Ezekiel stung my ear with his finger. "Go ahead, follow the man, ass hole. See what it gits ya."

I knew better than to let on and we slipped beneath the branches into the black woods like ghosts. I followed as best I could until Snake pulled me down.

"Pickets."

I saw nothing but dark shapes and deeper blackness. His fist gripped my shirt. We waited for a long while, his face only faintly visible even up close, then he dragged me forward through a tight tangle of wet saplings. I made too much noise, but Snake pulled me along maybe another one hundred yards or so. In mid step his hand pressed over my mouth and he turned my head to the right and whispered. "There."

He let go and slipped away into the blackness as it began to drizzle harder. I dropped down into soaked leaves and pine straw and didn't dare budge.

Rosealee cried quietly nearby. "I'm scared Conner. I wanna go home. Please take me home."

A light breeze rustled the trees and distant wagons rumbled over a plank bridge far away. Then very close, the tin clinking of a cup or canteen and the snap of a branch. Someone coughed maybe twenty yards away but it sounded closer.

"Who's that?" A man whispered. "Who's there?" His voice cracked, then something bolted through the saplings. Legs smashed into my shoulder and bodies thrashed close by in the pitch black. Then sudden stillness. Just a faint gurgling like water boiling, then a crunching sound.

"That boy sure got his surprise." Snake whispered close to me.

I could just make him out, kneeling over something in the leaves and working with his hands. He pulled back and held something close to my face.

"See this here. Can y'see?"

"What is it?" I held my knife ready, not knowing what Snake might do. I could hear him panting, catching his breath, as he fumbled for something. Then a match struck close to the ground and for an instant of brilliant clarity I saw what he had done. Snake's fist clutched a mat of black hair. A yank's severed head. The headless blue-clad body lay in the leaves, neck still pulsing blood. Snake smiled.

"See here. This here's how it's done. Something precious Conner!" He wiped off his knife. His eyes flickered yellow in the match-light "More precious dead than alive. A man can savor what he's killed."

The match went out and a canopy of darkness descended deeper than ever, like despair come to smother me. Snake fumbled with the corpse.

"Got to put his head on backwards. That'll git 'em. Mess with Carolina boys an' this here's what ya git. Remember Conner, a buzzard don't land fo' no reason. When he sets down, somethin's daid."

He became still and quiet and I wondered if my eyes had played tricks, then he pulled me back quickly through the woods until we came to the edge of the field where we waited. I held my rifle ready.

"Why?" I caught by breath.

"Cause a what they done to Reeves. Cain't let that go." Snake wiped his blade with a handful of leaves.

"But why bring me?"

"Cause you got to learn, shit hole. Someday it'll be up to you." He laughed quietly. "Don't say nothin' to nobody boy. You hear me. Wouldn't be somethin' I'd forgit."

He held up his blade and pretended to lick it clean, then slid it into his belt.

Jacob and Rosealee chanted softly in the darkness, "Don't say nothin' 'bout the buzzard, an' de' buzzard won't be landin' on you."

Ezekiel cursed them, "Shut up damn it. The buzzard lands where he damn well pleases."

I knew I'd never say a word. It was murder pure and simple. Damn if I'd tell anybody. We crossed the field silently and climbed back over the logs without being noticed. I quickly wrapped myself up in a soggy blanket, gladly listening to the chorus of snores and trying to believe it never happened. The earth itself spoke in my ear.

"Just sleep while you can. Hold tight to the ground."

Jacob and Rosealee hummed spirituals for a while then Rosealee whispered to me. "I don't like that backwards head, Conner. Not one bit. Don't let 'im do that agin. Please?"

Ezekiel kicked my foot. "Told you, didn't I. Christ you is dumb. Dumber than a roly-poly."

Jacob giggled. "Roly poly Conner. Got a hundred feet all movin fast an' goin' nowhere."

# XII

First light brought us rain but no breakfast. Heavy rifle fire ebbed and flowed in the distance, but no one seemed to care. The earth had turned completely to mud in the night. It clung to all of us like a soggy hide, weighing us down. Mud- covered jackets, trousers and blankets blended into the earth. Sleeping men seemed invisible. Only movement gave them away.

Rosealee whispered in my ear. "Cover y'sef Conner. Dat mud's y'friend. It be tryin' to hide ya."

"It'll be alright." I whispered back.

The twins smiled at me and nodded. Both had socks stuffed into their rifle barrels and whistled as they groomed each other with the bowie knives. Peter stood above them, silently on guard. Everyone else seemed to be grumbling and the brigade was on the move. Getting up wet and hungry didn't help. Everyone was soaked. Up and down the water logged trench men did their best to keep rifles and cartridge boxes dry; but the worst part was giving up what we'd dug with our own hands.

"I ain't budgin!" Snake squatted down in the mud. "Ya'll go if you want. I'm stayin' put, Major Asshole can drag me off."

Mr. Clement wrapped his soggy blanket roll and shouldered his rifle. "Better we dig the second hole than fight in the first."

The rifle fire continued to grow louder.

"Hell no!" Snake propped his feet on the logs. "They can court marshal my ass if they want."

Mr. Clement laughed, "They can shoot yo ass if they want. Stop gripin! Major Clyburn might just have a burr up his'n."

"Hell you say. They'll be shootin' the bunch of us. The Major can go to hell."

Sir William sighed as he gathered his roll and rifle. "If we dig enough holes, we're bound to catch us a yank rabbit or two." He didn't seem the least perturbed and I tried to fake the same.

Ezekiel laughed loud enough for everyone to hear. "He's scared shitless. Look at 'im tremble. Yanks gonna git ya Conner. Gonna git ya and chop you up."

Snake cursed the whole time and screamed once in Anthony's face. He was the last to follow along as we took to the road leaving our wall of dirt and logs behind. It hit me like a wave of homesickness. Anthony teared up.

"We built that wall. We build it. It's ours. They can't make us leave. It ain't fair. It ain't right."

Mr. Clement tried to shush him up for his own good but he wouldn't stop crying. Macfadden and Lady whispered and had a good laugh.

"Leave him be, damn it," Uncle Paul yelled from out in the cornfield. "Can't be helped if he's a coward. Conner's the one I'm worried about."

"I'm worried f' you too Conner," Rosealee whispered.

"Don't mess with his mind Rosealee!" Uncle screamed. "The boy's got to focus."

"Focus pocus" Jacob laughed. "Conner ain't never been much on dat."

"Quiet, damn it!" Mamere screamed.

Rosealee giggled. "Alright Mamere. We be real quiet 'cause we love you so much."

Jacob nearly choked. "Yep dat's it."

I ignored them as best I could. The snaking column hurried along toward the canvas-tearing and the barking twelve pounders. I hoped like hell we'd have time to dig the next hole. My stomach growled and my eyes searched the side of the road and the edges of the corn fields, but every stunted, half ripe ear of corn was already gone. The firing grew louder and closer and smoke rose above the line of woods to the west. A spent mini ball hit Anthony in the head and he jumped sideways like a startled rabbit.

"You ain't delicate is ya? Better git it in the head than git ya balls shot off." Lady grabbed his crotch and walked backwards poking Anthony in the chest. "Better daid than spayed."

Polecat followed behind wearing a cook pot on his head like a Viking helmet with the thick wooden handle sticking out front as the single horn.

"Best git you a pot my boy. Them spent balls is bad on the scalp. Yanks like head shots too. Justa' waste a' time for 'em with the pot though. Nothin' worse than a headthrobbin."

We passed a shattered artillery caisson. Dead horses crawling with flies and maggots thrust their putrefied legs in the air. The stench helped quell my hunger. Shells burst in the woods across the narrowing field. The gray sky hung low with clouds and prickly drizzle. Ground fog veiled parts of the field. The drizzle soon gave way to a steady shower and the canvas tearing sputtered into pops and crackles then died out completely as if muffled by the rain.

I checked my cartridge box under my jacket. Thank God it was still dry. At the edge of a stand of hickory trees, we passed freshly dug graves. Six in a row. I counted them twice. Each one filling up fast with muddy water and waiting on a row of stiff, blue skinned corpses. Each with an arched back, legs and arms flexed, and abdomen bloated with gas. One had already burst open, dripping black liquid and boiling with maggots. One hand twitched and pointed to me.

"Go back." The open fish-mouth didn't move but I heard it distinctly. The finger twitched again and followed me.

"Go back."

"Christ almighty," I whispered to Macfadden. "You hear that?"

He just elbowed me and shook his head. I looked back and Elliott's hand sank into the grave.

"Go back." The corpse looked straight at me.

"Jesus." I stumbled into Lady. Rifle fire drowned out the voice.

"Shit Conner. You havin' some kinda fit or somethin'. Stop ya damn fidgetin'." He kicked at me and it helped. The rain washed my face and Macfadden grabbed my elbow.

"Don't be talkin' crazy on me. Wait till all this here's over."

"Don't wait Conner," Rosealee pleaded. "Got to listen to a dead man. They's the ones dat make de' most sense."

The roar of rifle fire crept closer and closer. It sounded like a dozen trains rumbling in circles.

"That there's Gettysburg! You hear that!" Mr. Clement held his rifle over his head, jumped up and down and screamed. "They'll be comin'! C'mon you bastards!" He screamed until his lungs should have burst, and all down the muddy road men took up the yelling.

"Will they come right at us?" Anthony whimpered.

Lady blew his nose in the mud. "No Squirrel. They be comin' straight at *you*."

"Yanks! Yanks!" Men pointed through a gap in the tree line to a clearing shrouded with misty rain. On a little rise about a mile away a line of little dark shapes moved slowly from right to left. They didn't look like much but my chest felt tight. The rifle fire hadn't let up and there was no doubt we were in for it.

83

A battery of howitzers fired volleys from just off the road. Their wheels bogged down in the mud, jumping clear with each shot. Shirtless gunners struggled knee deep with heavy shells that disappeared over the tree line. The yanks opened up in return. Shells exploded across the churned field to the right and in the pinewoods to our left.

We plodded through smoky ground fog layered across a wide, mud churned hay field. The rain let loose and shells whistled overhead. Anthony shook so badly he could scarcely hold his rifle. Powder smoke mixed with the drizzle as volley after volley erupted close by. The mud sucked my shoes off and grabbed at my legs as men pressed forward. We ran into a muddy stream and men bunched up trying to scramble up the bank. Shells whined all around. Macfadden puffed and gasped for air as we ran up a gradual rise through calf deep mud. The mist thinned and a tree line reappeared to the right. Dead ahead, a low dark line of works stretched from the oaks and pines across most of the field. Gray brown troops lined the trench. They kept their heads down as minie balls and shells searched for us in the rain. We took cover behind the log wall just as a shell exploded right on top. Several men went down, the mud beneath them quickly turning crimson. One man's head disappeared. A mess of red and gray brain floating down over his neck. Arteries pulsed blood for a few last seconds. I looked up and saw a dark sphere and flattened in the mud. A solid shot clipped the head log and ploughed into the mud behind them, whirling itself out of sight faster than a mole. Two more explosions to the left had everyone hugging the works.

"Holy Mother of God, Conner!" Mr. Clement yelled. "You attractin' artillery?" His face was pressed tightly to the logs.

"Blessed art thou amongst women." My mother whispered in my ear.

"Never had no solid shot come that close!" He howled two feet from my face. "Not at Sharpsburg! Not at Gettysburg!"

"Blessed is the fruit of thy womb, Jesus." Mother knelt behind me dressed in black, her fingers working gold rosary beads.

Macfadden peeked over the wall. "Jesus Lord. Hell's goin' on up yonder."

"Pray for us, sinners. Now and at the hour of our death. Amen." Mother's voice turned into mine and she was gone.

Anthony stared at me terrified. "Why'd you say that?"

Sir William calmly wiped his face with his sleeve. "Don't be getting all red in the face, Squirrel. If it's your time, ain't nothin' to do 'bout it."

"I can hide," Anthony whispered just loud enough for me to hear.

"Conner keep y'head down." Mr. Clement pulled me down, and more shells exploded behind us. Someone yelled from inside my head.

"The bastards missed their one good chance!" It sounded like Dr. Tradd, but muffled through a hollow log. "You saw the damn shell! You know damn well what to do!"

"What? Do what?" I looked around as dozens of men jumped back over the works and sprawled behind us in the mud. Most had no rifles. A balding man fell on his side panting for breath and scooping up mouthfuls of muddy water that dribbled down his gray beard. He curled up barefoot, weaponless, covered in mud and muttering to himself terrified.

"They killed 'em. Shot 'em down. Hands up, white flag an all. Yanks is savages, I tell ya. Savages."

He glanced up at me and twirled his beard nervously. "Yanks be comin' son. Thousands of 'em just up yonder. Not half a mile." More shells crashed in and everyone kissed the earth. "They come out the woods like a wave. All over us 'fore we knew it. Befo' dawn. Ran like hell. Ain't seen my boys since." He panted for air. "Got t' run some mo, I bet"

I peeped over the logs and saw nothing but smoke and mist.

85

"Maybe he's just a coward like Anthony." Uncle laughed. "Make him admit he's lying."

The old man kept on. "They got thousands! Inside our work! I tell ya they's inside. Thousands! Ain't nothin' stoppin' 'em. Not today."

He couldn't catch his breath and sunk flat on his back in the mud.

Mr. Clement grabbed my arm. "Time to go." He stood straight up on top of the logs and screamed out, "Let's go boys! We ain't stoppin'! Let's go! Git movin!"

He yelled it over and over and started grabbing and pulling up crouching soldiers. Other men took up his yell behind the works. A twelve pounder fired over the logs and from a recessed battery. The gunners blackened hands pulled powder bags from underneath a board lean-to.

"Git up! Git movin!" Mr. Clement screamed. Most still hadn't budged. "Damn it boys, move! Everyone forward!"

Anthony cried, terrified. "Not past the wall. Not past the wall."

Mr. Clement fired his rifle in the air. "Follow me! We're goin up!" He jumped forward off the logs and a spring released. Dozens of men jumped over behind him. Sir William and Snake went with them, then Macfadden and Lady. The twins waited on me, gobbling beside me like agitated turkeys. Peter waited on them, moaning like he was in pain. The old man held up his hand as I climbed over the logs.

"Ya'll are dead men." He lay back down in the mud and so did Anthony. He flattened himself on his belly, covered up his head with his hands and refused to budge. We left him there and I could hear Mamere snickering, but she was the last of my worries. On the far side of the wall, the muddy field rose gently into the mist. We moved forward past a group of dismounted officers crouched around a young general with a mustache, wide-brimmed gray hat, and gold sash. He stood up, a bit wobbly, and waved his sword.

"Whose troops are those?" He called out, his words slurred.

"McGowan's South Carolina!"

It felt good to yell out. Maybe the yanks would think twice.

The general yelled back, "No better soldiers in the world!"

"Drunk crock of shit!" Ezekiel yelled from out in front.

Macfadden poked me. "That's General Rodes. By God his North Carolina boys'll give 'em hell."

I saw no other brigade, but everyone cheered some more and the rush of blood helped. The closer we came to the top of the little rise in the field the louder the firing and the closer the whining of lead in the air. Smoke rose from the far woods as balls whistled past and men fell to the ground. My hat flew off and Polecat fell backwards behind me. His neck erupted into a gushing crimson geyser. Blood pulsed from his mouth and torn throat. In a second he lay still. One hand still clung tightly to his rifle and one leg contorted underneath. His pot helmet sat upright in the mud ready to catch the rain. His clay jug was crushed, seeping a black stew of worms, slugs, horseflies and lightning bugs. A sturdy brown moth twitched convulsively in the slime.

Sir William knelt beside him trying to stop the bleeding but too late. Mr. Clement stared straight ahead stone faced as Snake and Lady yelled and pointed to the trees.

"God damn bastards. Lets git 'em. Git to the trees!"

I felt a burning like I'd gulped a large whiskey and strange things started to happen. Macfadden leaned towards me and yelled something, pointing his ramrod at the trees. I saw a distinct flash of blue flame beside an oak tree about fifty yards away. Silhouetted against the plume of powder smoke was a little black dot that passed slowly between me and Macfadden and just over Sir William, still kneeling beside Polecat. The line surged forward with a yell, across a wagon track and downhill to the edge of the woods. Another dot slowly passed Snake's head.

Everyone started running, and we left Polecat's body in the mud. Something told me that if I looked back, I'd join him.

We ran past a battered farmhouse at the edge of the thick woods. A broken sign post read 'McCoull.' Bullets tore through the shivering plank walls and the charred remnants of a barn next to a crumbling brick arch and chimney. Smashed beams stuck upright in the mud like the bare ribs of a giant carcass. Gray soldiers swarmed the ruins firing back at the yanks in the tree line.

More men went down. Benjamin too. On all fours in the black mud with his jaw blown off, cawing up a red slush. Jagged bone jutted out of his neck like insect pincers.

Jacob yelled in my ear, "I seen a crow with his neck torn off. Piece of meat hung out, but didn't much bother the bird."

Benjamin's green lizard hung obediently from his earlobe. Peter grabbed his Spencer and tubes and disappeared with the twins in the smoke. Blue jackets covered the far works and muzzles flashed continuously.

"The old man was right." Ezekiel laughed. "The yanks done broke through. Give it up Conner."

Men fell all around. Mr. Clement bled from his mouth and nose but never stopped yelling. Neither did I. A volley exploded from the woods and a dozen more men went down. I fired and the rifle smacked my shoulder. No time to reload. I covered the forty yards down to the trees in seconds, splashing a cross a little stream. Hundreds of others did the same. We pushed forward through an oak tangle taking cover behind larger trees where we could.

Sir William ran up and fired from behind a stump. He knelt down to reload and yelled something inaudible in the roar. The back of his head burst open and his left eye disappeared.

"William!" Macfadden screamed as blood pored across Sir Williams's face and his body fell backwards into the leaves. Mr. Clement jumped to his side and pulled him against the stump.

"Get up! Get up damn it! No, no, no…" He stood up with his back to the yanks and pulled Sir William up by the collar. "Stand up! Stand up!"

Macfadden knocked him down just as the stump exploded. It was a miracle they weren't hit. Mr. Clement sat stunned against the stump and Snake and Lady were nowhere to be seen. Macfadden crawled back to retrieve Sir William's bandana and crow feather. Mr.Clement gently laid them over his face and straightened his body in the leaves. Macfadden fired over him and ran forward, "Damn you bastards!"

It began to pour. I fired and reloaded, trying to keep my paper cartridges dry and pressing percussion caps on by feel. All the while scanning for targets, and there were plenty.

Bullets whacked into my oak and I knew I had to follow Macfadden. Sir William would have. We fired tree to tree and leap-frogged forward up and down little ridges and gullies to a muddy spring behind some chestnut stumps that gave good protection on three sides. Peter and the twins already knelt there, Gordon fired as Lucas crouched to reload. Peter fired over his head. All were smiling, playing the same game.

Macfadden and I volleyed with them then Gordon grunted and fell backwards into the water. A round red hole appeared in his forehead and another in his neck. His eyes were wide open and he still smiled.

"Gordy?" Lucas shook his limp shoulder. "No Gordy. No Gordy."

I fired again at the blue hats moving through the smoke. Lucas looked up at me and started crying. He tried to say something then stood up and ran forward firing from his hip. He made it ten yards. A volley knocked him down and in a second he lay motionless on the ground. I grabbed Peter's shirt and pulled him back. The stumps exploded bark and we fired back knocking down two yanks in the open. Muzzles flashed everywhere. Smoke clouds drifted through the trees. I yelled at the top of my lungs, "God damn bastards! Bastards."

Father Reilly chanted in my ear "You're the messenger of death. Just say the word and they shall be killed."

I could hear Mamere laughing in the distance. Uncle Paul yelled at me, "Pay attention, damn it!"

Our boys fanned out in the trees right and left and our gully seemed like a pivot for the whole line. To me it centered the universe. It belonged to Sir William and the twins. To hell with the yank bastards. A line of blue jackets came towards us from out of the smoke. The stump splintered and a yank came at me. Smoking barrel and bayonet leveled at my chest. I fired and he dropped just in front.

A yank pinned Macfadden on his back. A big, fat yank choking him with his rifle barrel. Peter swung his rifle at another yank jabbing at him with a bayonet. It all happened in an instant. I smashed my rifle down on the fat yank's neck and felt his spine crack. My knife appeared and I drove it with two hands deep into his back. The other yank stabbed Peter in the stomach and then half the yank's head disappeared in a crimson explosion. Peter's Spencer rifle splintered in mid air. He curled on his side holding his gut and crying, "Jesus Lord. Jesus Lord."

He kicked his torn pants back and forth in the mud for a while. Then he grew still.

Mr. Clement jumped in beside me and pulled me down just as another volley raked the gully. He handed me a rifle and grabbed my face. "Keep down and stop yellin'."

I awakened from a trance.

Dr. Tradd called out far in the distance. "Don't kill more than you need, Conner. You should have let Peter go."

90

Mr. Clement stared at me, face and lips swollen, two front teeth broken off. Blood dripped from his mouth.

Jacob yelled to me, "Watch out Conner. Lion's kill fo' fun."

"We'll git a mess of em for William! Or God damn my soul." His knuckles whitened around his knife hilt. His jaw muscles hardened taut.

Macfadden propped himself up. His forehead bled badly. "Bastards killed Peter and the twins."

Mr. Clement glanced at Lucas and Peter in the mud but said nothing.

Father Reilly whispered in the trees. "Say but the word and they're souls shall be healed."

"Maybe so but they's still dead as hell." Ezekiel whispered back choking and laughing.

"Shush your mouth Ezekiel." Uncle whacked his cane against the stump.

Another gray jacket joined us. Mr. Clement had me reload all the rifles and the stranger thanked me for one.

"Names Marshall. First S.C."

"You with Chisholm Mackey?" Mr. Clement asked quickly.

"Was." He answered matter of factly. "Dead back yonder." He pointed over his shoulder with this thumb.

Mr. Clement jerked his head down. "Shit!"

Marshall nodded. "Shit it is."

Layers of smoke darkened the trees. The rain continued steadily. Brown shirts moved to the left. Bullets cut into our stumps and whined overhead. I lay flat, nearly invisible in the bog with two loaded rifles, one with a bayonet.

"Stay down Conner" Rosealee pleaded. "Don't git y'sef shot."

Mr. Clement's hat flew off and the yanks charged again. Thirty or forty yanks came out of the thicket through the smoke and met a volley head on. Half went down. The rest kept coming, firing on the run.

I fired and smacked one square in the chest. They were on us as I fired the other rifle. A yank's spectacles exploded into his eye. Blood poured out of the socket then he knelt down slowly, bending forward like a moslem. Another yank came from behind and a blow stunned my neck. My rifle wrenched free and a weight smothered me.

I listened to my mother recite the rosary as Father Reilly chanted from the treetops. "Do not fear the shadow of death. God is with you. Blessed be His holy name."

"Dats it!" Jacob sang out. "Rise up boy! Rise on up like Lazarus man."

"Shush!" Mother whispered, finishing the decade. I lay there under a dead weight surprised that her whisper carried above the roar of rifles.

Macfadden pulled off the limp yank and crouched with Mr. Clement beside me. Both bled even worse. Five dead yanks lay across the stumps. One had a broken bayonet sticking out of the middle of his back.

I spat out a mouthful of blood and watched a line of black dots fly past overhead. A yank bayonet skewered my cartridge box in the mud. Mr. Clement pulled it free.

"Bastard speared your box, but you caught 'im comin' over. Skewered 'im like a pig. Like a goddamn blue belly pig." He winced and felt his swollen lip. "That'll teach 'em."

His shirtsleeve had torn away from his ripped shoulder. Raw muscle stuck out from beneath the wound. Macfadden tied it up with a piece of shirt and the red muscle contracted into a ball. Mr. Clement just worked his jaw vise tighter. He never made a sound.

Marshall knelt to reload as more brown shirts ran up past us. A thump on his chest knocked him on his rear. He dropped his rifle, stared at me and rubbed his chest then slumped forward, his long black hair hanging between his legs into the mud. Mr. Clement and Macfadden fired at the running yanks but Marshall was gone. I lay him down on a stump root so his head was above water.

Mr. Clement stared at me in a daze. "C'mon boys. Time to leave this hole."

I caught my breath and gulped a mouthful of blood-tinged bog water. "I ain't never leavin'."

"Thank you Lord!" Rosealee cried.

"Hell you ain't." Mr. Clement smiled, splashed water on his face, and shivered. "You're comin' with us. We're gettin' up yonder. Up there." He pointed to the gray brown troops darting forward into the smoke. "Follow me! It's the only damn thing to do."

He grabbed my shirt, shook me then ran forward with two rifles yelling as loud as he could. Macfadden followed quickly without a sound. They both fired their rifles then melted into the smoke past Lucas' body, the sound of their shots lost in the roar.

# XIII

Muzzles flashed in the smoke like heat lightning. The branches of the closest pine tree swung down with the weight of the mist. Rain dripped tears from green needles. It caressed my face. Pinecones fell in a line across the mud and Ezekiel's face appeared in the bog water whispering to me. "Why you let this happen? Tell 'em you got to leave. What if ya die? They'll never let me go."

Uncle Paul dropped a pinecone and the water rippled. "Leave him be Ezekiel. He can't just leave his friends. Conner's got a bit more on his mind."

Ezekiel's head surfaced next to Peter, dripping mud. "Doubtful. Ain't never had mind enough fo' much."

"Shush up." Rosealee reached her hand over the log and wiped his face. "Let's just watch what he do."

Uncle was right. I looked back at Gordon, Peter and Marshall dead in the mud and knew it was no use. Hiding in the bog grave wouldn't change a thing. I saw Elliott for a second next to Ezekiel. Then they disappeared. Laughter came from the mist up ahead. The bastard yanks were laughing. It was all I needed. I grabbed the yank's rifle and ran past Lucas' body over the next hummock into the far trees. I found Mr. Clement and Macfadden crouched in a thicket of oak saplings choked with brambles and creeper vines. A dozen other brown shirts waited prone in the muddy rot obscured by thick smoke. Volleys roared right and left. The trees rained bark and branches. More of our boys melted in and out of the trees. Six bodies lay right in front in a little clearing in the tangle.

One mud covered gray soldier crawled up next to me and yelled in my face. "Stay down! Yanks got us pinned!" His ears dripped blood. "Yonder deaders! See? Been movin' up, yanks been there first. Stuck ass! Stuck bad!"

Mr. Clement ignored him. He nodded at the clearing. I glanced around and saw a fireworks of muzzle flashes on both sides. The volleys churned smoke and chaos except for straight ahead. Our dead pointed the way. I loaded flat on my back and the deaf soldier watched me and did the same. Mr. Clement raised his hand. "Let's go!"

He plunged across the clearing with us right on his heals. The ten yards across to the bigger oaks seemed a mile. A line of blue soldiers staggered out of the vines and saplings flanking us on both sides. Then the whole woods exploded. I fired and dropped the closest blue jacket. The man next to me fell backwards with two holes in his chest that sprayed red mist. I grabbed his rifle as a bald, toothless yank came at me with his bayonet. My blade easily parried his but the bastard kept coming, swinging at me with his blade. I jumped forward sticking my bayonet into his stomach up to the hilt. He bent double and dropped to his knees. The bastard slashed my arm before he fell dead on his side. Another bayonet stabbed me in the chest knocking me down on my back. I threw my rifle forward with all my strength. The bayonet caught the yank in the throat as he came over me. The blade stuck out the back of his neck pumping a red fountain. His dark eyes squinted into slits and he fell dead on top. His last breath spurted blood out of the ripped gristle of his windpipe. His bayonet stuck in the ground next to my head. I tore open my shirt. There was no blood at all. Just a dent in St. Sebastian. Another crease in the Caesar face.

"Kyrie Eleison. Kyrie. Kyrie. Christe Eleison." The choir roared. Incense burned thick in my nose. Holy water drenched my face.

"Blessed be the meek for they shall inherit the earth." Father Reilly whispered in my ear.

"Conner's meek alright," Ezekiel laughed. "But he ain't gonna inherit shit. I'll see to that."

"Kyrie, Kyrie." The choir drowned him out.

The yanks rifle was still cocked. He could have killed me anytime. I grabbed it and the barrel swung of its own accord toward the yank on top of Macfadden. The muzzle flashed and the yank flew sideways. Volleys erupted from both sides of the clearing. Men fell everywhere, but I was untouched. I screamed out Hail Mary's as loud as I could.

"Good my boy." Father Reilly yelled above the roar. "It's the Glorious mysteries that keep you alive. Recite them quickly."

Then the yanks were running. The congregation in the trees applauded. Macfadden lay on his back bleeding from chest and forehead. He held his hands over his face. Blood dripped through his fingers. He moaned and moved his hands away. I fell to my knees. A bloody crease marked where his eyes had been. His eye sockets, just jagged red holes. He was just aware of it and pawed at the sockets trying to wipe his eyes.

"No, not my eyes." His hand recoiled away and hung in midair for just a second. A bullet ripped through his palm.

"That's enough. That's enough!" Rosealee cried. "He be suffered enough."

"Let 'im suffer." Ezekiel laughed. "Plenty others stood worse. I don't 'member 'im helpin' me. Deserves what 'e gits."

Father Reilly sprayed more holy water on us. "Better to pluck out the eye like the good book says."

"Nonsense," Tradd yelled from out in the smoke. "Get off your knees, Conner. Don't listen so much to priests. There's a limit to prayer. Too much is unhealthy for a gentleman."

A wave of nausea doubled me over. I splashed water on my face and looked up. A skinny yank aimed right at me down a lane through the trees. I jerked sideways as the barrel flashed and the black dot passed my head. I had no time to sort it out. The yank stood there calmly reloading by feel, staring at me. His hand in the cap box, his ramrod already thrown to the ground. I ran straight at him, bayonet aimed at his chest and my head surrounded by a scream. He fired from the hip as I swung my barrel. The flash burned my face, nothing else. He fell backwards trying to block the blade. His hands grabbed the bayonet and almost pushed it away. It cut through his fingers and punctured his chest between gold tunic buttons. The ground stopped his escape and held him firm. The blade ran through to his backbone and broke in half. His eyes met mine, and just a second before death, he bared his teeth like a dog. I felt nothing. Less than I'd felt for slaughtered pigs. Then he was dead and my chest groaned and I yelled until my throat scraped raw. I put a foot on his chest and jerked out my broken bayonet and knelt beside him.

Uncle Paul rapped his cane against a tree. "That ain't bad Conner. Ain't bad at all. You rendered him well."

Rosealee and Jacob yelled over the roar. "And we knew him when he was just a little white boy!"

Ezekiel screamed at them. "So did I. Ya'll remember what you want. Jus' cause he ain't whipped us yet, don't mean he won't. When they grow up they always use what they got. Mark my words."

"I promise I won't. I promise!"

"Bull shit." Ezekiel spat at me from high up, and then disappeared. Yanks fired from the trees up ahead. Gray and brown soldiers moved around them on both sides. Dead bodies sprouted up through the woods like mushrooms. I caught my breath, and a burning crept over my face. Colors in the trees changed rapidly. Streaks of yellow, orange, blue, and flashes of red. Thousands of black dots flew overhead clear as day.

A voice said very clearly, "Over there. There's a Spencer carbine over there."

I looked down at the skinny yank's face. His blue eyes opened up, and his teeth glowed red. "Why'd you do it? You shouldn't have used the blade."

A wisp of dark blue smoke rose slowly from his mouth. He looked up at me plain as day, then his eyes closed and he was dead again. I touched his face to be sure. His eyes reopened. "It's the hex y'see."

The hair on the back of my neck stood straight up, and I burned all over.

"You're dead you bastard!" Uncle yelled from across the clearing. The yank just laughed and blew more smoke. Uncle screamed as loud as he could. "You're dead, damn it!"

Finally, he was still. He was dead again for good. I spotted something else on the ground. I touched it to be sure it was real. A Spencer carbine with its hexagonal, leather cartridge box full of long copper magazine tubes. God had delivered a wonderful gift. He was showing me the way. I strapped my muzzleloader over my shoulder and picked up the light short Spencer and marveled at it.

"Hex all right. Hex on you." Ezekiel laughed. "You believe 'bout anythin', don't ya. Yanks jus' leavin' seven shooters all about? Sounds likely."

"No it's real. I've seen one before.

"Conner, you see what you want to see. " Uncle laughed. "I should know."

"Talk about seein'?" Mamere yelled. "I see a blind man and a crazy boy."

98

The carbine aimed itself, fired, and the colors immediately stopped. The burning became pleasant, like warmth from a winter fire.

More explosions erupted all around. I grabbed the cartridge box and ran back to tend to Macfadden. His arm lay across his face. Blood coated his neck. Mr. Clement had disappeared, damn him. I was on my own. I knelt down and opened my canteen.

"Macfadden, take some water. I'll go back and get some help."

He didn't answer, but the bleeding had stopped. The blood was a darker maroon, almost brown.

"Hold on. We'll get back to the lines."

I lifted up his head to give him a sip from the canteen. He was very limp and his arms slid down over his neck. I realized right then he was dead, but I refused to accept it. I bent over his bloody face and listened. Nothing. I put my ear to his chest. Silence. Macfadden was gone. He'd died alone. I'd been just a few yards away, but it might have been a thousand miles. I lay Macfadden's head back and told myself I should bury him but knew I just couldn't. I promised him I'd come back. Maybe he'd come back too. I looked around again for Mr. Clement, but he'd vanished. Dead lay sprawled about and wounded crawled in all directions. Some of our boys started moving up through the trees again, but Mr. Clement wasn't with them either. He'd left me. There was no one else to follow. No one to tell me what to do.

Rifle fire roared ahead like crashing surf. Gray and brown soldiers knelt behind trees, waiting, exhausted. The woods filled with smoke and dark shapes moved through the mist. A solid streak of brown fields lay to the left beyond the oaks and chestnuts. Our boys crowded a line of works, all hugging the muddy earth. Spent balls fell through the branches like acorns. The rain picked up again harder. I wiped off my face, drank some water, felt my lips sting. Shells burst close by then red flashes of explosions whipped fragments through the trees. Another

Spencer rifle lay in the wet leaves beside three of our dead. I wasn't even surprised. I strapped it on and tied the leather box of tubes to my belt. The woods sloped up and down into a jungle of vines. A hot steam of powder smoke filtered up through the dense foliage.

Ezekiel snickered at me. "What you gonna do Mr. Conner Dumont, take on Mr. Lincoln's army with y' make believe rifles? It ain't like fiddler crab killin'. Damn you is dumb."

"Go to hell Ezekiel."

"Tell 'im Conner. Tell 'im." Rosealee clapped.

"Shut up." Ezekiel yelled. "I'll whip y' ass, too."

Bullets ripped by me cutting into the vines and saplings. I hugged the leaves.

Ezekiel laughed. "Look at you. Ain't worth shit. Give it up."

"Go to hell."

"They'll kill yo ass soon enough, Conner." He stung the back on my neck with briars, but I ignored him and tried to clear my head.

"It's a miracle and must be tolerated." I said it over and over until I half believed it. The vines gave way to more tangled oak woods, which sloped back up another hundred yards or so to a torn and churned clearing where an earth and log parapet emerged from the ground. It looked like a series of hog pens. Freshly cut pines stacked four or five feet high, wedged against jagged stumps. Mud-covered soldiers crawled through knee deep water in the trench behind the logs, slipping over a carpet of dead and wounded. The pens formed an apex, facing a pine thicket and gully, curving down a gentle slope on both sides. Blue hats bobbed all down the right. Our boys held the front and left. The earth itself hissed flame and smoke. Bloody, drenched men squirmed in the pine log cauldrons.

"Like crabs in a pot." Rosealee cried. "See how they sizzle and kick. Don't let 'em boil you alive, Conner."

Gray and brown troops fired under the head log and over the right traverses at the pens down the slope. I ran as fast as I could and jumped down behind the logs. A soldier fell dead with a bullet to his brain right beside me. I peered around the traverse. Dead and wounded, mostly ours, littered the clearing. Yanks darted back and forth to the trees. Bullets whined overhead. Bodies, ours and yanks filled our pen, about twenty feet square. A man firing at the front wall yelled for a Spencer. I tossed him one. He jumped up on the parapet in full view of the whole world and fired down at the other side screaming all the while. He got off five shots then flew backwards, landing dead on his back with half a dozen holes in his chest. The other soldiers didn't even turn their heads.

I picked up the Spencer, wiped off the mud, reloaded and looked around. It could have been Hell itself. All of our dead had blackened mouths from tearing open powder cartridges. Most of them had holes in their foreheads or were missing part of their skulls. One was nearly headless with just a nose, neck, and ears and the top totally blown away. The rear of the pen opened to the narrow clearing that I'd just crossed. A wider field receded in the distance to the left rear, dotted with hundreds of bodies mostly gray, brown and butternut but some blue. The woods behind us flashed with rifle fire and a bullet dug into the logs close to my head. How I got across the clearing without getting hit was God's work to be sure. Two mud-covered men came quickly around the left traverse on all fours and knelt down in the pen. I didn't recognize Lady until he spoke up.

"Who's in charge here?"

Snake was with him. Both bloody, caked in mud and each with two rifles strapped across their backs. Black powder smeared their faces. Lady looked at me for a while then laughed.

"God almighty. Looky here. Got this far and still kickin', eh Conner? Got repeaters too. Give one here."
Snake shook his head and laughed. Blood dripped down his nose from a purple sack of skin dangling over one eye like a plum. "Maybe you ain't as wuthless as you look."

"God's up to something Conner," Father Reilly sobbed in my ear. "You don't have to wait long. It's that Wrath you've heard about."

A rifle with bayonet came flying over the wall like a spear, impaling one of our dead in the back. Blue caps appeared at the front wall. Rifles fired point blank under the head log. Snake and Lady jumped forward firing into the yanks. Blue jackets came over the wall and Snake went down in the mud. I blasted the yank beside him and Lady emptied his rifle at the top of the parapet and shot down four yanks. All a blur of flashes, screams, bodies, and swinging rifles. I fired at another blue chest on the traverse. A rifle butt barely missed my head. It thudded into the logs. Another bayonet cut into my side. Lady's rifle butt smashed the yank down. Another fired past me, burning my face. A blow knocked me off my feet into the mud. The yank dropped his rifle, jumped up onto the parapet and a red spray blew out of his back. He fell on his stomach and slumped over the head log. Rounds from a yank volley rippled his jacket and pants. His body oozed like a porous sieve. The last two yanks in the pen were knocked to the ground. A rifle butt to the head killed one. Lady shot the other blue jacket in the face.

Brown and blue bodies and crawling wounded lay in the mud. One of the dead was Snake. His face below his left eyebrow just a big red hole and his nose torn off.

I'd been death to him too. I was death to everyone.

"God is using you." I looked around at the bodies and saw Father Reilly wallowing in the mud. He reached inside his black shirt and called to me. He bled badly. "Conner, find the Holy Oil and cover yourself. Nothing they throw at you can penetrate the oil." Then he became just one of our wounded crying for water. The dots flew overhead, and laughter came from the yanks.

"Don't listen to em Conner. Jus' run like hell." Rosealee cried.

I reloaded and fired under the head log. The Spencer's lever snapped shut with the last round. Dr. Tradd clapped, "It's good to be alive isn't it son? A marvelous experience!"

"Asshole!" Ezekiel chuckled.

"Mind your manners, boy!" Uncle yelled. "He's a physician for Christ sake."

I ignored them. Snake's blood poured into the mud and Lady stood over him firing his Spencer, screaming. Another man fell dead over Snake's mangled face. I felt glad he was covered up.

More men crawled into the pen behind a sergeant who took charge. Two pens down our men were being overrun. Blue soldiers came at them over the front wall and across the clearing from the rear. Yanks were on all sides firing back and forth. More of our boys fired across the clearing from the woods behind us. Rifle fire hacked into the logs. Minie balls ate the trees behind us like a swarm of termites. An oak tree, maybe a foot thick cracked and groaned then fell over on a pen down to the left. Soldiers pulled a limp body out from under the branches.

"If that ain't a sign from the Almighty then I'll be damned." Uncle rapped the logs with his cane in rhythm with gunfire.

I watched in a daze until Lady's yelling brought me back. Blood covered my foot. I felt no pain but blood drained out into the mud from a deep slice down my ankle. Only a dull tingling like my foot was asleep. I hadn't even felt getting hit.

"Stop your whining." Mamere yelled. "At least you ain't draggin' intestines in the mud like them there. Watch 'em crawl." She started laughing and sounded like a flock of crows. "It's good to see a man crawl."

Dozens of them dragged themselves away. Some still on their feet, some stooped over, dangling torn useless limbs. A mutilated body pinned Jacob down by his good arm. "Don't worry bout me Conner. The string arm's growin' stronger. I'll be free soon. Better than most a' these here."

One yank right next to me lay on his side holding his hand over the bubbling hole in his ribs. He wheezed and coughed up blood. I pulled him over so he could rest his head on another dead yank's leg then scooped up some muddy water splashing away a clump of congealed blood. He sipped just a bit and nodded then started coughing again. Blood poured from his wound. He reached into his coat pocket pulled out a locket and chain. He tried to hand it to me, but his arm fell in the mud. I picked up the locket and looked at the picture of a clean-shaven man with a stovepipe hat holding hands with a plain looking woman, either fat or with child. Was this the same man? Mud covered, with black stubble and powder smears? His eyes were red and swollen and his breathing a rattle of bloody coughs.

"Take it," he hissed. "Take it. Patricia…Patricia Gould…Wellfleet, Massachusetts." Then he gurgled, choked up some blood and died. I shook him but he was gone. I reminded myself he was a yankee and deserved to die but it didn't help.

"He'll be alive in Patricia's mind for a few weeks maybe a month, then he'll be gone for good." Uncle sighed.

"What the hell you doin'!" Lady yelled. "Give me your damn rifle!"

"Go to hell!" I wiped away the tears. I thought of Macfadden and Sir William and the anger welled up again. He grabbed the barrel just as a yank jumped on the front wall and fired. Another of our boys blasted the yank off the wall at point blank range. Lady got hit in the thigh and crawled up against the traverse. He tied a strip of blanket around the bleeding muscle, grabbed one of my cartridge tubes and reloaded his Spencer.

"Keep your damn rifle, but use it or get the hell outta here! You hit in the head or somethin'?"

I felt my head. Blood congealed in my hair. My legs felt warm and heavy and my feet began to look smaller. I looked around and everyone grew distant like I was looking backwards through a telescope. The parapet began to recede slowly at first, then quickly until it was very tiny in the distance. The colors returned. Orange, purple, and blue-green. Little dots flew overhead in steady slow lines with larger spheres and cylinders filled with balls. Metal crashed and splintered the head log. A long sliver impaled a soldier through his chest. It happened slowly and distinctly like I was flipping the pages of a moving-picture book. He was dead before he hit the ground. The bloody tip stuck out his gray tunic like a giant specimen pin.

A dot came through a gap in the head log toward me. I leaned sideways and it dissolved in mid air. The strangeness was happening again. A shell exploded just beside me. Metal fragments hovered by my face. I wasn't touched. Men screamed and went down. One with the back of his neck torn open. He frog kicked for several minutes until he died. More shells exploded. Dots, spheres and colors disappeared, and everything returned to frantic speed.

"God damn mortar! God damn Coehorn mortar!" Lady yelled over the roar of the rifle fire. "Up front behind the crest! They'll drop 'em right on top of us, the bastards!"

Then I heard Sir William whisper. "Little mortar for close range. Yanks got ever' thing."

Ezekiel sneered, "Dat's right. They'll always git what they need, an' you ain't got squat."

Another shell exploded just outside the front wall. An arm flew over and landed at my feet.

Uncle sighed, "Stonewall and Elliott lost their arms but it's not your fault."

"Hell it ain't." Ezekiel laughed.

There was a deep roar from the pens down to the right.

"The yanks' breakin' through!"

Lady and five others crawled to the edge of the traverse and crouched with cocked rifles, fixed bayonets, and knives ready in their belt.

"Ya'll know what to do!" the Sergeant yelled.

Lady shrugged like it was nothing at all. I knew enough to stay low and follow the rest. I cocked the hammer, stuck in a fresh magazine and slipped a round in the chamber. I counted just four more magazines. A few yards away screams mixed with blasts of rifles.

"Now!" the Sergeant yelled. Men surged around the rear of the traverse past the next enclosure, where our boys were barely holding their own. Then into the blood-bath of the far pen. Most of the dead in the mud were ours, but five still swung rifles butts at yanks swarming over. Everyone on both sides was yelling and firing. The yanks, coming over the wall and us coming in the rear. The yanks got the worst of it. But they took a toll. The man next to me got shot in the chest. Three others got it, including the sergeant. I shot a screaming yank point blank in the face and his head exploded. The rest of the yank bastards turned and ran. I fired again under the head log and hit a yank square in the back as he ran for a gully. Other yanks crouched in the smoke firing back at us. The head log splintered right next to my face and I dropped down quickly. The boy next to me caught one between the eyes. He was dead before he hit the mud.

We cornered three blue jackets in the pen and clubbed them to death. One got off a shot just past my ear. Then a rifle butt crushed his head. Wounded from both sides crawled in the mud. No one said not to kill the crippled yanks but it was understood.

"Always a gentleman. That's my boy." Dr. Tradd called out from over the logs.

Father Reilly agreed. "He'll never kill a man who's genuflecting."

One yank pulled himself back over the parapet shooting geysers of blood from his groin as he squirmed over on his belly. He swung his leg up and dropped to the other side just before another yank volley rippled into the logs. One of our men jerked backwards and went down limp with a hole in his forehead and I felt whining bullets blow past my ear. I fired under the head long until empty then dropped to the ground and crawled over bodies back to the edge of the traverse to find the other cartridge box.

The fire slackened for a few moments while men reloaded and positioned themselves with extra rifles. A dozen or so reinforcements joined us, crawling up through the smoke from the woods behind us. Not one of them even got nicked. Lady started yelling like a crazy man. "God damn it's our now! You hear that you blue belly pigs!" His voice must have carried fifty yards even over the rifle fire. He was right. Hell if we'd leave what we'd won.

"Yanks can go to hell!" I yelled out.

Ezekiel yelled back, "Who's gonna make 'em? You can't do shit, Conner," he laughed "Nevah have. Nevah will."

Lady was laughing like a madman. "Come an' git us Billy! See if y'can! Some y'boys here don't look so good!"

"Don't tempt them damn it!" Mamere shrieked. "Another word out your big mouth and I'll cauterize your tongue!"

A dark bearded yank carrying a shiny lever action repeater and draped with cartridge belts appeared on the front wall firing. He hit one of ours in the face and another right next to me in the chest. I fired back and couldn't have missed.

Ezekiel agreed. "I'll give the boy that. He can shoot a rifle f' true." The yank kept firing and mud splashed between my legs. I emptied my magazine and knew something terrible was happening. The yank never budged. One gray shirt popped up right below him and fired into his guts. He staggered and blood poured out his shirt, but he stayed on his feet and fired back. Another of ours fell down with a hole in his side. The yank's eyes squinted into black slits. He fired again. A hornet stung my arm. Another of our boys stabbed the bastard with a bayonet from underneath. The blade stuck deep in his groin and the yank screamed and smashed the barrel down on the man's head, knocking him into the mud. I fired again right at his chest. It must have gone clean through. He jumped into the pen and clubbed another man down. Then Lady's barrel stuck right in his ear. The whole side of the yank's face exploded. He dropped into the mud. Lady put his boot on the yank's neck and shot him again in the chest.

"Cast iron bastard."

More screams came from the wall. Bayonets thrust through the cracks. More yanks jumped over. I shouldered and fired. Lady shot one in the gut, clubbed another in the head with his rifle butt. The man behind me got shot in the face and screamed with a piece of his jawbone sticking out his cheek. Another jumped up on the wall screaming and firing until blown off. His forehead disappeared and his legs propped vertically against the parapet. Another crawled on all fours, blood all over his face, part of his intestines in the mud. He must have been a yank since he tried to climb back over the wall. Just as his head stuck up over the top, it exploded into gray and pink fragments.

Hundreds of rifles exploded around our pen in just a few minutes, the smoke so thick I could barely see. Men crawled over the carpet of dead. All but one of the wounded was ours. No telling how many yanks were dead on the other side.

Two men came into the pen during the next lull dragging a tent flap piled high with loose cartridges. "We're from Harris' brigade," a Mississippi boy announced loudly with his distinctive drawl. "Here to save your ass. Hep y'sef!"

They even brought a few Spencer magazines which Lady and I shared.

Ezekiel snickered, "Magic bullets for the make believe." But I didn't have time to get into it with him. The yanks came again and we blasted them off the front wall.

"Like dem dogfish hoggin' Rantowles Creek." Jacob whispered. "Soon won't be no spot tail bass lef'."

Cannon shot sliced through the logs then crashed into the trees into the rear. The Mississippian's head blew off into the face of another man beside me and smacked him down. I reached over to help him up, but his forehead had crushed into his brain. A big piece of bone stuck out like a broken saucer. The Mississippian lay stretched out on his back, headless with his rifle muzzle where his chin would have been. A stream of blood pulsed over the bare bones of his spine. The remains of his head rolled back behind the traverse into the mud, already barely recognizable as human.

The yanks kept coming all day. Once I got grazed a across the forehead and bled so badly I couldn't see, even with a piece of shirt tied around my head. Lady and I used up the Spencer rounds and went back to the muzzleloaders. We took the rifles from the dead and wounded and kept up a continuous fire.

Father Reilly showered us all day with Holy Water and kept chanting, "May they live with their rifles after death."

"Amen." Rosealee answered every time. "An' Conner too."

Yank artillery opened up on us and splintered the front logs. It roared closer and closer. I knew we couldn't hold for long. Two more men got they're heads blown off. More blood and brains slushed in the mud. I sunk down to reload and waited to be overwhelmed

Another blast cracked against the front logs. Pieces of rifle barrels plopped in the mud.

"Yank bastards stuffin' cannon with muskets. Must be out 'a shells! Load up!" Lady screamed. "Fire over the front wall when I give the order!"

I listened and obeyed like everyone else. There was nothing else to do. We loaded and waited for a lull, and then Lady yelled.

"Now damn it! Now!"

Everyone leveled rifles over the top and God smiled on us. Out in front, a yank gun crew stood reloading their twelve-pounder at the edge of a deep ravine dropping to their rear. They must have been insane. I could have hit them with a rock. They stood out in plain view just beyond the tangle of our abatis. Yank dead littered the branches. One still knelt with his tongue stuck out as if taking communion. The gun crew never saw us. Our volley cut everyone of them down. We dropped back without a soul being hit. The rifle fire streamed black lines above our heads.

"Damn the bastards! Damn them!" Men screamed at the top of their lungs.

Mamere screamed back from the next pen. "Be quiet damn it. Can't a body git some rest! For the love of God, shut up!"

A mortar shell exploded just behind the pens and silenced her.

Rosealee cried out, "Mamere got it up her ass!"

"Serves her right, the old bitch," Ezekiel laughed.

"That it does," Uncle agreed.

I looked around the edge of the right traverse. The next pen stood empty except for a few of our wounded crawling in the mud over blue and brown bodies. Beyond that, sloping down the hill, nothing but yanks.

I caught my breath and listened to Lady while others kept firing.

"We're it boys. This pen's as far as we go. Too damn many of the bastards to push any more. This here is the farthest point in the whole damn army." He put his hat on a rifle barrel and waved it above the parapet for a few seconds until it was shot off.

"So what do we do now?" a Mississippian asked, reloading on his knees. He was bald with broken spectacles and a mud soaked red bandage tied over his ear. His nose was swollen and bloody. Dried blood caked his face. His tongue was pitch black from powder.

Lady smiled, "We hold 'em here. We're like a damn plug."

"Shit you say." The bald man spat blood and powder. "I done my bit. Ain't no plug neither. I say let's git. Maybe they'll do the same."

"Hell no!" I yelled loud enough for the yanks to hear. "Hell. If I'm leavin' what's been fought for?"

"Bravely said Conner," Ezekiel laughed. "And I won't be leavin' what I been whipped for."

"Go to hell," I yelled and Lady laughed.

"To hell is right. It's the bit dog that howls!"

"What do that mean Conner?" Rosealee asked.

"Nothin' you'll ever know, Sista." Jacob answered coughing. "White men talk like that, is all. It's kinda like a code."

Lady screamed then sucked a canteen dry. More of our boys crawled in from the left dragging blankets full of cartridge boxes. We found four more Spencer tubes.

"Christ you is lucky!" Jacob clapped.

"It's the Lord's work." Father Reilly splashed us all again with Holy water. This time, laced with incense. "Conner's Roman Catholic. God can give him a direct command."

"But how long do we stay?" one of the newcomers panted.

"Longer than those," Lady nodded back at the yanks. He calmly loaded a magazine, cocked his Spencer then stood up and emptied seven shots over the logs. He dropped down untouched.

"It's truly part of a miracle." Father Reilly chanted. "God's will be done. Hail Mary…" Mother followed him in the Rosary, her whisper visibly clear.

"We'll use the next pen for breathin' room" Lady laughed above the rifle fire. "We lay low. Wait till they come over, then take 'em flank an' rear. Clean 'em out!"

More newcomers joined us. One with his hands wrapped up in blackened rags. All covered with mud. They crawled over the dead and propped themselves up against the logs.

Lady ignored them. "Bastards can go to hell!" He yelled out for the yanks to hear. Then he patted my shoulder. "We'll turn 'em to rot, Conner."

The thud of lead was continuous against the front logs and bullets whirred above us like a thousand bees. I tried not to doubt.

"You've always been a bit cowardly son," Uncle said in a forgiving sort of way. "It's just your nature. No use denying it."

Ezekiel let out a howl, "Lucky he ain't shit in his pants!"

"Git ready! They're comin'."

Men crept to the right traverse keeping low, sloshing through the mud. The yanks deep baritone shout filled the next pen. Ezekiel squirmed through the dead bodies in the muck and grabbed my ankle.

"Come with me Conner. I ain't kiddin! Best come on home right now. We'll dump Mamere in the sound. Y'Uncle Paul won't care. What them Mississippi boys mean t'ya anyhow? We'll shrimp and fish and have us a good ole time. You can have Rosealee if y'want, since y'Daddy's dead. She might even want y'to. Best hide in the mud with me till it's over. Nobody's gonna miss ya."

Rosealee giggled. "Ezekiel's goin' soft. Ezekiel's goin soft."

"Shut up. I ain't neither. No tellin' when d'yanks'll come. A white boy might come in useful is all."

Another deep roar rose beyond the wall. Lady screamed for everyone to follow. Half the men went with him around the traverse. I struggled to pull myself up and aim over the logs with the rest. The yanks jumped over the front wall in a solid blue mass. Some were already inside. We fired a volley and blasted the yanks in the pen. The yanks at the wall fired back and most of ours went down including Lady. The yanks surged forward and Lady fell to his knees barely holding his rifle up. He fired and killed one yank just as another clubbed him down with a rifle butt. A third yank swung his rifle down full force on his head. His skull smashed open, squeezing out blood and grayish brain.

"Bastards!" I wobbled over the traverse and stumbled right into a skinny, smooth cheeked boy in a torn blue jacket reloading his Enfield. He looked me in the eye and opened his mouth to say something. My rifle fired point blank in his face before he could make the first word. His head exploded. Then a blow exploded against my neck. A weight smothered me in the mud. I waited for death, and in that fleeting instant before blackness descended, I begged God for forgiveness.

# XIV

I woke up in a dark barn that smelled of wood rot and termites. Rain water drizzled through the crumbling roof. Three dung littered horse stalls stood unoccupied. A blue layer of fog covered the first and stirred from something underneath. A severed cow's head, embedded on a sharpened stake, stuck up through the fog. Its eyes opened and stared at me unblinking through bangs of blood soaked hay. The remnants of the barn door flung open violently and a bright lantern blinded me for a second. Behind it a face shined white and round like the moon. A short man, fat as a cow, his abdomen protruding over his rope belt stumbled forward, his soiled shirt unable to hide the layers of stomach. For a moment he was my father. Then the stranger again.

"Knew it would happen. Knew it was wrong right off. Soon as the boy went down Charleston way. His Momma's to blame. Thinks ocean water's magical. Like them Papists'-Anglicans' Holy waters. Bunch a rich-boy, whiskeypalian slavers at St. Michaels. Papists just down the street. Got holy water sprinkled ever'where. The boy joined right in. Never had the backbone of a salamander."

Anthony cringed behind me. He shivered and whispered in my ear. "I'd rather fight for slavers than stay stuck on that shithole mountain."

"Don't sass me boy!" The man screamed. "I heard that Anthony! What the hell y'all did to my cow."

He held a rope tied to a sack of rotten chicken necks dripping a rainbow of grease. A trap door flopped open to a pit filled with black water teeming with bloated alligators. One jumped clear out of the water at the dangling chicken necks, its jaw snapping shut like a bear

114

trap. Anthony grabbed my neck in a vice, whimpering like he'd been bitten.

"Conner, you're the only one I'm gonna tell this to. I'm leavin' as soon as I can. I know they'll think I'm a coward but I don't care. There's another reason."

"Anthony, I don't really care..." He tightened his grip on me.

"Listen, please. Just listen." He was frantic. "He's gonna kill me. He's comin' right now."

"Who?"

Dr. Tradd walked into the barn. He was laughing and may have been drinking.

"How'd you do it Conner?" He was dressed impeccably in a purple silk waistcoat with a white linen vest and crisply pleated gray pants.

"It wasn't his fault." Anthony cried. "The cow's head just fell off. It didn't mean to."

Dr. Tradd and the fat man laughed and Dr. Tradd wiped his eyes with an embroidered neatly pressed handkerchief.

"I've never heard of a cow's head just falling off." Tears of laughter rolled down his cheeks. "That doesn't help the milking process much, now does it?" He slapped his legs and howled. "It wasn't a sacred cow was it?" He was laughing so hard he could barely breathe.

The fat man shrugged and walked away and for an instant a revolver hovered in mid air. Anthony reached for it but it disappeared. He pulled a Rosary from his pocket and blessed himself with the little gold crucifix tied to the end.

"The head is the worst part to lose, Conner. I just can't be responsible." Then he jumped through the trap door.

"Cow lost his head, Anthony lost his mind." Dr. Tradd wiped his face and picked up the cow's head. "He's still mooing." The tears of laughter stained his silk coat. He lay down in the blue fog and disappeared.

"Don't worry Conner." Mr. Clement and the other peered out from a dark corner of the barn. "We been watchin' the whole thing."

The whole group was there. A gray cloud of pipe smoke rose above them. Sir William dueled Macfadden in smoke rings. Macfadden's eyes were totally wrapped in clean white bandages. Snake shared his pipe with Lady who blew shaped clouds that could have been bird's nests. All their wounds were bandaged. Peter stood silent guard over the twins who whistled softly.

"Glad t'see y'all." I exhaled a pent up breath and felt my eyes watering up.

"Conner," Mr. Clement sucked hard on his pipe and sparks flew out his bowl. "It's alright. Sometimes people see what they fear. 'Specially in the dark."

"Here it comes," Sir William sighed. "The Cataloochee Hag."

Mr. Clement waved him off as a burst of rifle fire erupted just outside. It stopped just as quick and left a deeper quiet.

"People I know went up Pigeon River. Settled Cataloochee valley years back. No one there but some Cherokees. They saw what they feared too. Actually believed it. The Cataloochee Hag."

"Don't pay him no mind, Conner," Macfadden said, coming out from behind a dripping water barrel. "He done tole it a hundred times."

Mr. Clement may not have heard him and kept right on.

"Went up there with my uncle to trap mink, and bear hunt. Next day a Mr. Able Caldwell comes in half dead and crazy. Said an old hag on the next ridge killed his wife and boy. Said she lived in a shack with wild pigs. Could kill birds and crops with a wave of her hand."

Sir William pretended to snore, but Mr. Clement didn't seem to mind.

"Said she just appeared out of the deep woods and sprayed red oil on his wagon wheels. The wheel stones just exploded. Wagon rolled down over his boy bent down catchin' crawdads in the creek. Cut the boy's head off." He caught his breath and the twins whistled in rhythm with his breathing.

"Said he emptied his revolver point blank in her chest. Never even slowed her down. Said his wife took one look at this son's body then blew her head off with his shotgun. The old hag sprayed him with that oil."

"Had the smell of dead bear," Snake and Lady chanted.

Mr. Clement smiled and nodded. "Yep, kept him crazy with fever for weeks. Saved himself with a potion of gunpowder and honey."

Then everyone joined the chant. "Drew the poison out in boils behind his ear!"

Mr. Clement bobbed his head and raised his voice. "Wasn't sure how he'd got back to Cataloochee. No one paid him any mind neither." He cut his eyes at Sir William who ignored him. "Till he opened a tin box with a piece of his orange tainted shirt. Let me swear right now. God strike me dead if I didn't see it with my own eyes. Every bird in a hundred yards dropped dead to the ground."

Sir William laughed. "Told me one hundred feet. Hag oil gettin' stronger. Conner, you'll hear this ag'in. He loves tellin' it."

"The point is I saw it with my own eyes because I wanted to believe." Mr. Clement paused and took a deep breath. "Y'see sometimes the truth is like a dream and other time a dream is like the truth, but sometimes a dream ain't nothin' but a dream."

"That still don't make no sense. Never has." Lady shaved his neck whiskers with his bowie knife. Mr. Clement puffed a blue cloud of smoke that looked like chicken feathers.

"Swear to God, it's true."

I closed my eyes and followed him in the mountain woods. Chestnut trunks lay split open like long canoes. A red fox pranced through the maple saplings with a chipmunk in his mouth. A timber rattlesnake six feet long lay motionless across the trail, his head a fat triangle, wider than my fist, his open mouth sucking down a beefy kicking toad. Mr. Clement crept up to it and poked its rattles with a hickory branch. The rattler curled up to strike, rattling the alarm and startling a ponderous groundhog that squeezed his thick sides through a hole beneath a rock ledge.

Mr. Clement nudged me. "Hurry Conner! Maybe we can save the boy yet!" He rock-hopped boulder to boulder up a steep stream bed through the woods. I followed close behind slipping on algae and sending a huge salamander slithering off. I heard an axe at work then a woman scream. We made it to the top where the stream leveled off through a cleared swag between two stump-strewn ridge lines. A half-finished split log cabin stood at one end of the clearing and a crude hog pen at the other. The screaming woman knelt in the cabin doorway as if paralyzed, her hands reaching straight towards us. She was sun creased and haggard beyond her years. Her husband shirtless, darkly tanned and wiry, ran towards us with a revolver in hand. He fired past us towards the pig pen and only then did we see the boy and the hag. Both blended into the earth. The boy was three or four, dressed in a simple tunic of brown canvas with holes for his head and arms, cinched in the middle with a piece of rope. He knelt in the rock gulley below the hog pen, just downhill of a massive wagon loaded with cleared field stones. The hag stood just a few feet away. She appeared out of the woods behind the pen dressed only in caked mud, moss, and lichens. Her greased gray hair stood straight out in a complete halo around her head. She swung a wooden cup tied to the end of a six foot string. A little tin grate cap whistled as it whirled over the boys head.

Mr. Clement sprang towards her. She snatched the string and the cup coughed out a red oily mist that covered the boy and the rear wagon wheels. It all happened too fast to think. The stones bracing the wheels exploded and the wagon lurched back unstoppable. The boy bent forward playing. When he looked up, the huge wheel crushed his neck to the ground. Blood spurted everywhere and the boys guillotined head rolled down the hill towards his father who emptied his revolver at the hag.

The oily mist sprayed from her back. She sneezed a nose full at him then bolted over the ridge into the woods and disappeared. The man fell to his knees trembling so hard he couldn't hold the pistol. Mockingbirds, robins, and crows fell dead from the hickory trees at the edge of the clearing. The woman screamed louder and louder all the while. Mr. Clement shook his head and backed down the hill waving his stumps.

"Too late Conner." His jaw muscles tightened into knots. "It's always been too late."

The clearing disappeared and I found myself back in the barn.

"Coulda been a dream. Hard to tell sometimes. Once I walked all the way from Charleston to Charlotte. Back in '56. Sleep walk y'see. Helluva sleep-walk it was. Guardin' thirty five slaves freshly bought. Heading for Marlborough Plantation. That coulda been a dream too."

"You was a slaver?" Macfadden's jaw dropped and his bandage quivered like his eyes were still underneath and blinking.

"Don't git all riled," Clement scratched his head as unperturbed as always. "They paid me good money, an' them slaves was headin' up with or without me. Anyhow, I said it was a sleep-walk. Them slaves mighta been part a' the dream."

Macfadden shook his head in disbelief and Sir William just raised his hand as if to say leave me out of this. It obviously something he hadn't shared before and I wondered why now.

"Look here." Mr. Clement jerked around. "I didn't do nothin' 'cept make sure they didn't run off. Let the women and children ride the whole way in the wagon. Me walkin' the mules." He poked Macfadden. "Sleep-walkin' 'em that is."

He stared in odd silence for a while then listened to the canvas-tearing in the distance until Sir William spoke up.

"Well it just proves what I been tellin' y'all all along. A good man's the one gits tied up in a bad thing more'n a bad one gitten' tied to somethin' good."

Lady chuckled, "I ain't never understood that neither, but…"

"I know this here." Mr. Clement lowered his voice. "Hell itself ain't bad enough fo' some 'a them slavers. Shiner was the worst of 'em. Shot this here boy, tried swimmin' away cross the Santee River."

"Our Shiner?" I asked.

He ignored me. "Shot 'im dead right in front of all them little ones. I just 'bout blew his head off but there was four others. All with shotguns. I figured if he could git past all them gators, then just let 'im go. 'Specially in a damn dream. I mean what's the harm?" His jaw muscles ground his stubby teeth even smoother. "Hell with 'im. But no, Shiner rides right down out after the boy and shoots him dead. Shot 'im in the back. Pulls the boy's body back to mid river just to leave it for the gators. Made the others watch." Mr. Clement shook his head and sighed. "Shiner was a bastard. I ain't a bit sorry the yanks killed 'im."

I could hear Rosealee singing outside. Bloated gators slid quickly but quietly through the blue fog in the barn and disappeared beneath the surface.

"Can't hold it g'ainst a man f' doin' his job." Lady wiped blood out of his hair. "Slaves is slaves. Ain't nothin' else. Not yet anyhow." The rifle fire grew louder in the distance and the fog started to thin.

"Ain't we fightin' to keep the slaves? Ain't that what it's all about?" The voice came from under the trap door.

Mr. Clement squinted his eyes and wouldn't answer.

"That you Anthony?" Snake laughed. "Thought you was gator bait too."

"Shouldn't been there in the first place." Sir William stuffed gauze into his empty eye socket. "Just cause you got the right don't make it right."

"Like I said. Coulda been a dream," Mr.Clement smiled.

"Dreamin it's guilt enough," Sir William snapped.

"But ain't it what were fightin' for?" Anthony called out again from below.

Sir William slapped his leg. "Damn it. We're fightin' for our rights. Sometimes a wrong is right."

Anthony started to cry. "But I don't understand."

"We don't give a shit." Lady Laughed. "Squirrels don't fight no how. Not even in their dreams."

"Gator bait," Snake rubbed his bleeding jaw. "Hey Clement. You ever have one a them slave girls?" He elbowed Lady. "I mean in your dreams?"

But Mr. Clement just stared straight ahead and didn't say another word.

Ezekiel whispered to me, "I'll hold im down while squirrel boy cuts their dicks off. Make 'em both *real* ladies."

A loud screech made them all vanish. It happened in an instant. I found myself on an old freight car stopped somewhere in the Carolina lowcountry. Men climbed aboard to go back up north. Back to Lee.

Cattle cars, flat cars, old coal cars, freight cars, brimming with soldiers of all ages. Every car packed full and every roof overflowing with men, blanket rolls and rifles tied to roof slats.

My canvas pack wedged beside me in a straw covered cattle car sagging with too many men. Dust rose in the sunlight that streamed in between the rough boards. Dirt drizzled down from the caked boots of men squatting on the creaking plank roof. All strangers, gaunt and grizzled, in a variety of dirty gray and brown. Some bare foot, most trying to sleep with hats pulled down, slouched against plank walls or each other as best they could.

A canopy of emerald green water oaks stretched as far as I could see down the tracks over thick beds of palmettos. A fat cottonmouth water moccasin lay curled up in a patch of sun on a gum tree branch oblivious to the world. An alligator basked on a mud bank. Yellow marsh marigolds blossomed along a stretch of open water past a cypress stand. White water lilies waved like little flags of truce.

The train whistle shrieked. The alligator and moccasin slid quickly to water. Startled coots, a great blue heron, a black anhinga snakebird, redwing blackbirds and swarms of purple dragonflies flew off into the cypress trees. Little turtles stacked like sand dollars on a dry log spilled overboard. Soldiers fought in the doors of the freight cars. Others kicked at men climbing up the iron ladders. An agitated officer shoved his way salmon like through the unboarded troops yelling and throwing his hat down in disgust. He waved his sword above his head screaming, "Order! Order! Then he jammed the sword into the ground and fired his revolver in the air. The train jerked, forward narrowly missing soldiers scrambling across the tracks. We picked up speed, the engine hissing great clouds of steam as if trying to catch its breath. Rusty wheels grinding like a thousand screech owls, past collapsed boxcars, flatcars heaped high with bent rusted rails, an old engine with a burst boiler like a jagged metal crown. We headed north again as we'd always done. It was as if my life had begun on the train, but I couldn't remember why, and there was something raw and painful about it.

# XV

I became aware of the cold darkness around me and the incredible quiet. Water rose against my face and crept up to my mouth. I struggled to lift my forehead as waves washed into my nose. My arms burned and felt heavy, pinned to the earth by weights. All I could do was push with my toes and inch my head along. I could barely get enough air to breath. Water washed over my nose and everything was black. A buoy bell rang and awakened me. It rang for a long time then the water receded. Perhaps the turn of the tide or maybe God decided it wasn't right for me to drown. I don't know how long I lay there in the blackness, but it was so quiet that I had trouble at first remembering where I was. I struggled to get up, but a weight on my neck pressed me down and blackness came again. I wondered how many times God would save me before he decided enough was enough. When I awakened, a pain jabbed in my side. Some one kicked me.

"Can't you move?" a voice whispered.

"General Lee? Is that you?"

"They git you in the head son?"

"I don't know."

"You must be hit in the head. Get movin' to the rear right now. We're pullin' out from the muleshoe. Hell, most everybody's gone already. Yanks won't be waitin' too long."

He spoke quickly then moved on through the drizzle. It was still too dark to see much, but I could just make out a log wall close to my head. I was still in the pen. A dead yank was underneath me and one of our dead lay across my legs. Darkness draped over us like a funeral shroud. The fighting had stopped. The only sound was a long moan that came from further along the wall. Was it Lady? Maybe he was still alive. I wanted very badly to believe that. Maybe my eyes had deceived me, but deep down I knew they hadn't.

I freed myself from the stiff corpses and crawled towards the noise. A wounded soldier cried out in pain when I stumbled over him. I knelt beside him.

"Lady? Is it you? Can you walk?"

"Can't move my legs," He answered in a weak, raspy voice.

I bent over closer. "Lady, is that you?"

"Names Kusick. Reb bastards shot me in the back. Damn them. Can't move my legs neither." He strained to push himself up with his arms. "You a reb? I can't see so good. You sound like a reb for sure."

"I'm southern all right. They got you in the back?" I didn't really care. I just wanted to find Lady.

"Hell, you're probably the bastard that shot me! Least you could do is pull me up, get me a canteen." He started moaning again and coughed up some blood. I tried to think if I'd shot anyone in the back but couldn't remember.

"It wasn't me, I'm sure of that," I said, trying to convince myself. I grabbed him under the arms and dragged him out of the muddy trough to a solid spot against the logs. He cried out in pain every inch of the way. I groped around for a canteen that wasn't empty and he drained it dry in just a few seconds then threw it down.

"Better get movin' reb." He caught his breath and wiped his mouth with his sleeve. "My boys'll be comin' soon. They might just shoot your ass. That or send your ass off to Rock Island or Camp Douglas. Them prison camps is hell of a lot worse. Better to die quick." He coughed up more blood and his voice sounded weaker. "Soon as it gits cold you southern boys start die'n like flies. Bet we got more of your boys in the ground up yonder than we got here today."

125

"He's tellin' the truth Conner," Jacob whispered. "Don't let 'em send you up there. Younges Island boys die in the cold fo' sure."

"Don't you fret. I'm goin' all right. Whole lines pullin' back."

"No matter. Grant'll follow. Don't know nothin' but sluggin' straight on. Don't matter to me none. I'll be dead by mornin'." He panted for breath and tried to laugh. "You boys sure are mule headed bastards. War's been over since Gettysburg. Still fightin' like you got a chance. Shit. A chance in hell."

My head spun like a top. I knelt down and scooped up muddy water. My mouth felt sandy raw. I filled another canteen for the yank then groped my way out the rear of the pen. Time to run for it. The yank gagged and choked then caught his breath "Hope you make it boy."

"You too, yank." I made it about twenty yards and fell flat on my face in the mud. Maybe better to crawl. I figured it didn't matter how I got back as long as I was alive. It didn't make me nearly so dizzy and the nausea went away.

The field went on forever in the darkness, tilting back and forth until it came to a muddy stream bank. I slid down head first into the water. It must have been the same stream we'd crossed coming in. A river now, since yesterday. But that had been an eternity ago.

I struggled for footing on the slippery bottom and for a minute thought the stream was alive and trying to kill me. It took me three times to get up the far bank. When I finally made it, I lay down in the mud. Only then did I begin to feel safe. I heard voices ahead in the darkness and the sounds of axes chopping wood. I started crawling towards them until my arms began to wobble and the ground turned around and around, so I propped up against a tree stump and waited there for a long time.

Macfadden appeared out of the drizzly mist and nudged me. He lay down next to me short of breath like he'd been running. I was glad as hell to see him. Glad that he was alive. But I knew he was worse off then he let on. He poked my ribs and smiled.

"Gotta get through all this Conner. That's what counts. Get back to whatever." He furtively shared a piece of hard tack and tried to catch his breath. "I got a cousin back in Shreveport. Name's Sam. He's a character now. Got his leg shot off at Shiloh ridin' with Bedford Forrest's boys. Least ways he's alive." He adjusted his eye bandage, and for a second I got a glimpse of his mangled face. I looked away. "Got a cabin on Caddo Lake. Property line right on the Texas-Louisiana state line. Got his own cypress swamp. Plenty of high land too. Caught a fifty-pound catfish off the point, just before the war. We was skinning it..." He laughed for a while rubbing his fingers under the bandage. Blood dripped down his hands. My stomach turned, but I didn't let on. I didn't want him to stop.

"Big ole redback comes loiterin' out. Saw each other 'bout the same time. Comes full charge, head down and tusks flashin'. Sam put a shotgun load right in his head. Dropped dead at my feet. Now that was an evenin'."

I heard Jacob sniffling. "Why he got to kill somethin' to have a good evenin'? Dat ain't right."

"If white boys love an animal, dey gots to kill it," Rosealee laughed. "It's in they blood."

I listened for Ezekiel but he stayed quiet. Jacob whispered in my ear. "He's watchin' an' waitin'. He don't mind killin' either. Thinks he's gonna kill some white boys. I tole him he don't got to. White boys is killin' theysev's fast as lightin'. Fallin' like raindrops." He blew his nose, "I sure don't mind y' killin' y' selves, jus' wish y'all would leave dem pigs alone."

Macfadden nibbled the last of his hard tack and sipped his canteen. As he tilted his head back, I could see the oozing red tear where his eyes had been.

"Went down the road to Marshall, Texas. To a horse race. Got drunk. Tangled with two Cajun boys from Bayou LaFouche. Had some mulatto girls with 'em. Let me tell you…" He pulled his hands out from underneath the bandage and flicked a piece of bloody flesh past my head. He sighed deeply. "Let's jus' say they had talent. Went down to a tavern called Gustaf Billy's. Funny name eh? Bunch 'a free blacks all drinkin' and singin'."

Ezekiel groaned. "Bunch 'a bullshit to me."

Macfadden must not have heard him. Or at least he pretended not. "We done sang ev'ry song we knew. Stood on a table signin' 'Now thank we all our God.' Top of our lungs. Fine drinkin' song eh. Woke up hurtin' bad. With the mule nibblin' on the church lawn."

A red lantern swayed closer and closer. Its sphere of light seemed to form a little stage. A curtain lifted and the tavern scene was playing. A plank bar offered a dozen or so dirty green bottles filled to different levels with dark brown liquid. A fat, aproned Mexican bartender stopped sweeping the floor and stared at us.

The old banjo player stopped strumming. The place went dead quiet. Three blacks with patched jackets and two drunk Mexicans half hidden by sombreros froze. All eyes stared at us. Macfadden put a gold piece on the bar.

"Two bottles for us. Four for them."

The bar tender laughed, the banjo player started picking and the table erupted with melodia. Two Mulatto girls appeared. Both with low cut white cotton blouses. One pretty, a white camellia pinned to black hair. The other plump, beaming gold teeth, jiggling a full brown bosom.

Sam jumped on the table, moccasin feet sliding back and forth with the music, shoulder length blonde hair tumbling out from a straw hat sporting a stuffed armadillo head. He danced shirtless with an open cowhide vest painted with yellow dots and a huge bowie knife in his belt. Everyone was up and singing, two or three songs at once. Liquor flowed and we were all amigos. Macfadden danced wildly with the plump girl, smashing right through the door into the night. One of the Mexicans stood up laughing then threw a clay jug into the back of Sam's head. In an instant he flew over the table top, pounding his face. His compatriots fell out of their chairs laughing and the bar tender threw a boot through the greasy, yellow window into the alley.

Macfadden elbowed me. "You awake Conner? Anyhow, Sam was in love with that one girl."

The tavern faded away reluctantly.

"Said he didn't give a damn how many blacks she'd been with. Didn't matter none. Talked 'bout her for weeks. Went back for her but she'd run off with the Mexicans to Galveston. Never saw her again." He stopped for a while and nodded his head. One drop of blood dripped onto his nose. "Sam never got over it. Hadn't been signed up with Forrest for six weeks 'fore he got shot bad in the leg. Some 'a Bedford's boys drug him back from the Hornet's Nest. Been lyin' there most all day just thinkin' of her, so he said." The blood on his nose trickled down his cheek. "Said he didn't feel nothin' when the surgeon cut the leg off. Thinks he watched the whole thing. Said he might a dreamed it. I tell ya' Sam's a character."

"Sounds like a fella I'd like to meet."

"That's an excellent response Conner." Dr. Tradd tapped his steel wound probe with a scalpel. "I'll let you watch too. But later." Two orderlies picked up Macfadden. They disappeared into a surgeon's tent.

I lay there a long time until I fell back asleep. A dream quickly had me on the *Aleta* running before the wind on the ebb tide. White caps stretched for miles across Charleston harbor.

Elliott stood in the stern. We watched the yank guns on Morris Island puff smoke above a white strip of sand in the distance. The marsh grass of the James Island sound waved in various undulating, ever changing hues of green. The sky glowed a deep brilliant blue. Not a gnat or mosquito spoiled the breezy, cloudless morning. The Atlantic pounded the distant bar with roaring breakers. Sea gulls followed our every move looking for scraps of food, swooping low to fight for a piece of bread or shrimp, soaring motionless behind us in the breeze, heads constantly moving to spot any dropped morsels.

Then a dead pelican splashed next to the starboard bow. Then another and another. All drenched in turpentine. The water began to reek. Flames raced towards us across the harbor.

"Elliott the fire's coming!"

The mast shattered. Elliott screamed as fire roared from the hold. Flames curled over my foot and Elliott's arm. Then a butcher appeared with an apron and knife. Pain surged up my leg, and my calf muscles contracted into a ball. Fire raced over my chest and face then I fell into a dark hole.

I found myself on a canvas cot with a blanket over my legs and a burlap pad under my head. A woman's voice whispered close to my ear. She had a beautiful voice, soft and smooth. She called my name. It might have been Rosealee, but a bright light made her leave. My foot ached. I lay covered with a blood-stained rag, alive with flies, my right eye bandaged shut. The light went out again and everything grew quiet in the darkness. The voice whispered to me again and a blue light surrounded me.

"Wake up. Wake up. It's over. You're going to be fine." First she was my mother dressed in a nun's black habit then Rosealee, naked except for a purple stole.

"Your foot was very bad. The doctor cut some of it off. All your toes and half the foot. I told him to go ahead. He said it was that or the whole foot, maybe the leg. Had it off in less than a minute."

She faded away into a tunnel and blackness came again and there was hazy time of pain and chills and sweats, and then a lady's face, like the Virgin Mary. Her voice, like a dove's coo. Just little soft noises. I couldn't tell what she was doing or how long I lay there. Darkness fell for a while, then light, and more pain.

Elliott stood there laughing at me. He shook his head catching his breath. "You're a sorrowful mystery yourself, Conner. Best say another decade."

Father stood behind him, his big belly, taut and shiny. A little girl with yellow skin, yellow eyes, and ruby red lips held his hand. Elliot patted her head. "She's my sister, Mary Aleta, the one who died of hepatitis. You remember? We mighta been six. Found her back yonder. Sharing a pork pie with your father. Gotta take her home. Boy, will momma be surprised." Then they vanished without saying goodbye and it irked me. Mary Aleta reappeared and floated to the ceiling chanting. "Saint Clement and Saint William, ora pronobis. Lady, Snake and Macfadden, ora pronobis. Shiner, the twins, and Anthony, ora pronobis."

"Ora pronobis," I answered with her.

Rosealee stuck her face through the window, still covered with pluff mud. "What be pro nobis? What dat is?"

Then she vanished and Mary Aleta sifted vapor like through the plank ceiling. She left behind a yellow glow that slowly began to fade.

"There stands Jackson like a stone wall!" a voice yelled out. But I realized it was just me.

"Shut up Conner!" Mamere rattled her snake stick. "If he's dawdlin' then tell 'im to git a move on!"

"Don't be sacrilegious you old shrew! You know nothing of tactics!" Uncle whacked his cane bravely against the wall near my ear. "The great Stonewall never dawdled. Hell, his men were called foot cavalry for God's sake."

Mamere giggled. "Is that why they shot him?"

Uncle smacked the wall hard. "Go to hell you leathery bitch."

"Damn right, Uncle Paul."

"Hush there. You're just feverish. You'll be fine," said the soft voice.

"Is that you Rosealee, is that you?"

"Hush there son. I'm not your Rosealee."

She wiped my face and really was Rosealee for a second longer, but then her face changed and she became a stranger. An old lady with gray hair and a mass of wrinkles.

"You'll be fine. Your fever's breaking and there's no pus.

She pulled the bandages away and another wall of pain fell on my leg. It grew dark again. I was alone and cold but when the light returned I found myself in a muddy, untended field with men on the ground everywhere around me. Hundreds of men, maybe thousands. Most silent, some coughing blood or groaning with pain. A few screaming out in agony as a doctor made his rounds with two assistants. When they came to me the doctor poked at my foot. I jerked back with pain.

"Hurt much?" he laughed with squinty blood shot eyes, and he staggered a bit like he'd been sampling the ether.

"Damn right it does," I tried to push his hand away.

"Don't curse me son. I'm tryin' to save your foot. Want me to cut it off?" He had dark creases in his face and across his forehead. He spoke with a thick Irish accent. He pulled out a bloody knife and his eyes turned into red slits.

I waited to be pounced on, but he just grunted then changed the bandage roughly while I grit my teeth and took it. I didn't dare complain. He conferred with two others for a second then nodded and wrapped it up tight with another bloody cloth.

"We'll leave it. You're young. It just might heal up. We'll give it a chance." He laughed and slapped the bandage. Pain tore through my leg and I bit my tongue. Then they were gone to torture someone else.

A wagon pulled up and wailing started all around. I managed to get up on one elbow and take a look around. Hundreds of men with bandaged limbs and bodies lay on the ground beneath a line of oaks. Most missing a leg or an arm, and some perfectly still, possibly dead. All hollow cheeked, filthy and exhausted. They formed a carpet of gray and brown rags around a little roped area covered with straw with square tents made of frayed blankets tied to boards. Each blanket tent covered a wounded man. A surgeon's orderly moved from one to the next with a bucket of bloody water. The rest of us had gray sky and dirt. Two young men sat playing cards, one arm each, their bandaged stumps a matched pair. Another older man on a wooden pallet was missing his lower leg and lay propped on the elbow watching. Behind him a boy hissed as an orderly rewrapped an oozing chest wound. Others hobbled to the rear on crutches made of boards and branches, but most lay on blankets calling for water or swatting at the swarms of flies that covered everything. A bloody pile of amputated limbs grew ever larger just past the trees. Orderlies added to it as quick as they could, tossing up arms and legs like firewood.

A split railed fence snaked through some dogwoods on the far side of the field. Lashed to it every few paces with twine tied to their belts were the blind soldiers, turning their bandaged heads like owls trying to figure out what was going on. One was Macfadden for a second but he quickly disappeared.

A soldier closer to me lay on his back with both arms amputated just below the elbow, his bandages coming loose like white flags, as if he were trying to surrender. My skin crawled. How could he go on living with no arms? But there was something else. A voice called my name and the hideous amputee flapped his stumps like a bird.

He called me by name. His stumps moved in quick circles of whirling cotton bandages. I closed my eyes and waited for the apparition to vanish. God kept tormenting me, but I knew I could wait Him out.

"Conner! Conner! You alright?"

I refused to open my eyes.

"Conner, that you?" The voice quivered as if about to cry. "Conner, you hit? You alright? Conner?"

God was merciless. The nightmare wouldn't go away.

"Conner, that you?" He tried to push himself over with his stump. "You made it. You alright?"

I crawled towards him knowing that something had to be done. Maybe the colors would return and bring a miracle. Maybe he'd disappear if I touched him. I crawled up and put my hand on his shoulder, but God refused me.

"Mr. Clement."

"Conner!" He called out my name and flapped his stumps faster. "You're alive. Thank God. Your foot? Still there? Just part of it? You can make it all right. You can learn to walk, see? No arms, just stumps, but I'll be all right...can just reach...hold a cup...just barely." He sobbed and talked too fast. "Another inch and that'd be a shame, wouldn't it. It ain't bad. Ain't as bad as it could be...Could be a lot worse...Mose runs the ferry.. git some barrels. No swimmin' with stumps..lighter wood helps...best tie 'em tight...straps'll work...No ridin'...git some long hooks…Conner, you can help. Pole the creek…cast the net…Oyster shells and pluff mud. Got to balance…Mose can pole…"

"Well yes, but he didn't say Ora Pronobis did he." Mamere's ammonia overwhelmed the stench of excrement, pus, and amputated limbs.

"Go to hell Mamere."

I knelt with my arm around his shoulder, listening to his babbling and cursed God too. Only a bastard would do this. I told Him straight to His face and then prayed for a miracle. It was the least He could do. But there was nothing. Mr. Clement caught his breath and looked around suddenly aware.

"Caught a shell 'cross both arms. Bad luck…Like I went deaf. Couldn't hear it comin! Couldn't hear nothin' all of a sudden. Like God took my ears and was just waitin' for me. Waitin' to take my arms. Had to take my ears first. He knew I'd hear Him comin!" He tried to laugh. "This one wanted to hang on for a while though." He wiggled his right stump. "A big piece of meat on the inside held it tight. Surgeon cut it off quick with a big knife. No ether." He smiled and rubbed his face on his shoulder. "Bit through my belt. That piece of meat was real tender." Tears filled his eyes. "You alright?"

"Conner's fine. He's not a smart boy but he's tough." Uncle Paul waved his blind stick from under a wagon. Mr. Clement caught his breath.

"Yep. We made it out. We'll be all right. How 'bout the others? Macfadden? The Snake and Lady? You see 'em?"

My head swam in circles.

"Yes he still sees them. They're right here." Uncle Paul's stick pointed to the blind owls who for a second were the entire group.

"Did ya?" Mr. Clement held his breath, and I spat out the bile.

"Dead. All of 'em."

"Shit." Mr. Clement flapped his stumps and winced. "You sure? Lady too? Not Lady!"

I nodded and felt green. My stomach turned. "Lady too. Up in the pens."

Mr. Clement worked his jaw muscles and stared off across the field. Tears rolled down his cheeks. Two orderlies came and lifted him a canvas stretcher.

"Conner, it don't matter now. You made it. We made it. You git on home. Won't be long now."

They carried him off to a waiting line of wagons and loaded him inside. He yelled something as the canvas flap closed but I couldn't hear.

"Says he'll get new arms, if you keep your promises." Doctor Tradd whispered in my ear. "Says keep your vows and the whole earth will heal."

The wagons rolled away through the trees and a bandage waved between the canvas flaps. I waved back, but if I'd had a gun I might have put him out of his misery. Maybe me too. I crawled away as fast as a coward could.

"It's all right Conner," Rosealee cried. "I been crawlin away from stuff all my life. Y'uncle mostly. Thank God, he's blind. Ya daddy 'fore 'im."

"I'm sorry. I swear I'm sorry."

"It's all right. It'll be alright."

More wagons with stretcher-bearers rolled up close and orderlies culled wounded from the field. They chose me ahead of men with chest wounds, men with no legs, gut shot men, blind owls. Truly a miracle, but it shamed me. I hid my face and tried to ignore the wailing as they picked me up.

Twelve more were squeezed on board. I sat up bracing against the sideboard.

"Maybe they should shoot the lot of you." Uncle Paul tapped the wagon from underneath. "Wouldn't be missin' much."

The nurse came over and climbed in behind the wounded. Her brown hair, up in a bun, her white cloak smeared in bloodstains. She ladled water for us from a bucket that dangled off the side. Each man waited his turn. The water tasted of blood, but it might have been my own. Dr. Tradd trotted by quickly on a black stallion.

"Taking communion Conner? Not a bad thing to do. Water to wine and all that. Everlasting life my boy. That's the prize. Keep your eye on it."

Father Reilly brushed past, his surplice rustling against the wagon, his gold chalice sparking in the sun. "This is the blood of Christ. Just a sip will do. Never mind the others."

Mamere laughed and ammonia filled the wagon. "Ain't never had much mind one way or other."

"Leave him be, Mamere." Uncle sighed.

A shirtless soldier lay next to me with his chest and head wrapped in bandages. His left ear just a piece of cartilage and blood. A slash of torn muscle creased the side of his jaw. His severed lower lip wriggled like a bait worm. He coughed and gagged. "I just want some water for God's sake." He lisped.

"Now, now. Don't worry. We have plenty more." The nurse dipped the ladle for him and he gulped it down.

"Blessed are the peacemakers for they shall inherit the earth," Father Reilly chanted as he moved off through the field of the wounded.

"Inheritance? Ain't gonna be no inheritance..." Ezekiel laughed. "Damn well see to that. Like the prophet says, 'if he makes a gift of his inheritance to one of his servants, it shall be his to the year of liberty'."

"Bullshit." Uncle rattled the wagon. "Won't be liberty for you Ezekiel. This year or ever."

"Ezekiel, don't leave!" I cried out but he didn't answer and the nurse shushed me.

"He ain't leavin." Jacob whispered. "It's y'all be leavin." His voice drifted away across the field and I fought back tears.

"Not Conner," Rosealee cried. "Don't make 'im leave."

The mass of wounded moved slowly past. The men on the ground, begged for a place on the wagon. Most were worse off than me. I had to lie down and hide.

Maybe with sleep, all would be revealed. All would return. For a while I couldn't tell if I heard gunfire. Or was it just clatter and creaks from the wagon wheels? Was the battle over? Had we won? We must have won. Mr. Clement and all the rest couldn't have been destroyed for nothing. God was not that cruel. He wouldn't inflict pain without reason. But the pain came with each jolt and a cold rain came with it. I slipped in and out of touch, half awake in a hazy fever.

I found myself on a straw mat under a tree. The bandages were still there tied tight. My foot ached and the blood spot grew bigger. Gauze still covered my eye. A young boy ladled out water and laughed at me. There was something quite funny about my bandaged eye. A farmhouse served as a field hospital where wounds were redressed just before dark. The pain woke everyone up. I had the first good look at my foot and it was startling. Half of it was gone, including my toes. A swollen red and purple ridge marked where the skin was sewn back. It drained blood and watery fluid, but no pus. Thank you Lord, for at least that.

A surgeon's orderly unwrapped my head bandage. The darkness didn't change much except maybe a little lightening into gray. I still couldn't see out of my right eye. I felt for another bandage, but there wasn't any and I made sure my eyelid was open. The gray darkness persisted. I thought of Macfadden blind and dead on the ground and the tears came. Was this the end of it all? Punishment for what we'd done? For what others had done?

A spasm shook me and breath came hard. Elliott was dead. So was Macfadden and all the others. Mr. Clement even worse. I had to block him out of my mind. I didn't want to think about any of it, but the vision of Lady on his knees grabbed me and wouldn't let go. He'd been brave. No doubt about it. That's why he died. It was a curse. Bravery killed.

"Then you must be gonna live forever!" Mamere screamed in my ear until it hurt.

"Leave the boy along, bitch." Lady called out. "I can still whip yo' leathery ass."

"Ain't Stonewall Jackson dead?" Mamere shouted even louder.

I knew it wasn't supposed to be that way but it was. Anthony was alive. Lady and Stonewall Jackson were dead.

"Conner and Anthony! What a pair!" Mamere's foul odor had everyone coughing for a while. Then she was gone.

The thoughts poured in even more. Did Lady feel the rifle smash his brain? I wanted to know when I was about to die. I wanted just one second to close it out with God. Just one second would do. Just long enough to be aware it was over.

A man cried again for water and there were flies on my lips. I flicked them off with my tongue, but they'd just hop to another spot then circle back. Lazy bastards. I swatted at them and a red-hot poker stabbed my face from eye to jaw. It ended as fast as it had come, but the flies didn't bother me anymore. The floor moved again. Through a slit in the planks I saw things passing by. Trees, a fence post, a wooden gate, oak woods, the remnants of a cornfield. The floor jerked hard and the movement stopped. Everyone cried out for water. Cursing erupted all around. It might have been Uncle Paul and Ezekiel but I couldn't tell. Then a leg and cavalry boot in a stirrup. The pants were gray.

"Git the wounded off the wagon into the field." A hoarse voice yelled.

I pressed against the crack to get a look at the stubble field covered with canvas tents and litters of wounded. The pain lanced my face again and wouldn't stop until a cloth covered my mouth and noxious ether assaulted my nose. I tried to pull away but hands held me down and then it went black again.

# XVI

I stood on a sandbar under a crescent moon. Lanterns flickered. Dark shapes jostled on the wet sand. Long boats lay faintly visible in the shallows. My father called out from somewhere in the darkness. "Carnal knowledge will come in good time. Behave with dignity!"

Elliott holding his severed arm ran past me pursued by two hugely fat women. Both buck naked. One black, one light skinned. One had him by his good arm, the other, by the raw white bone. They held him down on his back. The black one sat firmly on his head and pressed her face down on his groin. His pants descended magically. Soldiers gathered round in a circle laughing and chanting, "C'mon girl. Use that white boy up."

They wrestled for a while until Elliot lay still then she jumped up light as a feather and came at me yelling.

"Hold still while we teach you some manners!"

I fell on my back and the sun blinded my eyes.

"The boy's lucky it's a short night."

I recognized Doc Sarah's voice. She dangled her pendulous mahogany breasts over my face. Her immense abdomen pressed against my chest.

"If you sass me I'll sit on yo' face. Squish yo' little white hide thin as a sand dollar."

Pale, naked Rosealee giggled beside her so pregnant she might burst any second.

"If it's a boy, Father Reilly says I can name him after you. But a girl's gonna be Helen. Couldn't have been no other father, remember?" She waddled off down the sandbar.

"Wait Rosealee, I don't understand." But she was gone.

"How *could* you understand? You ain't female," Mamere heckled. "Even a slave girl's got more sense than any dirt-brain man."

"Leave him be, woman," Uncle sighed. "He's not the one who did it, and you know it."

"No, he didn't. That's true. But he *would* have, given the chance. Ya'll all do." Her voice rose into full fury. "Leave a woman alone with a man an you know what's comin'! Her belly's soon gonna bust open!"

She screamed with the gulls until her voice faded into the distant breakers across the river at Kiawah Island. I could see the red painted tin roof of Vanderhorst plantation barely visible over the distant jungle of live oaks and palmettos. Uncle Paul stood in the shallows fishing with a hand line, catching one spot tail after another. One hand rose up as if taking an oath.

"Blindness gives you the touch. Just close your eye. You'll be surprised." His scarred opaque eyes quivered horizontally and the line went taut again. "Go ahead Conner, try it. Don't mind Mamere, she's jealous, is all. Don't y'know that?"

The yanks across the inlet opened fire on us. Bullets sucked into the mud at the edge of the bank, splattering us with black clumps. Uncle kept right on fishing. Dr. Tradd appeared and wiped off his splendid yellow waist coat.

"There's absolutely no justification for the splattering of pluff mud. It's certainly not a gentleman's behavior." He cleared his throat being careful to cover his mouth then pointed across the marsh with his riding crop. "Those people are not gentleman."

Bullets kept sucking into the black pluff mud, inching closer to Elliott's hand, which stuck out of the mud. A clicking swarm of fiddler crabs scurried sideways in and out of their holes with tiny pieces of flesh.

"Git away. Git away from it." I stepped forward with a paddle to scare them off but sunk hip deep.

"It's alright Conner. They can have it. I've got another one." Elliott struggled to pull his pants up with his good arm.

Jacob ran up swinging his string arm and yelling. "I'll take it! I'll take it! I could use a hand. Even a white one."

I tried to ignore him. "But it's your right hand, Elliott. Don't you want to save it."

He shook his head 'No' and Jacob knelt and begged, "Please. Please. Give it to me. Please let me have it."

"No, it's his right hand."

I touched the skeletal hand with the paddle and it shattered into dust. "Damn. Sorry Elliott. I swear I just touched it."

Elliott grit his teeth and tried to be decent about it. "It's not your fault."

But we both knew otherwise. Jacob started to cry. "Ya'll got more hands than y'can use. I just wanted one good white one, an' look what y'done. It ain't right. It just ain't right."

I woke up in a smokey trampled cornfield. Virginia again. Jacob, Elliot, and Uncle were gone. Dozens of wagons spilled their loads in a big circle. Hundreds of wounded lay in brown and gray clumps of raggy canvas and mud covered burlap. I sat up and felt remarkably better but guilty for a while too. My foot oozed blood, but still no pus. I couldn't see from my right eye but still had good vision in the left. I could live with it. My stomach growled and I figured it had to be a good sign.

A dark bearded man on a litter whispered something to the others around him. A youngster with both legs freshly cut off above the knee pulled himself across the broken corn stalks to hear. It spread like wildfire across the crowded field. The man next to me, with a head and face totally wrapped like a bloody mummy, turned and shouted in my face.

"Jeb Stuart's dead! Yanks killt 'im at Yella Tavern!"

He lay back, raised both arms straight up and prayed. I knew it was true as soon as I heard it. It didn't even surprise me. Jeb Stuart had to be dead. There could be no place now for Jebs and Stonewalls. Just the likes of Anthony and me. The war was lost. Everything was lost.

"Well of course it's lost." Uncle sighed. "No Stonewall on their flanks with his foot cavalry. No Jeb Stuart chargin' the rear. Nothin' left but the likes of you, Conner," he groaned. "I love you my boy, but it comes as no surprise that you've been up there hidin' behind a pile of logs. Guess that's about the best we can hope for now. Hide behind logs and harass the bastards. But enough whinin'. Git' up an git movin! Maybe we can salvage something yet."

I stood up with the help of a hickory sapling that lay abandoned in the corn and took a look over the wagons. Smoke billowed across the road from a burning plank cabin. Fire burst through the roof as I watched. The wood shingles collapsed in an orange ball of flame. Black smoke that smelled of turpentine surged out the doorway. A woman emerged as tendrils of fire reached for her from behind. She wore a blue dress with bloody sleeves and a long white nurse's apron, bloody from neck to ankles. She might have been a butcher's apprentice. She drifted right down the middle of the road like a feather in the smoke past a gap in the trees where a line of soldiers shouldered rifles at a man tied to an oak. The smoke swirled around them. The woman turned and bobbed up and down as if caught in an eddy. The soldiers didn't seem to notice.

"Ready...Aim" A deep voice called out. "Fire!"

A dozen rifles volleyed and the man slumped against the ropes. His hands tied behind his gray jacket. His smooth shaven face partly covered by a bloody bandage. Firing squads shooting the wounded. It had to be

144

an act of God. Retribution perhaps. I hobbled closer. Thick smoke obscured the woman. She seemed to disappear.

"You're lucky they ain't shootin' you Conner." Ezekiel laughed from far off. "I still might tell 'em what y'been thinkin'. You know what I'm talkin' 'bout."

"Now's not the time Ezekiel." I answered as patiently as I could. "Please let me concentrate."

"Hah!" He toad-croaked as loud as thunder. "That'll be the day."

I refused to get into it with him and he just snickered at me for a while.

The rifle squad moved a way. An old timer in their midst hung his head.

Long wisps of gray hair dangled beneath his yank cap. For a second he was Sir William then a stranger again.

"Now we done it." He wiped his eyes with his sleeve. "Now we done an awful thing."

"He killed the sergeant and he ran. He deserved to die!" A young officer with an empty sleeve pinned against his gray jacket held his sword towards them, nodding his head. "You did your duty men. You did your duty."

"Who ain't run sometime or 'nother?" The old timer snapped back. "Sergeant Jeffrey's dead alright, but I ain't seen who done it. Y'all seen who killed the Jeffrey?"

He lapsed into a fit of coughing and took a seat on a tree stump. The rest of them looked away, shaking their heads and murmuring as they shuffled heavily up the road past the flaming cabin. The old man sat alone, panting in the smoke. The dead man sagged against the ropes while two soldiers with shovels dug a grave at his feet. The woman reappeared and seemed to float right by them as if invisible. She took the dead man's head in her hands and kissed his face. The gravediggers cut the dead man's ropes and gently slid the flaccid corpse into the hole. The women hovered over the grave watching quite matter of factly as shovels of dirt flew just past her head. The soldiers didn't seem the least bit concerned.

"Of course they don't!" Mamere screamed from the woods. "No man ever cared squat for a woman. 'Cept when they want that one thing!"

Ammonia drifted through the oak trees and the girl held her hands to her nose and coughed. Her face pale, thin, slightly wrinkled around the eyes and mouth, but pretty, even beautiful. Her dark hair pinned erratically under a starched, white triangular cap. Her knees shook and she gripped them tightly then pitched forward on the grave sobbing.

"Not my Thomas. Not my Thomas."

I hobbled over, sat down behind her and watched her cry.

"Didn't do nothin' wrong. He was just a boy."

Uncle Paul laughed at her from behind the wagons. "For God's sake Conner, can't y'see she's just usin' your mind. It always the honey tongues that do it. Wait and see."

Tears rolled down her cheeks on to the fresh dirt as she wailed.

"Watch fo' the tears Conner," Sir William said close by. His voice drifted through the trees like a fresh breeze clearing the haze. "Once they touch you, they git right inside. You'll never know ag'in f'sure. That there stuff 'bout Thomas sounds fishy don't it?"

The woman's chest heaved and she wiped tears off her face with her crimson sleeve. Then she lay prone on the fresh mound of her Thomas' grave.

Macfadden yelled at me from the trees. "Conner, if we had to die then he does too. If God wants to raise the dead, then Thomas can git' in line."

I watched shadows move under pine trees and a squirrel scampered up close and stared at me curiously.

"God owes us. Sure as hell," Macfadden called out farther off, heading south, and he was right. I sure as hell wouldn't let God off the hook. Why Mr. Clement's arms? Why the others dead? I knew He heard me but He wouldn't answer. The girls back moved up and down as if the grave was breathing. Her hands clutched the dirt. It may have been hours before she moved.

"Jus's cause a man's dead don't mean he ain't still real," the old timer wheezed short of air. "Got to have faith. Jeb an' Stonewall jus' as real too. Won't never really die." He caught enough breath to move on, but left his Enfield behind.

"That's true enough." Uncle agreed. "Jeb and Stonewall won't be needin' rifles for the next fight, just fightin' words. It's the one battle that'll never end. Just call their names out an' watch the yankees run."

I watched the woman rise up on her knees and rub dirt and tears off her face before noticing me.

"Who are you?"

"Name's Conner."

"Please go away. I don't need you."

She caught her breath. "Maybe so," Uncle laughed. "But Conner sure as hell needs you."

"Go away." Then she welled up again. She looked around at the wagons and soldiers as if they'd just appeared.

"Where they goin'?"

"Richmond, I guess. We're headed south."

"Now you've done it Conner," Uncle sighed. "Watch what happens."

She started laughing. "I need to get to Richmond too. You can help me. My name's Helen." She started talking softly, but quickly, about her

147

Thomas, like she knew me, like I was an old friend. How she'd found him at a dressing station after the first days of fighting at the wilderness. She started crying again then stopped just as quickly.

"See what I mean," Uncle laughed. "You can't put the cork back in the bottle."

She smiled at me. "The bullet tore up his mouth. Went through the cheek and disappeared inside. The surgeon never could find it." She pulled off her cap and long brown hair fell on her shoulders.

Mamere snickered. "She's practiced. The hair fell jus' right."

Helen smiled and brushed it back. "Nobody could understand him, y'see. The swellin' an' all. Just gibberish for the longest."

I smelled incense and heard Father Reilly clear his throat to interrupt. "If it's not Latin, then the speaking in tongues is forbidden."

Helen shook her head. "But not for me. I could understand everything. I knew just what he was tryin' to say."

Snake hollered out Catawba yells then caught his breath. "Course she knew. He was a man weren't he. Christ! She'd heard it a bunch 'a times. Seen a bunch a swellin' too."

She started crying again and I held her hand. It felt ice cold. "Will you take me with you?"

"Be careful Conner," Uncle Paul whispered in my ear. "It's a ploy. Feel sympathy? Don't you?"

"Yes." But it didn't seem the least bit strange. The last of the burning cabin caved in and flaming embers flew across the field. Men stamped out small grass fires near the wounded. I guided her to the wagon and she held my hand firmly. A soldier with a bloody shirt and his head bandaged on one side crawled out from underneath. He looked like Shiner. His face, pale yellow with splotches of light green and dark blue. He brushed past me, put his lint wrapped hands on her breasts and tried to kiss her. I grabbed his bandaged head and slammed it hard against the wheel.

"What the hell?" fresh blood poured from his bandage. "You gone lame in the head Conner? Everyone shares golden girl. Goddamn it, I'll whip your ass."

"Go to hell Shiner."

"Please! Don't damn him," Father Reilly chanted from the tree line. "It makes for a protracted confession. Tell Shiner to say the Hail Mary's with you. It'll save you both some time. Remember, God loves brevity. He hates being bored."

I could smell the holy incense, but I felt no temptation to confess. I didn't much like Shiner alive, even less dead.

"He ain't improved with death?" Mamere laughed. "Most men do y'know. It's a fact."

Blue jays screamed in chorus with her.

"Hell with y'both." Shiner spat on me.

I backhanded his jaw as hard as I could and probably cracked his teeth. My strength came surging back in a rush of blood and fight. He ducked back under the wagon and crawled off into the cornfield yelling.

"I'll git you Conner! Git the girl too. Use her like you don't know how."

Ezekiel called out laughing, "Poor Conner, he'll have to get in line. Behind all of us."

"Shut up Ezekiel," I called back but he kept on laughing.

"Shut up y'sef," the wagon driver snapped back. He was shirtless, irritable and may have been drinking. He cursed the whole time, never offering to help the walking wounded climbing back aboard. Helen and I found a spot just as he cracked the reins. The horses jolted forward and bodies tumbled over raw wounds.

The driver laughed. "Best hold on! Ya'll never rode a wagon before?"

"Bastard." I crawled forward, pulled myself up behind him and slapped the hell out of the back of his head.

Rosealee cried for help. "Slap Jacob, Conner, long as you slappin' ever'body. He been mean too."

The driver turned quickly with a short wooden club. His bare arms rippled with muscles. "Lie down you idiot. You crazy in the head?"

He turned his back and Helen restrained me from hitting him again.

"Just ignore him. He'll leave us alone." She giggled like a little girl.

"I'll make her giggle." Lady laughed, and I heard Snake slapping his leg.

I ignored them and held my tongue.

We went on as if nothing had happened. No one in the wagon stayed riled too long. We were alive and that's what mattered.

"Speak for y'self," Ezekiel laughed. "What matters t'me is land, an' naked girls. White girls, Conner. Know any?"

I knew it wouldn't do any good to get mad, so I hummed as loud as I could to drown him out. He laughed for a while but left me alone for the rest of the day.

# XVII

That night we slept in a peanut field north of Richmond, on straw mats circled around a big fire. An old couple who lived in a decrepit farmhouse at the edge of the field brought us fresh bread with hunks of moldy cheese, hoppin-john, and collard greens. Being full felt wonderful and I relished the quiet. Most of the men felt better despite their wounds. Only one soldier grew worse. He lay on the mat right next to mine and went delirious with fever after dark. The stump of his arm oozed pus and smelled awful. He became quiet later on and by the looks of his wound, it wasn't a good sign. I tried to give him a sip of water but he could hardly swallow and the orderly shook his head and held up another full canteen. There was nothing else to do. I stood up with the help of my hickory stick and limped off. I just couldn't lie there and watch another man die.

Macfadden sang out. "Maybe the colors will come back. Maybe he'll live. Maybe we all will. God can do it if He wants to."

"Damn right," Lady yelled. "Maybe Snake won't be such an ass."

"Doubtful." Mr.Clement laughed.

A nurse in a clean apron and gray calico dress walked up and touched my head. "Thanks for helping me. You're the one who helped me back there? Right?"

I wouldn't have recognized her. Clean dress, freshly washed face, long brown hair tied in a ponytail. She was truly beautiful. We sat down near the fire and she told me her story like she was going to confession. She'd singled me out as her priest and I didn't resist.

Father Reilly sighed. "I guess it's alright, but be firm with the penance. Confession does no good without suffering."

151

Helen let it flow out.

Chimboroza Hospital at Richmond, then north with the ambulance wagons, the Wilderness and Spotsylvania, then surgery that never stopped. She finally paused and caught her breath.

"Dr. Kennedy took good care of me." The firelight flickered in her eyes. "Every dying soldier called me by a different name. They just wanted to go home. Except you?" She sighed "To you I'm just Helen. But that doesn't matter anyhow. I couldn't stand it anymore. That's why I left with Thomas. The yanks have Fredericksburg now. Thomas said he had a place... No matter. How 'bout you?

"Silky sweet," Mamere laughed. "She's good."

"From Charleston. Just got up..." I tried to remember when. "With McGowan's brigade."

"McGowan's? You swear. McGowan's South Carolina?"

"That's it."

"You know my brother? Emory Macfadden?"

She saw the startled look in my eyes and grabbed my collar.

"He's with McGowan! Have you seen him? Is he all right?"

She held my shoulders and trembled. It was impossible. It couldn't be just chance. God was breathing down my neck. Macfadden's sister! My brain went numb.

Ezekiel howled. "God you is dumb! Can't y'see what's happenin'?"

"Leave him be Ezekiel!" Rosealee shouted. I'd never heard her raise her voice. Ezekiel hadn't either. He was stunned silent. Helen's fingers dug into my collar-bone. "Is he alright? Tell me!"

"I swear I don't know." I looked away. He was still alive in her mind, just like the yank from Wellfleet was still alive up north. Damn if I'd be the one to kill them.

"My God, tell me!" She clawed at me. "Tell me the truth!"

"I don't know what happened to him." I lied as calmly as I could but she didn't believe me. She stared at me then grabbed my hair and shook my head for a while.

"Don't tell her Conner." Macfadden was in the distant piney woods. "It'll mess her up bad. Don't risk it. She'll disappear on ya!"

She walked off and was gone until right before dark, then reappeared with a cup of sassafras tea. She sat down on the ground in from of me and watched me choke it down.

"It's all right. I know he's dead. You can tell me the truth now." She smiled with an air of serenity. But what I told her was pure fantasy. That he was all right when I'd last seen him. Wounded but safe and moving to the rear for help.

"Good Conner," Macfadden yelled out from the dark. "Not a bad lie on short notice. But I *am* all right. That part's not a lie. Movin' south, away from the bad things. Got to stay hidden in the woods. Trees keep a man alive."

"Not forever," Ezekiel chuckled.

Helen rested her head on my knee and her cheek glowed red. Her skin began to feel like soft wool. She sighed and rubbed my leg. Maybe she knew the truth but she didn't let on. She held me tight for a long time then pulled at my hair until it hurt.

I closed my eyes and smelled the dry husks of Uncle Paul's cornfield. I found myself back home. It was good to get away even if it was just a dream. Just a hint of breeze rustled stalks heavy with ripe ears baking in the sun. Elliott and Ezekiel led the way through thick rows that climbed above our heads. The sun cooked us and crickets roared. Elliott beat the unsuspecting stalks with a thick bamboo stick.

"Y'all scared ain't ya," Ezekiel taunted. "Beatin' stalks 'cause you scared 'a Plateye. Ole demon snake got you all twisted up, ain't he?" he laughed. "An' he don't even exist."

He carried a dead rooster by the neck, but no snake stick like Elliott and me. "We'll leave the rooster on Rosealee's porch. You jus' watch. She'll wash in the creek four times a day and powder herself with corn meal." He laughed and twirled the bird by its neck. "Only way to fight a dead rooster's root. Don't y'all be tellin' on me neither. Mr. Dumont don't whip white boys. Ya'll ain't had the bull on the back. But I got my own ways. Just wait and see." He shook the rooster in my face. "When I'm free. I'll remember ever' damn one. Ever' time I been so much as slapped. Ya'll been bad too. Yes you have. Got to pay someday fo' true. Ya'll jus' wait." He kicked the dead bird in the air and caught it by the spurs. "Damn bird's still fightin'." He laughed sucking blood off his hand. "Plateye can kiss my ass. Don't exist. Never did."

Elliott smiled back at him. "If Heaven exists then Hell exists. If angels exist then demons exist, and you tell me one demon worse then Plateye."

"Haints, you ain't mentioned haints," Ezekiel laughed.

"I believe in haints. So do you. That's why you paint the windowsills blue."

I nodded in agreement. "There's more haints than demons for sure, but there's only one Plateye. Twelve feet long with six-inch fangs. One swipe, he gulps you down. You're a lump in the fat snake for a week. The juices dissolve your flesh."

Ezekiel laughed. "You white boys believe jus' 'bout anything, don't ya."

Elliott stopped dead in his tracks. "My God! Its Plateye!"

He dove past me crashing through the stalks.

"Plateye!" he screamed, pointing his stick behind him. Ezekiel fell backwards kicking and grunting in terror, squirming on his rear through the corn faster than I could run. Then he was up and cutting a bullet line through the corn all the way to the road.

"Where?" I held my stick ready, heart in my mouth.

Elliott stopped and caught his breath, laughing. "Mostly in Ezekiel's mind."

# XVIII

clean blanket kept off the morning chill. A barefoot orderly in a fresh yank uniform brought me bacon, a roasted sweet potato, and a cup of ginger beer sweetened with molasses. I'd never had a better breakfast. Helen found me under a huge chestnut tree. Ezekiel hid high up in the branches but wouldn't even say good morning. He just whistled and made crow calls. It made Helen smile. The morning sun sought her out and shined a determined beam on her face. She changed my dressing as carefully and gently as she could but it still hurt like hell.

"No pus still. The sutures are holding tight." She wrapped the fresh cotton bandage with a strip of blue cloth. "Is he still up there with McGowan? Or did you bury him?"

"Watch out Conner," Dr.Tradd spoke out. "She's on to you." Branches snapped as he moved quickly behind the tree, disappearing into a large hole in the trunk. She looked up at the tree and smiled.

"Tell me please."

I tried to picture Macfadden's face but all I could see was the bloody crease.

"I didn't bury him. He's still up there." It was the truth, but felt worse than lying. She tied the cloth in a knot to keep it tight.
"Maybe I can find him after it's over. Take him with me. Maybe back to Fredericksburg. Let him have a view of the Rappahanock. He always loved that river."

"Of course. When it's over…"

She shushed my mouth with her hand. "It's over now."

She had it all figured out. How to get a wagon. How to get past the pickets and sentries. What to take. Where to go. It was as if it had already happened.

"Of course she's got it figured out." Uncle called to me from the ambulance wagon. "Women always have it figured out. They think men don't know shit."

"They don't!" Mamere screamed loud enough to send the crows flying.

"Dat's f' true," Rosealee laughed. "Uncle Paul, why you think yo' custard always sticky? Ezekiel made my stomach turn. Said you'd eat it no matter what he do t'it." She laughed harder.

Helen straightened her dress. "I did more than my share. Plenty enough. Anyway, I volunteered. I can leave anytime I want. Emory and Thomas are dead. I refuse to go back."

"I didn't say he was dead." I held her soft glowing, hand.

"You didn't have to say it." She started crying again, and I let her.

"Be careful." Macfadden coughed loudly in the woods. "She's trying to trick you Conner. She's messin' with you."

I watched her cry and felt the honey glow warmth of her skin. She put her hand on my shoulder and smiled as if she'd just thought of something. Little crow's feet landed on the corners of her eyes. "You can leave because you're wounded. I can leave because I've got to take care of you."

"I doubt that'll work." Dr. Tradd laughed from inside the tree. "There' plenty worse off than Conner. The boy can still walk. One eye works. Not as bad as most."

"The boys mind is the problem." Uncle sounded irritated. "Been weak his whole life."

"Of course it'll work! Take the girl seriously Conner!" Mamere yelled from behind me. "Typical man," she hissed. "Never grateful."

157

"But first go to confession, my son." Father Reilly whisked by, his black robes rubbing against my blind eye. "Beware the sins of the flesh. Better you live the monastic life with men who know how to ignore women. But…."

"Monastic my ass!" Snake growled. "Conner's Papist but he ain't a crazy man. Got to be touched in the head to wear a hair shirt an such."

"Hair shirt. Hair shirt. Conner wears a hair shirt," Rosealee ran by squealing.

"Git outta here you black devil 'fore I wash your mouth out with lye." Mamere nearly fell out she was so mad.

"Better lye in the mouth than a lie from the heart or lie in the grave." I could smell the sweet tobacco of Sir William's pipe. "Damn. Now I done it. Dropped the porcelain eyeball. Where on earth is it? Conner, help me find it."

Helen grabbed my chin. "Pay attention. We'll leave tomorrow. Dr. Kennedy's brother is in Richmond. He'll give me all we need." She smiled confidently, "And then there's Thomas' farm."

"The plan remains intact," Uncle laughed "With Conner, the substitute."

"Sound alright t'me," Snake laughed from under the wagon. "I'll go if he won't."

"Hell you say." Lady yelled. "I seen her first."

"No sir," Macfadden called out from the woods. "She's my sister, ain't she Conner."

Ezekiel grunted his toad-fish from high in the branches. "You white boys is crazy. Still thinkin' y'all is first. Them days is over. Mr. Lincoln seen t'that. First y'fight for a pile 'a logs. Kill each other off. Now y'want the prize. Like y'deserve it. Like nobody else matters. Bullshit! It ain't never gonna happen!" He dropped a handful of chestnuts that just missed my head. Helen picked one up and put it inside her dress.

"See what I'm talkin' about?" Ezekiel laughed. "It's the day of jubilee f'sho."

She gave me a sip of water then drank the rest of the canteen.

"I need to tell you something though." She hesitated and took a deep breath. "I'm with child." She looked up at me and waited for a reaction. I think I disappointed her. I just nodded and quite honestly felt nothing. Her being with child wasn't hard to believe. Not as hard as Sir William's head exploding. Certainly not as hard as Mr. Clement without arms. I didn't try to reason it out, but it seemed to fit. It seemed right. They were all dead, except Mr. Clement, and the thought of him made me sick. It all had to be God's work. I sat down beside her and put my hand on her knee.

"Might as well."

"Might as well? That's all you can say? Might as well?" She was nearly in tears.

"See how fertile she is Conner?" Uncle called from the milling crowd of wounded. "Fertile as your mind."

"The boy ain't got no mind," Mamere hissed from inside Dr. Tradd 's tree hole. "But I like the girl. She's doin' just right."

"Lord preserve me," Dr. Tradd muttered. "What on God's earth have I done to deserve an Irish hag."

I could hear Mamere choking herself speechless.

Dr. Tradd groaned. "Christ almighty, Conner. If this shrew's your grandmother, there's no wonder your mind is gone!"

"The boy's mind ain't as bad as you think," Mr. Clement answered calmly. "I seen worse. A man who can't see beauty when it's in his face ain't got much mind. Ain't that true, Sir William."

"It's a fact. Beauty's born every day. Gotta look hard for it up yonder though. Mule shoe work'll eat it up fast. Hard to see beauty in a man's head explodin'."

"God works in mysterious ways," Father Reilly chanted. "Faith is the last true mystery."

"Boy's brain is a mystery. That's evident," Uncle laughed. "It's a miracle he can dress himself."

"No sir", I called out to him. "A miracle would be Mr. Clement whole and the others alive."

"What?" She stared right through me. "What are you talkin' about?"

"I'm talkin' about miracles." I snapped back. She stared at me then started laughing until her side hurt.

"You are somethin'. Miracle man."

"Miracle man. Miracle man," Rosealee sang out laughing. "How 'bout bring me some a dat miracle, Conner. What dat is anyhow? Like whiskey?"

Ezekiel cursed her and told her to be quiet. "God you is dumb Rosealee."

"Leave her be!" Jacob snapped back. "She just acts that way. Conner ain't so bright neither."

I ignored them and the others were quiet. Helen went to sleep in a wagon next to a dying man and I lay on the ground with hundreds of others. The stars aligned themselves as if trying to spell a name but I couldn't quite make it out, then sleep came racing towards me.

# XIX

Charleston harbor. On the *Aleta* with Elliott.

He shivered and bled badly. I pulled the tourniquet tight. Jagged bits of bone stuck out of stump of red muscle. Dangling, bleeding skin ended where his elbow should have been. I had to get him back to shore before he bled… My brain stopped. Uncle Paul whispered his warning.

"Don't think about what happened. Don't acknowledge it had happened at all."

"I agree. Best not to think," Father Reilly called out. "Just row as hard as you can. Try not to wonder too much. Just pretend. It's always best."

"That's it all right," Sir William agreed. "The Priest knows what he's talkin' 'bout. Wonder 'bout this. Wonder 'bout that. Pretty soon yer wonderin' 'bout God knows what all."

Elliott's eyes stayed wide open and coal black. A splintered stump of mast jutted up from the deck draped with a ripped, flapping main-sail and a tangle of halyards and stays. The boom stuck out four of five feet through the fractured transom. I couldn't move it without water pouring in, so I tied the tiller amidships and rowed. My brain froze. Thank God I had hard rowing to do. Even with incoming tide, it was a long pull across the harbor to the wharf. I watched the leaks closely. Thoughts bombarded me. If only I hadn't made him come. If only I'd hadn't talked him into going to Sumter.

I tried not to think. I didn't want to remember the words. It wouldn't help any way. All that mattered was that everything just hold for a while. But what a fool I was. Elliott could have said "No" but he didn't. If he died....There was a shock at even considering it.

"He will not die! He will not die," Farther Reilly chanted. "The Lord will not let him die."

"Maybe He will, maybe He won't." Ezekiel laughed.

"Go to hell Ezekiel." I rowed too fast and lost my breath. Something grabbed at my throat. My chest heaved, my heart raced. I splashed water on my face until it passed. I tried to calm down.

"Pace yourself, damn it. Get back to rowing. Hard and strong. Row harder than you ever have," Dr. Tradd's voice cracked. "Take care of my son."

The pain in my shoulders and back felt good. Each pull on the oars pushed us ahead of the incoming tide. The jagged hole in the transom skimmed just above the surface. Each time I swung the oars forward water spilled over. I counted thirty pulls, and then shipped oars to bail. The tide was coming in fast and each pull took us twenty or so feet closer. Thank the Lord for incoming tide. The sun sank lower behind my back and fell brightly on the yank monitors past the breakers. At least they weren't shooting at us. Maybe the worst was over. Elliott was wounded but alive. He'd live. Doctor Tradd would think of something. Maybe his arm hadn't really been cut off. He lay limp against the transom with his arm covered by a piece of sail. Maybe my eyes had played tricks. May be his arm was all right.

"Arms are tender things, Conner," Mr. Clement sighed. "Just do the best y'can."

Jacob laughed "One's better then none. Even a string arm's got its uses."

A sloop struggled against the tide towards Sumter and Mount Pleasant a mile or so to port. I looked around for other boats. Any faster boat. But the closest, another sloop, drifted backwards along the James

Island shore. The black shapes of more federal monitors dotted the horizon out to sea. Our gunboats lurked up the Ashley river. Elliott lay totally quiet. Thank God. I didn't want him to move and start bleeding again.

Ezekiel chuckled. "He ain't pious, but he do pray."

"And it's the form of a prayer that matters." Uncle sounded irritated. "How well was it delivered?"

"No 'Et cum spiritu' and such, but satisfactory," Father Reilly chanted.

A breeze picked up from the stern and I pulled harder than ever. Over my shoulder a thunderhead moved slowly westward over the city drenching it with gray sheets of rain then sprouting dual rainbows. The harbor rippled with prisms. Elliott stirred once and turned his head, then sank back into oblivion. As long as I rowed time was stuck. The world just a little sphere of air and water around the boat. The oars scraped the wooden locks, biting into the water with each long pull. My hands moved symmetrically so each oar moved in the same arc. Both blades cut the water the same depth. Both became extension of my arms. The *Aleta* part of my body. When her sluggishness increased, my arms tired as if connected to her by flesh. My shoulder and back muscles tore.

I stopped and bailed and renewed our joint strength. Another volley landed. Shells hit Fort Sumter in quick succession. Damn them all. Damn them. I swear if Elliot dies….I stopped the thought as quick as it came and pulled as hard as I could.

"Damn if he will." Dr. Tradd cried. "He's my son, and worth a lot more to me than you, Conner."

Ezekiel laughed, "There ain't much that's more worthless than Conner, that's for sure."

I focused on the oars and listened to more explosions echoing over Sumter. Water sloshed over my feet. The city wharfs crept closer. Masts and spars of coastal schooners, sleek gray blockade-runners, and harbor steamers rose above the rooftops. The black granite seawall capped with bleached white timber railing stretched nearly half a mile down East Battery to White Point. Heavy guns protruded from three tiered grass mounds. Soldiers sat up top lounging in the breeze without a care in the world.

"Help us damn it!" I yelled.

"They hears ya!" Rosealee cried. "They hears ya, but they ain't gonna hep. Nobody gonna hep, Conner. Don't y'know dat?"

"Cause white boys always expectin' ever'thing. Ever'thing's gonna be jus' fine. Nothin' gonna spoil their life." Ezekiel sounded almost sympathetic. "I do feel some sym'thy. Got to be ign'rant or crazy man t'be expectin' much in this life. White boys is usually both."

"Hell with you."

The last hundred yards hurt the worst. My shoulders and arms dissolved into painful jelly. The *Aleta* settled lower by the minute. Water covered my ankles. But damn if we'd sink this close. I pulled the final stretch with my last wind and we lumbered into the wharf.

Elliott's head flopped limp over the transom. His chalky white body lay still. The bells of St. Michaels rang. Dr. Tradd and Uncle Paul stood above me on the brick and tabby quay. Dr. Tradd blew his nose. "You did your best son. It's not anyone's fault."

Uncle put his hand on his shoulder. "It couldn't have been any other way."

Elliot awakened and pulled himself up stiffly. Blood dripped from his torn sleeve but he managed a smile. He crawled up a wooden ladder slippery with seaweed, moving quicker that I thought possible with just the one arm.

"He ain't dead yet but the boy is still quick." Ezekiel laughed from the shadows along the wharf. Elliott raised his good hand for quiet than pointed his shattered bone to St. Michael's steeple, "Once white, now blackened against yank siege guns. St. Phillips in the natural brown."

"He's obviously feeling much better. Now that he's back home and all." Dr. Tradd put his arm around him. Tears filled his eyes.

"See. One arm's plenty. He don't even miss the other." Jacob was there swinging his string arm.

Ezekiel come out of the shadows holding Rosealee by the hand. He held up a rifle. "Mighta saved y'sef from rowin' so hard. He might be fakin'." He laughed. "Anyhow, it's too late now."

"Behold the blackening," Elliott called out hoarsely like he was on stage. "Confederate brown and slave black. 'Til death do they part. Time to keep your vow Conner. If one dies, the other goes north. If one is fish bait the other fertilizer. Bobby Lee is calling."

Uncle Paul and Dr. Tradd smiled and applauded. "Excellent rowing Conner. Excellent. See how much it's helped him."

Elliot stared at me with hollow eyes and I wasn't so sure.

Dr. Tradd waved his riding crop. "We'll find a way to fix the arm. Don't you worry." He unbuttoned his vest and checked his watch. "It's not easy though. It takes a long time when a limb is severed, it doesn't mend easily. It's like the two parts want to go their separate ways."

Ezekiel laughed. "Oh please! More bullshit for a dead white boy!" Uncle waved his cane above his head and cried out "It'll never be the same!"

Jacob and Rosealee chanted with him. "Lawd it won't nevah be de same."

Ezekiel fired into the air. "Good riddance."

Rosealee winced and covered her ears then opened one eye and cautiously looked around smiling. "Whew. That was close.

# XX

"Conner. Wake up. Stop feelin' so damn sorry fo' yosef. I found my glass eye. See? I'll find you one too."

Sir William played with his painted porcelain eye for a little while then vanished with daylight. My foot throbbed, but the pain had weakened and all the dizziness was gone. We rode south all that day in a long line of wagons full of wounded, under a dust cloud thicker than incense at High Mass and through deep woods that gobbled us up like insignificant morsels. The warmth of the sun on my bandages felt curative. We made it to the outskirts of Richmond late in the afternoon. At a stop for water Helen told me to hide in a field behind a stable and wait there. Like an obedient dog, I did just what she said. I lay on my back in the weeds between the rows of corn and watched the low gray clouds roll by, one ridge after another. I drank out of the horse trough and washed my face, ignored by the old man in the stable with his three young blacks fixing an old buckboad.

Ezekiel called from inside the stable. "You can run Conner. But you cain't hide. I'm tellin' on ya'. Tellin' the yanks' zackly what ya doin'." He laughed. "But what is ya doin'?"

I ignored him. Wounded soldiers hobbled on crutches. A pretty common nuisance in Richmond about then. The old man didn't say a word. He looked through me like I was invisible. Helen didn't come back for a long time.

"Should've gone to Chimboroza," Mr. Macfadden yelled from inside the stable. "Git y'wounds checked. Got half a foot, one eye. Doubt they'd want ya back, but never can tell. Army takes 'bout anybody these days. They ain't picky."

166

"The boy ain't never even considered it," Snake laughed. "Why should he? Goin' with the golden girl."

The afternoon slowly disappeared. More wounded soldiers walked by down the road with defeat etched in their faces. Mirrored in the face of the old man too, and the women in the road. Only the children smiled.

A little boy ran through the road in front of the stable pulling a toy cannon on a string just a head of the squealing girls with sticks. They caught him and kicked his cannon into the ditch then ran off behind the stable giggling. The boy threw a dirt clod that skimmed the taller girls head. Thunder rumbled. Lightning flashed in the blue-black thunderhead darkening the sky to the north. The boy didn't look up. Storm clouds at the end of the road didn't concern him. He cleaned his cannon then stacked pebbles and dirt clods in case the girls tried sneaking back. He glanced occasionally at the stable to make sure. Long straight black hair framed his sun browned face. Thin, barefoot, with a rope belt cinched up, cut off trousers, and holding a carved wooden knife. I fingered the leather cord around my neck and pulled out St. Sebastian. His upside down Caesar face seemed to smile. I pulled him off and walked over to the kneeling boy who eyed my approach carefully.

"What's your name?" I smiled at him and he frowned back. His hand was on his cannon, ready to snatch and flee. He stared at me a while before he answered.

"David." His eyes never blinked.

"Take this and wear it. It'll protect you." I held it out for him, but he didn't budge or say a word. "It's St. Sebastian. He'll give you four lives."

"Well, hell then." Snake yelled from the stable. "I'll be first. How 'bout Lady and Clement. Just four? That ain't right. Need one fo' Macfadden and Sir William both. Cain't St. Sebastian make it five?"

"Don't forgit Benjamin, Peter, and the twins," Sir William lectured gently.

The boy stared at the medal for a minute or two then shrugged and let me drop it in his hand. He looked at it carefully then put it in his pocket.

"I guess so." He squinted his eyes into slits then whispered and pointed past me. "You gonna steal that buckboard?"

I looked around. Helen walked up the road leading a fully loaded wagon. "The buckboard? No. I'm with the nurse."

He squinted at me a while then looked over at the stables.

"Who?" he cocked his head and rubbed his chin.

I leaned against my hickory branch. "It's all right. I don't expect you'd understand. See, I'm wounded. Got to heal up a while."

He stared at me perplexed. "My daddy lost his arm last year. With the Rockbridge Artillery. He's still up with the army. Why you git to go home?"

"He's got a good point, Conner." Uncle Paul called out. "Snake here's dead. Mr. Clement lost both arms. You just got 'a hurt foot. You could still fight some more."

"The boy lost his eye, Paul!" Marguerite laughed. I could smell her whiskey breath. It was good to hear her voice. "Don't make him lose his mind. We've got enough of that in the family."

"It's all right Conner," Father Reilly chanted. "A Papal dispensation avoids the desecration."

I tapped my foot bandage with the stick, and the boy smiled.

"I'm gonna heal up first. Then I'll go back."

"Hell you will," Uncle Paul laughed. "You'll be loungin' on that damn *Aleta* in no time flat. Alone, mind you. Remember Elliott's dead. Gonna step a new mast by yourself?"

I couldn't think straight. "I don't know."

I glanced back at the boy holding the medal with both hands as if in prayer. He looked at it intently.

"Wear it. It'll protect you. Like it says."

"Yep, it sure protected Conner," Sir William agreed.

"Did a helluva job."

The boy glanced up then put it back in his pocket eyeing me suspiciously until I walked behind the horse trough.

"I won't tell," He called out. Then he gathered up his things and ran off. I waved to him but he never looked back. It seemed odd that there could still be children in the world but I felt relieved there were.

"We won't tell either." Lady laughed. "Runnin' off with a nurse. Can imagine that too. Might just come with ya."

Marguerite laughed with him until the last of the sun dropped behind the trees.

Helen whistled to me with the sun behind her back. "Come here. See what I've found?" She giggled like the little girls. Two mules harnessed to the half rotten buckboard flicked their tales. They looked old, sickly and thin. The wagon looked worse. Patched with scrap wood, wheels and axles so worn I figured it couldn't make more than a few miles. One of the mules stared at me with a withered blind eye. A fellow Cyclops. Sores covered the other more than hide. His flank, branded with 'McCoull'. I knew it was some message from God. The name the stars were trying to spell. My dreams would show the way. I felt the old reddish scar of raised whelps gently with my fingertips and the Cyclops mule turned and wiggled his scarred stumpy ears like he approved.

169

Uncle Paul called from the stable. "When you're blind, you can see what you want forever. Everything's always beautiful."

"Bullshit," Ezekiel spat over my head. "White bullshit."

Uncle just laughed at him. I pretended not to hear and busied myself rounding up corn and carrots behind the old man's back.

Helen took my arm. "Now they're charging $300 dollars for a barrel of flour! Count your blessings. We've got enough food for two or three weeks if we're careful." She smiled, talking more to herself than to me.

"It ain't food the boy's after," Lady laughed.

He made me smile. Helen too. I helped her align boxes and sacks in the back of the rotten wagon. It was so overloaded I expected the whole thing to collapse any second. The mules didn't look any livelier even after food and water but managed to get us going down the road, slowly pulling along at an even pace. For the first time in days, I felt awake, alert and pain free. I ate raw carrots until my stomach ached, quite content with a narrow view of the world, as long as Helen sat on my blind side.

"It could damn well be worse, Conner!" Mamere hid under the boxes. "Complain one time and I'll break hickory on your back side. I swear to God I will."

"Fear not Conner," Dr. Tradd chuckled. "Your grand mother suffers from Irish inheritance. She can't be held accountable. That's why we have the Church of England, remember? A narrow view makes not a narrow mind. Or is that backwards?"

Lady laughed until he choked. "I just love whiskey-palians."

I laughed with them and Helen joined in. "What's so funny?"

Tears rolled down my cheeks. By all measures, I should have felt better, but tears came again and again. Just a trickle at first, then a torrent with chest heavy sobs. They came so fast Helen thought I was still laughing. She stared a few seconds then gave me a cloth. I hid my face and cried. It lasted for several minutes then came and went for a while. She didn't seem to take much notice though.

Only Snake made fun of me. "What now? Another Anthony?" But even he was subdued. Sir William didn't need to rein him in.

We clattered slowly down the road past clumps of old men, women, and children walking beside overloaded carts and wagons, mostly headed the opposite direction, towards Richmond. A few headed west like us, but no one paid us any attention either way. Just another pair of refugees with dying mules. Every person had plenty enough burden already. We made ten miles or so before we camped in a field all alone. After a supper of bread and stale beef out of a tin, Helen conjured a real cigar from a box in the wagon. I lay in the rough grass and smoked, watching the sunset of pink and purple and marveling at her magic. She decided to finish her confession and I did my duty and listened . . .

## XXI

"Our place was up at Hamilton's Crossing up the old Richmond stage road from Fredericksburg. Sixty-two acres. That's what Momma said. But she never set foot off the porch 'cept to ride in the wagon to Fredericksburg to drink, so I doubt she really knew. She had a stroke y'see. Couldn't talk or move one whole side for 'bout a year till she died. Coughed herself to death with pneumonia. Took her four days." She stopped and smiled.

A woman wrapped in an orange shawl appeared at the edge of the field. She limped with a cane. Her croupy cough startled a flock of sparrows.

"She couldn't get down the road no more any how, so I bet she was ready. More than ready. So was I. I felt sorry for her though. I really did. Even after all she'd done. She was a bitch, pure and simple."

The woman limped closer. A sparrow perched on her shoulder. "Had four husbands that I remember. Maybe more when I was little. All of 'em came and got me at night. Momma knew it too. I wasn't but nine or ten the first time. "

"Don't believe her Conner" Uncle Paul whispered, close by in the darkness. "She's still working. Trying to get to your mind."

"That ain't all she's gonna git." Lady chuckled.

"Just *findin'* the boys mind is hard." Mamere's ammonia drifted in the breeze. The woman coughed louder and the sparrow took flight. She stumbled along closer still.

Helen laughed and shook her head. "God, they musta been hard up. Momma liked a man to buy her a drink but God help him if he tried to touch her. Am I boring you?" She looked me in the eye and paused.

"No. No. I was just listening, that's all." I watched the woman pull a bottle from her belt and take a sip.

"No you weren't" Father Reilly scolded. "Please light the candles and prepare for your own confession."

"The boy ain't never prepared fo shit." Snake kicked the wagon and walked off.

"You were smiling." Helen looked puzzled.

"I didn't mean to."

"Well it wasn't very funny. They hurt me. I was real little and they were all big men. That's what I remember most. They were giants. And how they smelled. All of 'em foul as asiphetida and sweaty." She shuddered and clenched her jaw.

Macfadden laughed. "Bet ya one of 'em was named Lady. Biggest of the big. Ask them girls in Richmond if y'don't believe me."

"That's a fact," Mr. Clement agreed.

"They got to Momma enough though. She had four others after me. Three girls then Emory."

The four children ran out into the field from the far trees then dropped down and disappeared behind an old oak stump. Helen glanced over her shoulder at them and smiled. The woman ignored them.

"I took care of 'em all by myself while Momma lay up in bed for days with men and whiskey bottles."

"Don't sound too bad t'me." Snake hocked a wad into the fire. "I seen worse."

Helen seemed quite annoyed. "Rosealee, Sarah, Marguerite. All dead before their second birthdays. Emory was the only one to live."

"It's always the women who suffer." Mother said the Rosary with Jacob and Rosealee. Their Rosary beads rattled inside the wagon.

"Rosealee with jaundice. Just over nine months. She'd crawl so fast I'd…" She stopped and bit her lip, crying silently for a while. She wiped her eyes with her dress, caught her breath, and then went on deliberately.

"She had the strangest eyes. One brown and one kind of yellowish that matched her skin. Momma said her father was the biggest drinker in the county. Said his liver was bad enough to pass bile on through his seed. Rosealee never had a chance." She cocked her head and swiped her hair behind her ears.

A tall man with white hair dressed in a buckskin shirt and butternut britches came out of the woods. He stood motionless for a minute or two rubbing his pot belly, then took a deep breath and screamed.

"You little bitches! Git your little shitasses home!"

The children ran back to the woods quickly and silently. Emory stopped at the edge of the field and waved, but the old man cursed and chased him behind the pines. The woman turned and watched them. She took a long swig then dropped the empty bottle in the dirt and limped closer towards us.

Conner, don't you have a sister named Rosealee?" Helen watched the children disappear.

"No."

"Sure you do.

"But I don't, I swear."

"You told me so."

"No I didn't."

"Don't argue with her Conner," Sir William called out from a dry gully in the red clay hillside at the other end of the field. "No use arguin'. It don't matter if it's a lie. When somebody like her makes her mind up firm and fixed, there's just no talkin' her out of it. Just a waste of time."

"Shut up damn it!" Mamere screeched louder than the biggest barn owl. "How else did her skin git so pale? Your father will never admit it. Just like a man to ignore what he's conceived. And wasn't Sara sick for a while? Was that your doin' Conner?"

Mamere flew close overhead and snatched at my hair. I sprawled flat on my stomach and covered my head. Helen kept right on.

"Sara with diphtheria. She lived the longest. Would've been two in a month. Marguerite with yellow fever. She was still a peanut. Maybe six weeks. She would just lie there and stare at me. Her eyes would follow me all around the room. As long as she could breathe." She stopped again and rubbed her eyes.

"See? See? Crocodile tears," Dr. Tradd laughed. "Your mother can say the Rosary from now to the Second Coming. Some women were born to whine."

Mamere screeched louder, but Helen didn't raise her voice. "Momma never once got outta' that bed. Had to bury each one myself. Emory was maybe ten or so. No man around when you really need one." She shook her finger at me.

"Tell 'em Helen," Mamere stopped screeching to clap. "Tell 'em, and you listen Conner! Listen like you never could!"

"They stayed around just long enough to git Momma drunk and pregnant. And me. Anyway, I dug each grave. Out back by the oak trees where you could look down to the river and back across the fields. Emory made little stick crosses and lined each grave with stones from the creek. It's a pretty place to be buried." She paused and touched my arm. "Promise if you're with me when I die you'll bury me in a pretty place. A place that's open, with a view. Promise?"

"Every man has a cross to bear, Conner." Father Reilly drizzled holy water down my back. "More often than not, its wife and child."

"Christ, priest. What you know about that?" Snake yelled.

"He's celibate, but well versed," Uncle replied.

"Cel-i-bate my ass!"

"Leave 'im be, Snake." Lady laughed. "He'll put a hex on ya'."

Father Reilly sprinkled more holy water and chanted. "Forgive them Father, they know not what they do."

Snake spat back. "I know what t'do, I'd cut your balls off if you had any, you black-robe piece of…"

"Blasphemy!" Mamere screamed.

"That's enough," Mr. Clement stopped them. "Conner's got a mind of his own."

I took her hand, "You're not gonna die. I promise."

"Well, I did come pretty close once. I miscarried. One of Momma's men. I was fourteen. Nearly bled to death." She stopped and laughed. "Momma came into the room with me lyin' there bleedin' all over the floor. Told me I better clean it up. She was somethin'!"

"Blame the mother? That's what a man would do! Shame, girl!" Mamere yelled.

Mother recited another decade and whispered to me. "It's not just the sorrowful mysteries. Do you understand?"

Helen grabbed my face and laughed. "She got real crazy after the last of 'em left. Drank worse than ever. Steady for a solid month. Some old timer up the road brought her a jug everyday. She turned yellow and started seein' things. Said I was tryin' to poison her."

The woman hobbled up to us smelling of feces. She produced another bottle and gulped it down. She stared at Helen, but didn't say a word. Helen smiled at her then laughed.

"Well, I did consider it. Anyway she fell down and stayed paralyzed for about a year till she got pneumonia and died. Had to bury her too. Didn't have a box for her not like the babies. Emory covered her up in a flowered curtain."

"That's it my boy!" Dr. Tradd sang out. "The illuminated society of the flowered curtain. She's the founding member."

The woman coughed on us, finished off her bottle, then walked away. She made it about five yards then fell in ditch hidden in a blackberry tangle and disappeared.

"Stop looking away Conner." Helen pinched my nose. "I'm tryin' to git this out. Now listen." She sighed, exasperated.

"I like her more an' more," Mamere giggled.

"Had to throw dirt right on top of her, but can't say it bothered me much. Emory cried a little but not for long."

"I swear, she's lyin'." Macfadden pleaded.

Snake and Lady laughed and threw dirt clods at him. I thought of Shiner covered with dirt behind the fence rails and Ravenel Meggett in a hole back in North Carolina.

"Wouldn't mind bein' in a hole," Uncle hiccupped. "But for God's sake, not in North Carolina. Get me back to Younges Island."

I could barely hear Ravenel and Shiver calling out in unison. Their voices were faint from the grave. All I could make out was "... not the last hole..."

"Kinda seems a coincidence don't it Conner. Them girls' names. Might be she's got some kinda hold on your mind there boy." Sir William's voice was gentle but firm. "Don't let her knit you in too tight. Might never git out."

"Don't mind 'em Conner," Macfadden called from the night woods. "I'm alright, myself. Was a bit mad at ya' leavin me an' all, but....What the hell. Better than bein' buried. Easier movin' about. I'll be catchin' up with ya later, when it's your turn."

Helen squeezed my hand. "I left there for good. Walked all the way to Fredericksburg with Emory. We lived with My Uncle Loundes for the last few years. He was nice to me. No one's ever been that nice."

Macfadden whispered in my ear, "Nothin' special that *I* remember." Helen frowned, "He got shot at Manassas. Right in the eye. I nursed him back. What was left after the doctors finished carvin' on his head. He stayed in the hospital in Richmond for a long time."

The old man reappeared at the other end of the field like he skirting the edge of the woods. He called out from behind a pine tree.

"See what I got here? See? Ain't puttin' up with little shits like this!" He lifted little Emory by his leg and held him upside down. The boy cried, but the old man swatted his head. "Ain't enough women in the world worth this."

He swung Emory hard into the tree and his crying stopped. Snake yelled from out in the darkening field.

"You gonna take that Macfadden? I'd slit that big belly open, quicklike. Let 'im watch his guts run out. Betcha he don't mess with baby's no more."

"I ain't no baby," Macfadden answered patiently in the dark.

"Well go do it then!" Snake called back, but the old man set Emory down and retreated deep into the woods out of sight. Helen glanced back and shivered.

"Got real mean there, too. Would smack me for no reason. Came at me once with a chair leg. That's when the doctor told me to leave. Said I just riled him up."

"That's the truth Conner," Sir William called. "A bullet in the eye will rile a man. Make him mean. 'Specially when the skull breaks open.

Hurts like shit. Cain't say I blame the man for hittin' somebody. Hell maybe she deserved it."

"Bet she's riled quite a few men," Lady laughed.

"Went back to Fredericksburg. Helped tend to wounded there too. It wasn't long before the yankees came. Can't remember exactly when. After the big battle. You remember?"

"The boy weren't with us then," Mr. Clement laughed. "He's just a new boy. Weren't there when Maxcy Gregg got killed. Now he was a fine Brigadier. Showed them yanks somethin' at F'burg. Tried to break our lines but we whipped 'em good. Easier to do with two arms. Me and Stonewall. Your Elliott too."

"They took me across the river over to Stafford Heights one night. Reb deserters and yankees. Kept me there for three days." She bit the back of her hand and looked away. "Tied may hands together. Each had his way with me. The others held me down."

"Don't believe it Conner," Dr. Tradd laughed. "She's just playin' for more sympathy. What's she really after? And don't try to reason with her. Reason won't work at all."

"I'd like to kill them all. Tie each one up like they did me, then cut their privates off one at a time. Let the others watch and wait their turn, then stuff each mouth with fresh cut balls."

Snake howled. "My daddy calls that makin' a man so-prawn-o."

She laughed. "Let 'im watch me squeeze the trigger. Right in the eye, one soldier at a time." She held her hand out like she was gripping a pistol.

"Damn, I like the girl. She's a cold one," Mamere smirked. "Like to see that myself."

"We'll do it fo' ya, won't we Snake." Lady held up a revolver and laughed, fiddling with his head bandage.

"Hell yes!" Snake jumped up with a Spencer and grabbed my hair. His nose and eye were wrapped in gauze. "You too Conner-boy. Got t'hep the golden girl." He pulled me far out into the dark field before he let go. Lady tapped my head with the revolver barrel.

"Don't worry Conner, you ain't been scalped."

Snake flashed his knife in my face. "Not yet anyhow."

Helen called back to me, "Where you going?" She seemed to glow by the fire.

"I'll be back directly."

"I guess I'll wait then." She seemed cross but curled up in her blanket and didn't say another word.

"C'mon boy." Lady led the way down a bare hill, across a rocky stream, then up through a patch of oak and pine woods. We stopped at the edge of a sloping cornfield, taking cover behind a thick granddaddy oak. Across the field stood a rough plank cabin. It might have been a dairy at one time since it was dug halfway into the ground in the back and surrounded by a wooden water trough fed by a spring just uphill. Light came out the two windows and we could hear men's voices but couldn't make them out. Lady and Snake pulled their knives and Snake handed me the rifle.

"You shoot the first one who goes f'somethin'. We'll do the rest." He snatched at my hair again but I grabbed his wrist.

"No more a that Snake. I'm quick as you now."

Snake laughed. "Quick an' the dead, eh. Don't git y'sef riled. Jus' the seven of 'em. It ain't nothin'."

Lady told him to hush and we followed him across the field to the door. They caught a quick breath then charged inside before I knew what to think. I followed and covered the men with the Spencer. None of them showed any surprise and none were armed. They seemed relieved in a way.

"'Bout time y'all got here," A short heavy set soldier sighed. "Been waitin' some days." The three others were white-haired and sun shriveled. All dressed in remnants of confederate gray. One with a stump arm, one standing on a peg leg, and one sporting an eye patch and a huge scar across his face. They all nodded in agreement with the speaker, the only one unscarred and intact.

"Commissary corps," he smiled at me. "Never missed a meal. Even at Gettysburg." He sat down on a hogshead of molasses below a kerosene lamp that swayed from a crossbeam. The others stood in front of a rack of curing hams. A little brick stove glowed with a tiny fire and smoke drifted up behind them. The speaker nodded to three young, mud covered yank soldiers kneeling behind a split log bench across the room.

"Captured at Spotsylvania. Surrendered real quick, Said they was sick of it all," he laughed. All three mumbled the Rosary together. Their forage caps remained perfectly aligned.

Snake stood behind them and tapped each cap with his bowie knife. "Could be altar boys, eh Conner? But are we sure these-here's the ones?"

Lady nonchalantly waved his revolver around "You boys all know why we come. Time to pay fo' the golden girl."

The speaker shook his head. "Nope. War done changed that. Mighta been that way back in '60. Maybe '61. Not now. Not in '64. We done served. Done worse than that thar." He flicked his thumb towards the open door and the far woods. The wounded men nodded.

Lady took a deep breath, held up the revolver then emptied it into the ceiling. It nearly split my ears.

"Got t' least make it look good," He nodded to Snake who cut each yank on his ear before they knew what happened. They winced but stuck fast to prayer as blood dripped down onto their folded hands.

"Conner it's up t'you." Lady stuck the revolver in his belt. "The old man has a point. They done served in the gray. That gives a man leeway. Hell, I done worse mysef'. Don't think we should shoot our own, do ya?"

"But she was just a little girl." I aimed the rifle at the speaker, "No excuse for that. Worse than those." I nodded to the yanks who were still hard at the Hail Mary's.

"Well…", he nodded and raised his hands. "Yep, you're right. I did wrong. We all did. We admit it. Cain't take it back. Do what y'got t'do. But I seen an' done plenty since. Seen plenty a' killin' on both sides. Boys 'bout as young as her." He blew his nose into the dirt floor. "We ain't much f'beggin neither. Nobody never gave us shit. You got a seven shooter, don't ya'? Well, we won't put up no fuss. Won't blame ya neither. You been in it too, ain't ya? Up yonder mule shoe way?"

The four of them stared at me but I already knew I wouldn't do it. It felt like the decision had been made long ago. There was nothing that absolved what crimes they'd committed or made sense of who suffered what. There just had been enough killing.

Lady patted my shoulder. "Its alright Conner. Don't got t'kill jus' cause y'can. Lettin' 'em go feels good, don't it? Admit it now." He poked my ribs and Snake sheathed his knife, rubbing his head like it really bothered him. The yank boys all cried and bowed their heads still not believing.

"See there," Lady laughed. "It's catchin'. Even blue-belly shits git t' walk free. This ain't somethin' natural, I tell ya."

Snake climbed out the back window mumbling to himself and disappeared into the dark. Lady called after him.

"You too Snake. Y'got t' admit it. Makes y' feel full in the belly, don't it." He laughed and sheathed his knife too. "Snake ain't one t' go soft f' no reason. This here's somethin'. Somethin' nobody cain't never understand if they ain't been in it up yonder."

He backed out the door and I followed still keeping them all covered just in case. But I should have known by the tears in their eyes that none of them meant harm. We were quickly gone through the woods and back to the field where Helen's fired burned.

Lady took the rifle from me. "Jus tell golden girl they suffered like hell. That they all paid the price in full. Won't be too much of a lie neither. Hell, tell her we cut their balls off like she wanted. Take her a few if y' wanna'." Gunfire rumbled in the distance. "Plenty of 'em rottin up yonder if she wants proof. Better git back to her Conner. She's the way home." He lay down in the weeds, pulled his hat down over his bandaged forehead and fell fast asleep. I crept back to Helen, gently placed a few sticks on the fire then wrapped up in a blanket and watched the stars. Before dawn she woke up and I told her just as Lady had said.

"Well, I wish I could've seen 'em die." She threw a rock against the wagon. "Hope they suffered like hell!"

"That they did. That they did." I wasn't even sure if it counted as a lie.

"She certainly justifies the killing doesn't she Conner," Dr. Tradd laughed.

"That's it alright!" Mamere laughed bitterly. "A woman's got to *justify* it! But a man don't! Y'all should be ashamed. Lettin' them bastards go."

"Kill 'em y'sef, hag." Lady yawned. Mamere choked until she passed out.

"Let he who has not sinned cast the first stone." Father Reilly shifted his weight in the wagon. "Bless yourself Conner, say one good glorious mystery."

"The boy ain't smart enough to sin!" Uncle Paul called out. "Couldn't find a good sin if it was mapped out for him. Not even the original variety."

"Conner's never been original about anything that's a fact," Dr. Tradd laughed. "He's quite honest about it though. Stronger in the arm than in the mind. Can flat throw a stone. Its his mind that's the weak link."

Everyone agreed laughing while I said a few Hail Mary's to myself. "Now y'done it Conner." Mr. Clement chuckled close by. "Got 'er all riled up again. You'll both be seein' dead yanks in y'sleep. Ain't nobody tole' ya not to rile a woman at night. Best wait 'till y'be leavin'. A woman likes to dwell on things a while. And dwellin' ain't the same as dreamin'. Y' done mess up bad."

Helen rambled on. Her voice seemed visible. The words were little downy feathers that floated past my face and covered the grass. Lady bugs congregated on them. Helen disrobed and nothing covered her bare skin but her long brown hair.

"Watch out Conner!" Mr. Clement yelled. "Remember what that mayor warned about in the Richmond paper? 'Soldiers preyed upon by rouged streetwalkers'. Remember?"

Snake howled in the distance. "She'll give ya powerful prayers Conner. Mighty powerful. Cans she pray on me too?"

"It ain't p-r-a-y you ignorant ass. It's p-r-e-y," Mr. Clement laughed hard enough to choke.

"You done tole me already. But it don't matter." Snake came walking across the field. "One little letter don't make no difference. That girl's legs might be bout as prayerful as you can git. She can pray on me ever' damn night. Cain't blame a man for dreamin'."

Mr. Clement puffed on his pipe and blew a cloud of smoke. "Could be a damn fine night if she'll let us, but we'll be decent about it. We're gentlemen ain't we Snake?"

"My ass," he snorted back.

Uncle laughed, "Conner, it makes me think. You remember the time your cousin Sarah came to visit with her mother?"

Helen kept on talking. Her words still visible like sparks above the fire. But I remembered all right. No one ever explained how we were related. Uncle and Sarah's mother disappeared all day and all that night. Uncle told me they had business to discuss.

"Sarah was a red head, remember?" Uncle teased. "Didn't she follow you out on the marsh path?"

"Yes she did."

Everyone laughed, and Helen stopped talking. She lay back down and covered up with the blanket and put her fingers in her ears.

"Tell us Conner, tell us," Snake croaked and grunted. "We got t'know."

"It was nothing."

Howling erupted for a while.

"Quiet, damn it!" Mr. Clement yelled, "Please continue, Conner. I bet that ain't all."

"Well... she did ask if I'd like to see her 'God given moss'." I tried to smile, but couldn't.

"Weee-dog!" Lady yelled from the dark field.

"Everything happened so fast. I remember thinking it was a miracle."

"For you? Damn well was a miracle," Snake laughed. "Doubt lightnin' strikes this time. Not even with the golden girl."

Helen jumped up and lit a match, cupping it beneath her bare breasts. "Well look at this."

185

"Cover your eyes my son." Father Reilly blessed me with incense that drifted above the dying embers. "Don't fall into the den of iniquity."

"Iniquity my ass," Snake yelled. "How 'bout milk and honey?"

Helen pulled out yellow-green vase from a sack. It was inscribed with the words "Aide-toi et Dieu t'aidera."

"What is it?" Sir William blew clouds of smoke across her face.

She kissed the vase and smiled. "It's the Naval officer's. From Richmond. Dr. Kennedy's friend. Says 'God helps those who help themselves'. Least that's what he told me."

"The girl knows everybody," Uncle clapped.

"Your turn Conner. Go on. Git t'know her," Snake laughed. "I'll be next."

She set the vase carefully in a box in the wagon then sat down with her chin on her knees and watched the last embers die out. Guns rumbled in the distance. She stood up, patted my head, then shoved me on my back and sprawled on top of me pushing my arms apart and pressing full length against me with her fire skin.

"Help yourself." She pressed her lips against mine.

Father Reilly called far away. "You're certainly covered with mortal sin, my boy. Penance is due." I felt another sprinkle of holy water.

"Wash away your iniquity. Behold the work of the human hands."

I felt paralyzed, suspended with her in mid air.

"New boy's doin' alright," Lady yelled. "Ain't no law 'gainst it."

The rest laughed and applauded. I tried to ignore them, but they sang "Yellow Rose of Texas" until Helen started laughing too.

# XXII

I woke up to the snapping sounds of a breakfast fire and watched Helen brew root tea and toast cornbread over the flames. The mules were in no hurry and neither were we. Mornings became idle and lazy as we drifted slowly westward through unmolested countryside of rolling hills and forest. I felt better each day. Only the visions bothered me. They'd be gone before I could say a word, but always brought a shower of sweat. Mostly of Macfadden with no eyes, Mr. Clement flapping his stumps, and Lady's head splitting open. I told her about them afterwards but she'd just nod her head and tell me it was all over. I tried to believe her. No use thinking of it. The past was damn well gone.

Ezekiel would answer each time. "Bullshit it is. I ain't never gonna forget. Won't let you neither."

I tried not to let on, but night made it worse especially after the fire died down. Shadows became yanks with bayonets. Several times I woke up thrashing against a nearby tree. In the dreams the yanks always came over the stumps in the bog. Macfadden's eyes dangled out of the sockets, Mr. Clements arms lay in the mud, and Lady's head exploded. Each time Helen's voice came from far away and made the yanks retreat. Then there'd be a soft thing, my face in her hands and her pressing herself against me. Once I'd knocked her down thinking she was a yank. I'd straddled her neck and dug my thumbs in her windpipe until she hit me in the head with a rock. I'd damn near killed her but it didn't seem to bother her much. She just kept the rock under the blanket to pound me again if need be. She even laughed about it. So did the others.

187

"His head is harder than most rocks," Uncle Paul laughed. "Always has been."

"Don't fret Conner. You can't kill the golden girl," Dr. Tradd chuckled. "Not a chance with your brain the way it is."

"She should be chokin' you!" Mamere gasped for breath. "You leave that girl alone or I'll..," she wheezed into a fit of coughing.

Snake hocked a wad over my head and sneered. "Most times when a man wakes a woman up in the middle of the night, it ain't to stick his thumb in her neck!"

"The boy ain't right, I tell ya," Uncle laughed. "Might as well imagine something better than that."

"Leave him be." Mr. Clement spoke softly. "He's killed a man. More than one, up close. That does somethin' to a man. Like somethin' inside dies."

Lady laughed, "Must be dead from the waist down if he's usin' his thumb."

I took their teasing with renewed patience. The farther down the road we went the easier it got. She told me of an apple orchard and a cabin outside of Charlottesville, close to Monticello. I surmised it was her dead Thomas' destination but she wouldn't say. Maybe the head wound caused me not to care, but wherever we went seemed plenty all right with me.

One night we camped in a clearing by a brook. It churned through a little gorge then fell over a ledge into a deep pool of cold, calm, darker water. Green streamers of algae dangled from the rocks providing cover for minnows. Larger fish, deeper in the pool, glided slowly under a submerged shelf.

I rolled up my pants, took off my bandage, and waded into the stream across the shallows with the help of my hickory branch. It was damn cold. My foot burned fire hot on the slippery stones before the

188

water numbed the pain. A tree leaned over from the far bank providing shade to the deep pool. The one eye made for terrible depth perception. My head twitched side to side to see worth a damn. A big trout darted back under the ledge out of sight, just as I got close. Wary old codger. I waded back across the stream, slipping on algae, jarring my nub foot so bad that pain surged to my knee. The scab in the purple ridge bled a little. I looked back at a swirl of water in the pool. The old trout laughed.

"You gonna take that kinda insult from a damn fish?" Lady crept above the ledge just out of sight.

"Leave the boy alone!" Mamere threw a handful of pebbles into the stream. "He ain't fit to talk and fish at the same time."

Lady crept away laughing. Mamere cursed him until he slid out of sight, then she held her tongue.

I liberated a cord in the wagon while Helen lay on a blanket on the grassy bank smiling at me. I stuck my finger on a hairpin and drew blood.

"Got y'sef wounded agin Conner?" Snake laughed. "Dumb ass."

Helen propped up on her elbows. "My hairpin? To catch fish?"

"They're as good as gutted and scaled."

"Only thing the boy's good at. A blade in the belly eh Conner?" Lady yelled from upstream.

I pretended I couldn't hear him. The hairpin bent itself into a hook and the cord cooperated nicely. Bait was ample. Slugs, worms, and two grasshoppers. The worm went first, impaling itself on the hook. A swirl of rifle fire and smoke rushed over my head.

"Don't think about it Conner. Don't think anything. It's all over." Mr.Clement's voice cracked. "Just focus on the fish."

"Conner?" It was my father. His voice rolled down the bank from far in the past, weak but critical. "It'll never be over. Y'know that. Don't let 'em think you're simple minded."

"You've been gone too long Dumont," Dr. Tradd called out. "The boy's free now. His mind is all that's left." Dr. Tradd was right. I did feel free.

"Feels good does it?" Ezekiel grunted with disgust. "Tell me what its like."

"Find out y'self," Uncle Paul yelled.

"Don't you worry, crazy old man. Soon enough."

I ignored them all. I found another sturdy branch long enough to keep me away from the edge of the pool and stay hidden in the shadows then tied on the cord, put my bait in a cup, waded back across, and let the worm drift down with the current. I held the line out from the snags and watched as it went over the falls into the pool. My line went taut with a whirl and a splash. A fat trout came flying by over the rocks flapping about furiously. For a second it was Mr. Clement with no arms.

"Like a damn penguin. Cain't fly. Cain't grab nothin'. No use to me at all. Cain't even touch em, see." He strained to touch his stumps together.

I pounced on the trout and he disappeared. It was just a fish.

"Them yanks was just boys. Don't be worryin' too much bout a damn trout. A fish ain't a boy." Mr. Clement called from upstream unable to hide his irritation. He flapped his stumps. "See? This here's worth worryin' 'bout."

"Leave him be, Clement." Sir William replied calmly, "He's just a boy."

Rosealee giggled, "I like 'im when he flaps. He do it like a duck."

Jacob laughed with her. "Yep. Least I got one good arm."

I could hear Mr. Clement grinding his teeth as I waded back with my prize. My foot throbbed and bled along the suture line. Helen dried it off with her dress and dabbed the bleeding spots until they stopped. She touched the trout and it made a sound like Lucas and Gordon. It made me smile.

"Can you clean them too?"

"And cook. This is just the beginning." I threw the fish into an empty sack and tied it to my belt. I took a knife from the box in the wagon and wondered why I hadn't taken it with me from the start.

"It's just a knife," Sir William whispered. "And a rifle's just a rifle. Won't bother nobody on its own."

"He's right my boy", Dr. Tradd was downstream. "What happened before was in another world. Another time. There's no connection to this. Don't let there be one."

Macfadden laughed. "Course there ain't no connection. Killin ain't connected to nothin'. A dead man's connected to the ground maybe. To worms an' such. Not much else. Maggots maybe." He cleared his throat. "That's why I ain't gonna let em bury me. Plan t'keep headin south. Live in the trees. Rustle about on windy days. No maggots gonna eat my face off." He threw a stone above the falls but stayed hidden.

Helen laughed while she nursed my foot.

"Stitches need t' come out. Git y'foot clean an numb."
I did as she said, setting my foot in a deep pool while I readied the next worm. Smoke swirled for an instant with movement in the sack. It wouldn't stop until I opened it up and looked.

Helen called to me. "Make sure he didn't fly away?"

"Just looking. That's all."

"Lookin at what ya killed?" Snake teased in a girl's voice and hocked another spit wad that plopped close by in the current. I vowed not to look again. No matter what.

191

"My ass! You'll look every damn minute. Gonna find a yank's head in there yet," Snake laughed loudly. "Dare ya to look."

"No thanks." I cast out the worm and waited. Supper time boys. Come and get it. Another hit and the line pulled hard. In a few seconds, I had another fish up on the bank and pinned against the rocks. It was working out quite nicely. The last two worms brought close misses. One fish thrashed about on the bank in another cloud of smoke and then slipped away to warn the others. I laughed and felt glad he'd gotten away. Next came the fat juicy slug contracting into a tight ball when the needle stuck through his middle. Bayonets flashed at me.

"Its only a slug Conner," Mr. Clement called out.

"True enough. But Gordon nor Lucas weren't no genius neither." Sir Williams pipe smoke drifted close by. "They mighta got along decently well with that thar slug, if'n polecat ain't et im. Member them lightnin' bugs?"

The slug didn't wiggle as much with the pin through his middle and made a nice splash when he hit the water. Polecat's jug lay broken in the rocks and blood spurted down the falls.

"Pin a man to the ground an' he'll wiggle a bit too," Polecat's stench turned my nose. The slug lay still in the water. "If the fish don't eat 'im, I will. Best keep a blade ready if he comes loose."

Another hit and a fish jerked the line. Polecat disappeared. Another big trout flapped on the rocks and I straddled him with my knees. My foot jarred on a rock ledge and throbbed terribly. Helen laughed and applauded as the fish thrashed in my hands. For a second it was the yank boy with the red teeth then just a fish again. My foot screamed.

"The pain is penance. But you know that already." Father Reilly sprinkled holy water over the rocks.

"The boy ain't as guilty as he looks", Lady called from far across the stream. "Penance is hair-shirt talk."

Helen clapped as I held the fish up and yelled to her to clear my mind. "No earthworm for the big boy! No sir, he wanted the slug all along!"

Uncle Paul sighed. "You should be ashamed of yourself Conner. Killin' yanks with rifles is tolerable, but slugs and insects? Sign of weak mind, my boy. A weak mind."

All the while the two grasshoppers waited their turn patiently, going over the falls kicking with all their might. Smoke swirled about then disappeared with the first bite. I pulled up another big one and Helen nodded.

"Four's enough for now. Catch more in the mornin'."

"It gits easier don't it Conner," Lady yelled from beyond the far rapids. "Once you kill one, the rest is gravy."

I waded downstream and dispatched all four with the knife in an eddy of rifles and smoke. It finally went away when I refused to stop.

"Better to forget if y'can." Mr. Clement stomped his feet. "Even no arms ain't worth stayin riled about forever. What's it gonna hep? Make 'em grow back?" He laughed then drifted off in a spasm of coughing that sounded like a flock of crows.

Helen stood up smiling. "I'll cook. Not that I don't trust you. But you've done enough already."

Sir William, Macfadden, and Lady clapped and tossed rocks downstream. The twins chanted, "Done enough. Done enough. Done enough." Then they whistled their best mockingbird songs. Snake laughed, "Nope, the boy aint done yet. Not till he does the golden girl."

Lines creased Helen's forehead and radiated out from the corners of her mouth as she smiled. Her eyelids squinted in the sunlight but the coal black of her eyes could still paralyze. She pulled her white dress so tight I could see the distinct curve of her breasts. Her body, a dark silhouette behind thin cotton. She stared right through me. Her hands closed behind my head and pulled me against her face. She kissed me hard with her tongue. I dropped the sack, pressed her against me and we fell on the grass. Clothes came off as if they had a mind of their own. We rolled on the bank and made love with her legs engulfing me, her fingers digging into my back.

I lay immobilized on top of her for a long time like a beached jelly fish feeling her body wrapped around mine and her breasts and stomach against my skin, all softness and pleasure. The breeze cooled my exposed bottom and there was a splash in the water.

"They're comin'?" Mr. Clement yelled. "Git down!"

But it was only a trout escaping downstream. I lay on an elbow and felt Helen's bare breasts and reassured myself that we were safe. The others didn't make a peep. She held me for a long time, then made love again in another delirium of pleasure. When it finally ended, we swam naked in the deep pool and turned blue and screamed together with the cold. We dried off with blankets and gorged on all four fish baked over the fire.

Afterwards she propped my foot on a log beside the fire and took a good look at my wound. She told me to be still while she cut out black, encrusted threads with the knife. It hurt like hell. I yanked my leg away each time, but she was patient. The wound oozed a little blood and just a bit of pus, but nothing too bad. The pain subsided tolerably. I was alive and there was no fever. Something the others would have traded for gladly. I'd lost half a foot and honestly couldn't remember how. The rest I remembered in painful detail. I wanted badly to conjure up a miracle for them, but it seemed less likely with each passing moment. Still I prayed as hard as I could, settling beside her under the blanket watching streaks of orange, red and purple descend into the black horizon. Hovering pink clouds waited patiently for the twilight then gradually faded with the breeze. Sparks flared up from the fire until it burned down to red coals then darkness enveloped us under a million stars. I watched them dance about until they'd exhausted themselves and started falling out of the sky by the hundreds.

# XXIII

Sir William appeared, passing out the last crumbs of stale cornbread and gristle of cold salt pork. Rumbling gunfire came in waves from far to the west.

"Goin at that Muleshoe. Told ya they would. Betcha them New York boys is in it. Heard it last night. Yanks got fresh brigades, thousands strong, from up New York way." Sir William lit his pipe quite pleased with himself while everyone listened to our artillery open up all down the western end of the line. "Bunch of them boys over yonder right now. Won't be easy neither."

Volleys crashed continuously and everyone looked up. Mr. Clement lit his pipe and nodded.

"Billy Joyner been up to New York City. Made it in three days on the train."

"Three days? Doubtful." Sir William shook his head and chuckled.

Mr. Clement raised his hand. "I swear it. Said there was more kinds a people than he ever knew. Greeks, Italians, Poles, Chinese, Germans. Lots he couldn't make out, and crowds everywhere. Said there was buildin's one hundred feet high. Ten, twelve, fifteen floors. Said the land was too valu'ble to have just one floor."

"Why's it so valu'ble?" Snake sneered. "Gold or somethin'?"

"Nope, just a big rock is all. Whole city built on a big rock," Mr. Clement blew smoke rings.

"So why live on a damn rock. Plenty good land all 'round." Snake waved his arms at the field and the tree line.

"Don't you fret none Snake," Lady laughed. "Yanks done figured that out. Why you think theys comin' south? Just to free a bunch a slaves? Don't think so."

"Shit on 'em. They deserve what they got." Snake winked at me. "Conner here bloated up a bunch of 'em."

Mr. Clement ignored them and puffed his pipe. Everyone listened to a pause in the fighting. "Said it had to be least a million people. Least a million." I stared at him in silence. If he was trying to punish us he'd done a good job. Volleys erupted fresh and loud. Sir William poked at the embers. His head was scabbed over and crusty with dried blood.

"Some a them New York boys comin' from up Elmira way. Up by them Finger Lakes. Been up there once y'see."

"What's a damn finger lake?" Snake laughed, rolling up his blanked out in the darkness. Rifle fire crackled continuously in the distance.

Sir William ignored him. "Them boys is hard, too. No soft city folk. Good shots, all of 'em. God fearin', hard workin'. You boys would like em. If... well."

"How you know bout New Yorkers?" Macfadden turned over, covered in a blanket. His eyes still bandaged.

"Went up to Elmira in '55. My uncle's funeral y'see. Uncle George moved up yonder when I was a boy. Never saw him agin'. Had to take Momma up. God rest her soul. He died of pneumonia at a little place called Watkins Glen. Up by Seneca Lake. One a them Finger Lakes. Momma died as soon as we got home. Just went to sleep an' never woke up." He wiped his beard softly.

"What's a damn finger lake?" Snake snorted and spat at his feet.

Sir William pretended not to hear. "Uncle weren't one to take a bath, but somebody told him 'bout a waterfall called Glen Eldridge. Said if you washed in it, it was like a fountain of youth. Uncle stood in it all day. Ice cold too."

197

"Was your uncle a drinkin' man?" Lady chuckled. He was just behind us and out of sight. A huge volley erupted to the north, past the shadow of the far woods.

"Yes he was. Just like Conner's daddy." Sir William sat in the glow of the little flames and smiled. "Had his own winery on the hill between the lakes. Keuka and Seneca. Indian names. Long lakes, like fingers. Cold and deep. No one's ever touched bottom. Glacier's made 'em years ago. So it's said."

"What's a glacier?" Mr. Clement asked. He stood behind Sir William with his bandaged stump arms just visible in the dark. The twins appeared beside the fire and mouthed the word "glacier" simultaneously. Peter as always stood guard over them, his red pants shimmering as if on fire.

"A big chunk of ice come down from the North Pole. Somethin' like that." Sir William shrugged. "Anyway, that's what I was told."

"Don't seem too likely," Snake crunched twigs with his moccasin feet. The twins nodded in agreement. Cannon fire erupted all a round.

"Well I ain't no professor but them gorges is somethin'. Five or six water falls stacked one above another, all runnin' down to them Finger Lakes."

The rifle and cannon fire faded away and I could see the gorge dropping precipitously below a narrow path to a series of five glens each carved out of sheer rock cliff. Waterfalls tumbled down from one glen to the next, then to a rocky stream that emptied into vast Seneca Lake which stretched for miles to the northern horizon. The narrow path clung to the side of the cliff above the tallest waterfall. Sir William trotted along far ahead jumping across the flat boulders above the stream. The air smelled as crisp as the North Carolina mountains in October.

"Uncle George drinks most a what he makes," Sir William yelled. "It turns his face all red and his eyes yellow. He'll catch pneumonia from that there waterfall and we'll bury him close to it." He paused to listen to the roar. "Your daddy don't look so good neither."

I spotted father in the gorge. Flat on his back snoring on a rough plank table and naked other than a canvas loincloth. Even after so many years I knew it was him. His huge abdomen bare, bright yellow and taut as a ripe watermelon. A bowl of wine wedged tight between his knees. An empty clay jug dangled off the table on a leather cord tied to his wrist, swaying and twisting in the breeze just above the stone floor of the glen. Sir William grabbed a handful of crayfish out of a tin bucket by the stream and dropped them in the bowl.

"Gives it some bite. Good for your innards, see." He nodded to father who stirred briefly. "It'll hep 'im I swear. Might be one more chance yet. You too Conner. Drink Some. It's a long way home, ain't it. A long way from black pluff mud and salt air." He handed me the bowl and I took a wary sip as a crawdad tried to pinch my nose.

"Tastes better than communion wine, don't it," he laughed. "Clean an' clear as this here waterfall. Red as fresh blood. It'll hep y'yet, I swear. Y'daddy too. Take one more."

I did as he said and got nipped on the lip by a quick claw. The wine and blood tasted better than I could imagine.

"Like nectar ain't it?" He drank the bowl of wine in one gulp, and one of the crayfish latched on to his top lip. He let out a howl and ripped the crayfish loose leaving the pincer claw stuck on his bleeding face. "Conner, when the war's over, git on up here an' cool y'sef off. This here cold water's like a damn miracle. A man cain't stay riled for long. Water's too cold for that. Best git up here, quick as y'can."

The glen roared louder in approval. Rifle fire roared in return, and I was back in Virginia before the echoes stopped. The gorge was gone.

The twins flanked me. They nodded and whistled their mockingbird songs. Everyone else had left. The fire had burned down to embers. Seneca Lake disappeared.

Helen sat up, pulled a heavy cotton coat over her head and buttoned it up tight. "It's about time Conner. What took you so long? Sir William's been back for hours, waitin' on you. Don't you have any manners? Makin' an old man bide his time…" She shook her head and wagged a finger at me. "Shame on you. Now come on. Quick!" She led me as if leashed, through the dark woods then across an open field to a cabin of pine logs with a tent roof and tent flap door. Sir William stood inside. His face an ashen gray mass of leathery winkles and brown splotches. He nursed his swollen lip. His ill-fitting porcelain eye dangled precariously out of the eye socket. His head and hands trembled coarsely in rhythm.

"No harm done my boy. Don't mind ya dawdlin' .Especially at Seneca. One of my favorites. Anyhow…the war's made me a patient man." He smiled and raised his hand, nodding towards the gunfire to the north. "Cept fo' that , its hard to tell there's any war left, ain't it. Partly why I like it here. Noise don't delight me no more. Been too much talkin' in camp."

Anthony appeared on the path through the scrub oaks at the edge of the field. He waved then slowly faded away as if absorbed into the woods.

"People mostly leave me alone now. Y'all see who that was? Our lost boy? Gone quick eh? Well, an old, one eyed man ain't much to look at." Then he began to cry. Not loudly but suddenly with no attempt to hide it. Another rumble came over the breeze and he looked at Helen. She shook her head at loss for words. Sir William fiddled with his eyeball, stopped his sob, and just as quickly resumed his normal cheery voice. "Damned peaceful 'specially at night with a full moon." He smiled again just slightly and wiped his face. "Y'all seen a man cry ain't ya?"

"I thought maybe you were touched by the solitude." Helen whispered.

"Touched in the head. That's what you thought. But I ain't much. Just too damn old. Cryin' for no reason ain't so bad. The Lord ain't seen fit to give me much else to do lately. The yanks ain't exactly swarmin' the piece a field." He started crying again and sat down on a rickety wicker chair. His cabin stood seven or eight feet at the peak with a center pole holding up a canvas roof. A cot, another canvas chair, a small barrel with a board table top surrounded the pole. A knife and scabbard hung next to a fine leather-bound field glass with the inscription "Hidden in the veil of distance." A rusting tobacco tin lay under the cot next to a pile of books and a bundle of candles tied with a string. Unfolded on the cot rested a book and a large hand-painted canvas map of the confederacy from Virginia to Louisiana. Each state's border painted in red, the coastline and rivers in blue. Black X's dotted the map, names printed underneath. Gettysburg, Sharpsburg, Chancellorsville, Manassas, Seven Days, Fredericksburg, Chickamauga, Shiloh, Vicksburg. Smaller x's without a label sprouted everywhere.

"Just as important to the boys buried there but no room on the map. Just ask Ravenel Meggett our lost newboy. Come on in son." The flaps opened and Ravenel appeared. He looked all cleaned up, wearing a starched white shirt and a fresh gauze head bandage. He put his hand on Sir William's shoulder and pointed to his own X in North Carolina.

"See this Conner? My vows worked after all. This here X means I'll live forever. Granddaddy was dead wrong."

"That's a fact Conner." Sir William agreed. "Give a man his own X and he's damn well immortal. They'll remember Ravenel long after you're dead an' gone."

"We all got to die sometime or 'nother." Helen whispered, her hand in mine. "I sure don't mind."

"Well I do!" Ezekiel called out from across the field. He came closer as he spoke. "I ain't dyin' 'fore I live free. Ya'll don't know shit, do ya."

"Enough of that." Sir William held his hand up, but didn't lose his patience. He wiped his eyes with his sleeve, slapped the map and pushed his finger down hard on a spot in Virginia. "This here's the whole war. This here. This here river. That right there. You don't believe me, do you." He sighed. "Why should you? I'm just an old goat who cries too much."

"Oh no. No sir, not at all." Helen cooed.

"It don't matter. But believe me or not, this here's the whole war. Right 'cher." He pointed to the same spot on the river in Virginia and started crying again. "They done tried ever'where else. See these here? Here in Virginia? Here in Tennessee? Here all along the coast...Got Ravenel right 'cher." He pointed to Ravenel's X and just about every other X on the map. "Grant will attack west of Fredericksburg. He'll cross the Rapidan and the Rappahannock Rivers, straight on down to Richmond. Then it'll all be over."

"We don't give a shit 'bout that." Ezekiel croaked and grunted just outside the tent. Rosealee and Jacob laughed with him. "White people all worked up 'bout battles an' shit. Don't mind sellin' blacks like cattle. But God forbid a yank shoot a rebel boy. Hope y'all choke on them X's. Just a bunch 'a dead whites to us. Confederate pipe dreams."

Sir William wiped his face again and tears abruptly stopped. He smiled and chuckled to himself ignoring Ezekiel. "But that's enough of that. It's the tactics that's over y'see. Strategy and tactics is what they'll remember. Not a man's skull breakin' open." He rubbed his purple head scar, and Ravenel adjusted his bandage.

"You mean when the wars over?" I asked.

"Well not 'sackly. Won't never be over. Not least to some. They'll be fightin' long after we're worm bait."

"I sure ain't forgettin nothin'." Ezekiel yelled, moving across the other side of the field.

"Someday y'all gonna pay."

Rosealee and Jacob laughed and chanted the response behind him. "Ain't forgittin, ain't forgettin. Somebody sho' gonna pay."

Sir William mumbled to himself and wiped his eyes. "They just might be right."

Ravenel pulled his bandage tight and nodded, "Yep, but I done paid my share."

He picked up a daguerreotype pinned to a piece of board on the table. It showed a dark haired girl holding a baby.

"Isn't that me?" Helen asked touching the girls face.

"It sure could be," Sir William nodded, sobbing again. "The child will be grown up when the war ends, but I'll be long since dead and gone." He put a bony hand on her shoulder, "And you'll soon be comin' with me young lady."

Helen shrugged like it was nothing, but her eyes watered up just a bit as she glanced back. The tent flap blew open and the three of them darted out and ran across the field into the trees and disappeared.

# XXIV

I rose at dawn and felt a sigh of relief. Helen was still there. Thank God. The trout had become wary overnight, so it took a long time to catch two for breakfast. I must have used up a dozen worms and slugs. Helen didn't say a word but whistled like the twins while she brewed up sassafras tea and baked corn bread in the fire with the fish.

After we ate, we hitched the mules and headed down the road towards Charlottesville. Leaving that little stream pained me more than I'd expected. Thank God a warm, bright day greeted us. A day of blue sky and blue butterflies that swarmed around us all morning celebrating.

Helen whistled to them, almost as well as the twins, and I could have sworn they whistled back. We laughed and God was with us. The radiance of the sun baked our heads and the butterflies rested for a while on the backs of the mules. They'd fly up just as the mules flicked their tails, then settle back down like a game of tag. Helen held a dozen brave ones in the palm of her hand.

"My little apostles. They're family now. Even if we never see them again." She blew softly over them and the twelve apostles fluttered their wings in unison. They took turns flying about, entertaining us all morning with their acrobatics.

About midday we turned off onto another road slowly winding uphill. The butterflies abruptly left us. Helen waved goodbye, tears in her eyes, "Don't forget us. Come back when you can."

They scattered off into the woods as the road faded into a withered cornfield. The stalks drooped over stunted and bare of a single ear of fruit. Across the field a charred ruin of a farmhouse smoldered. Part of a blackened beam stuck high out from the remnant of wall surrounded

204

by a bed of smoking coals. What appeared to be a ham dangled from the end of a rope. A lone crow perched on top tearing off little pieces, eyeing us warily as he ate.

About forty paces away stood the remnants of a weathered barn painted rust red with an intact wood-shingled roof. The sides of the barn had been stripped away as high up as a man could reach so that it seemed to perch on stilts.

"Like a big red bird," Helen abruptly laughed. "See? It wants to fly off too."

As we rode past, a pair of redwing blackbirds darted past us towards the far trees.

"They must've heard me," she smiled. "Conner, hate to tell you, that ain't a ham tied to that rope." She pointed to the hungry crow.

Twisting slowly in the breeze and partly covered with torn, matted, blood caked trousers hung a human leg tied by the bare ankle. The white thighbone protruded downward from jagged flaps of muscle congealed with a glistening maroon tar. The mules shied and turned their heads.

"I can't stand it neither." Helen yawned then faked crocodile tears and pretended to hide her face.

Father Reilly called to me from inside the barn. "Lamb of God who taketh away the sins of the world..."

"Pray for us." I answered.

"Alright," Helen blessed herself smiling. "Do you think it will help?"

"Maybe."

I had her hold the reins while I shimmied up the loose boards then out on the beam to cut the rope. I felt nothing at all. It was just a leg. Nobody I knew. Just something to bury which didn't take long. Helen did nothing to help, faking sobs while I filled the hole. "Poor lamb.

Down to his last leg. Leg of lamb." Helen giggled. "Conner, are you down to your last leg, too?"

I ignored her and she seemed a bit irritated again. I listened for the others but heard just the quiet rustle of the breeze and it seemed odd. We didn't linger. The mules were glad to get away, pulling us quickly to the far woods where the road sought the cover of the trees as if expecting trouble. We entered the deep shade, and a gunshot rang out. The mules bolted and in a matter of seconds we lay hidden in a little swag in the cedar and pine woods.

I dropped to cover and peered through the brambles on my belly, knife in hand. A black man walked towards us across the field. I recognized his stride.

"By God its Ezekiel." I whispered, not knowing if he was alone. Helen crawled up beside me.

"You want me to kill him?"

"Hell no. It's Ezekiel. How the hell did he get all this way."

He walked up to the trees, sifted right through a gap in a honeysuckle tangle, and stood before me dressed in a new blue uniform with sergeant stripes. He held a revolver.

"Ezekiel, what the hell?" I grabbed him by the shoulders and he pushed me away. "What the hell?"

"Conner I been followin' you." He pointed the gun at Helen and I pushed her behind me. "Put the knife down Conner."

"Ezekiel, you put that damn gun down. She's with me."

His mouth didn't move, like it was paralyzed, but I did as he said.

"For God's sake…what the hell?"

"It ain't fo' God's sake, Conner. Its fo' mine." He pointed the revolver to the sky and fired twice. It sounded like a cannon in the trees. "The Haint's with you?" His face was palsied stiff.

"Ezekiel…" I stepped towards him.

"No, Conner." He pointed the revolver at my chest.

"If she's with you then it won't matter. She'll be gone when the boys take you." He raised the revolver up again and fired twice more. My ears nearly split.

Helen whispered into the back of my neck. "Just say the word. I'll kill him like I did the others."

Through the branches, I spotted the first of the yank cavalry in the far woods. They milled about in the trees at the edge of the field like the open scared them. Ezekiel kept the pistol at my chest, glancing over his shoulder at the yanks.

Helen kept on whispering, "I'll use the magic on'em one at a time", she giggled. "Git' 'em roused up then cut it off."

"Time to go Conner. Time fo' all y'all to go." He raised the pistol to fire and glanced back again.

I swung fast and caught him full on the temple. He dropped to the leaves and I grabbed his neck and the pistol. Ezekiel jerked me back by the hair and tried to yell out. I squeezed the air out of his throat. He let go of my hair, dropped the pistol and smiled at me.

"Cain't hold my neck fo'ever, Conner." He whispered, forcing out a little air. "Soon as you do, I'll howl like hell, an' they'll come quick. Yanks, Conner, plenty a yanks."

"Shut up Ezekiel. Don't make me hurt ya."

"Is that it? I got t' *make* ya hurt me?" he choked trying to laugh. "Bullshit."

Helen sat down beside us and wiped my knife carefully on Ezekiel's trousers. She hummed softly as the horsemen came across the field. They weren't but a hundred yards off, slowly picking their way towards us. Ezekiel arched his neck to see. I pressed his throat down harder into the leaves. He smiled.

"Thems won't take kindly to y'chokin' me. Might carve y'balls 'fore they shoot ya. They'll take care of the haint sure as hell."

Helen laughed so loudly I just knew they'd hear. She pricked at Ezekiel's leg with the knife. "If you yell you'll be so-prawn-no too." She sliced open his trouser leg. "I won't exactly kill you." She giggled and flourished the knife. "Git what you deserve though."

Ezekiel kicked at her. "Be gone haint. Sizzle in the holy water." He wiggled his neck to force out a hoarse whisper.

"For God's sake shut up Ezekiel." I squeezed his throat harder.

He smiled at me. "Tell y' what Conner. I give ya my word they won't touch her in the flesh. Let her jus' vanish in thin air."

"Damn it Ezekiel, shut up." His arm muscles strained toward the pistol. His free hand snatched my hair and pulled hard. My thumb pressed his throat shut but he wouldn't stop.

"Got to kill me Conner."

His raspy breathing grew still and he went limp. Shots rang out from across the field and the blue horsemen bolted away yelling. I relaxed my grip for just a second. Ezekiel yanked my head back and had the pistol in his hand. The barrel came at my face. His arm strained against mine.

"Nevah beat you befo'," he grunted. "But it'll happen someday."

The gun-barrel trembled next to my head.

"Let go Ezekiel. Let it go. They're gone. We'll go too. Just let us go, damn it." I pushed with all my strength but the pistol inched towards me.

"Cain't," he croaked. "Cain't never let you go. You didn't let me." His arm muscles tightened into knots.

Helen plopped down behind him and sliced his scalp with the knife. "See? This here's just the beginnin'," she laughed.

Ezekiel grit his teeth and growled. His strength surged. He kneed me in the groin. I head-butted him back. Our foreheads knocked against the barrel and I never heard the shot. Ezekiel's head jerked and he faked a smile. Blood poured out of his ear. He winked at me as a gurgle rose in his throat like he was trying to make his toadfish croak one last time. I pulled away and saw his brains in the leaves. The gurgling stopped. Ezekiel lay still. Smoke rose from the woods on the far side of the field. The yanks were gone.

"You performed admirably." I could feel Uncle's breath on my neck. "Made it look like his fault. Same with Elliott. Well done my boy."

"I didn't mean to." I crawled away through the leaves. "There was nothing else I could do."

"Of course. Of course. That's the beauty of the mind. You can't be held accountable. Good work Conner. And don't worry, I didn't see a thing," he laughed.

Helen laughed with him and the mules bolted again. It took an hour or so to catch them. When I got back, Helen had already buried Ezekiel.

"It was real easy." She mopped her brow with the back of her sleeve. "Slipped into the ground like spilled coffee. Like he belonged there." She scuffed leaves on top the bare soil with her foot, but I couldn't look. I knew if I didn't look there was a chance it wouldn't be so. Ezekiel might still be all right. I just looked the other way.

I didn't want to look at her either. I let her drive the mules so I could close my eyes and keep my fingers in my ears to block out her humming. It took a long time for her to stop. Miles and miles of humming that I tried my best not to hear. When I opened my eyes we had stopped at a fork in the road. The lesser track marked by two stone posts. It rose too steeply for the mules to pull us, so I walked along beside the wagon with Helen. My foot hurt so badly I could barely keep up, even with the encouragement of my walking stick. I told myself over and over that Ezekiel would be all right. After all, I hadn't seen him buried. Him or Macfadden. Not like Shiner.

"Put him out of your mind. Put all of it out of your mind," Mr. Clement called from deeper in the woods. "It's the only way."

Sir William sniffed and blew his nose. "Don't worry he'll be roamin' about before nightfall. I'll bet we hear him callin' tonight. Might get up with Macfadden. Never know."

Helen nodded. "He'll be back directly, too."

I stopped to listen and it might have been him singing 'Glory Halleluiah' in the distance.

"Just the wind Conner," Helen smiled.

"I'll let you know if they call out." Mr. Clement yelled from far off in the woods, "They just might."

I knew Ezekiel wouldn't ever go anywhere with Macfadden. They'd kill each other first. Still it was a pleasant thought. One I was glad to nurture. It helped numb the scare.

We climbed through an apple orchard and helped ourselves to the green fruit, but McCoull mule was so tired he couldn't eat. I unhitched him and let him walk behind the wagon and unloaded the heaviest boxes and sacks so Cyclops wouldn't have such a hard pull by himself. He surprised me, though, having plenty enough steam to get to the crest where he had a great view of rolling hills and fields to the south and east. There were pine woods to the west and a smorgasbord of wildflowers. They covered the open hilltop. I tried not to think of anything else.

"See? Red cover, goldenrod, pink and lavender milkweed, Queen Anne's lace, and purple thistles." Helen laughed. "All the ones I like." A cabin sat at the edge of the field in a stand of sycamores that dropped sharply downhill into a maple and hickory woods.

"Sycamore makes a good butcher's block." Sir William yelled out from the trees. "Too hard to cut, y'see. Conner you listenin' t'me? Pay attention boy!"

"Leave him be William," Mr. Clement laughed, "The boys got more on his mind that butcherin'. He'll find it out in time. All in good time." They rustled off past a noisy brook that ran away to the bottom of the hill over a bed of glistening, smooth stones. I stared at the reflection of the cabin in the rippling water. It seemed to shimmer like a mirage. Log walls, plank roof, shuttered windows, and a red door, swinging open for us in the breeze.

The sun beat down on my neck, and I felt wobbly from the walk up the hill. My foot throbbed as we made our way across the field. The milkweed rustled against my legs and I began to feel strange. The ground surged and I lay down on a carpet of red clover and rolled on my back. The clouds spun around uncontrollably. I don't know how long I lay there. I sobbed like a baby and felt ridiculous, but I couldn't stop. Helen made me drink some water from the canteen, until it finally passed, but I felt embarrassed and told her to go ahead to the cabin. I lay back to rest and watched the clouds. They were big, puffy cotton balls, slowly changing shapes. I watched them for a long time. The last one was the head of a dead yank whose eyes slowly drifted out of the sockets and turned into rainbow colored humming birds that darted off into the cloudbank.

When I tried to stand up, I fell flat on my face. I didn't resist. I listened for the others, but they were silent. No one rustled around. No one said a word. The breeze came across the field and cooled my head. I sat up and realized that they were all gone. I don't know for sure how I knew, but I did. It was sad in a way but a relief of sorts too. I knew they had to go.

"It's the way of things," Helen called out from inside the cabin.

Finally, when the world stopped spinning, I limped to the door where Helen was finishing sweeping. She had the shutters open and the breeze whisked the room. Inside stood a log bed with a burlap mattress and thick patchwork quilt, a plank table, two slat chairs, a cupboard with tins of food, several sacks of cornmeal, and clay jugs of molasses and sorghum syrup on the brick floor. A big iron pot hung from a rusty hook over old ashes in the fieldstone hearth. Stacks of kindling and dry split logs stood ready.

Helen took my hand and pulled me to the bed. She pulled her cotton slip over her head, and stood in front of me naked, except for a silver locket around her neck. I pulled her to me and felt her arms around my back, the cold locket against my temple. I looked up and grabbed it with my teeth, but she squeezed my face to make me let go and pulled me into her soft middle.

"I found it in your shirt and put it on so you wouldn't lose it. Your parents?"

For a second I couldn't remember what it was or where it had come from, then it dawned on me. The yank in the pen, from Wellfleet. It came painfully clear.

"Let me see it."

She undid the tiny latch and opened the locket. I held it close and looked at the two people framed in silver between her breasts. A man with a stovepipe hat and a heavy woman, perhaps with child. For some reason I thought of my father and tried to remember what he'd said about my sister when she died. I wanted to remember very badly. I concentrated my thoughts as I lay against her skin, but all I could remember was him holding me, crying, and saying that he loved me. I wanted to hear his voice one more time but he was gone too. There was something else. Something about mother. I was little. Something bad had happened. I couldn't see what. Her voice was all around me, soothing, calming, reassuring.

"It's all right. God loves you." I heard her voice as clear as the brook outside the window but then she was gone. Helen pressed against me and I succumbed. There was nothing else I could do. They were all dead now in various routes to the hereafter.

Helen smiled. "Thank God it's not your job to sort it all out."

She rolled on top of me and we sagged together into the soft mattress. She stretched over to the shelf by the bed for a brown bottle and tin cup. "Its whisky. From the cupboard. Thomas thought of everything."

She poured me more than enough to burn my throat but it felt good. The sting renewed me. Her hands glowed with radiant warmth. I embraced her and a wave of pleasure enveloped us. All became softness and heaviness.

"Go to sleep Conner. I can't sleep unless you sleep, alright?"

I did as she said and slept for a long while. When I woke she was gone. There was a jasmine smell in the cabin and the doorframe radiated a soft honey-colored glow in the evening light. I didn't worry though. I knew she needed her time to wander about. I poured another cupful of whiskey and sat on the bed. My foot ached from the exertion and there was more blood on the bandage and some on the blanket. I reminded myself to be careful and not tempt fever. I tried to think out all that had happened, but it was just a jumbled mess.

Sweat poured off me. Elliott was dead. Macfadden and the others too. Mr. Clement even worse. I didn't really know what to make of Ezekiel, but I pretty much convinced myself he was alive and alright. It couldn't have happened like that. All I needed was to hear his voice again. Hear him cussing me out, bossing me around. I wanted to hear them all again. All just one last time. I closed my eyes and listened to every sound. Maybe they just blended in with the rustle of the breeze in the trees, the creaking of the shutters, or the undercurrent gurgling from the stream. I strained to hear every noise, listening for even fragments of a syllable. But they were silent.

Faint whistling came from outside the window. "Helen?"

I stuck my head out but couldn't see her. The whistling came from down the hill. It wasn't as clever as Lucas' and Gordon's. I half expected the twins to join in, but they didn't.

"Helen? Is that you?"

Nothing. Just the whistling. Maybe it was just a mockingbird. Helen had disappeared. I looked around outside. Cyclops turned his blind eye towards me, but McCoull mule was gone. Vanished with Helen. The whistling rose from down in the hickory woods. Then for the first time it occurred to me. She might not come back. I might not see her again. Ever. If not now, then some other unannounced time. The idea startled me, but less than I'd imagined possible. I was alive. If Helen disappeared for good, I'd still be alive. I'd figure out what to do tomorrow. I laughed. I couldn't remember how I'd thought otherwise. She could have faded away any time. That she'd stayed with me this long was a miracle of sorts. I thanked the Lord for it. I hadn't been alone yet, but I figured I could do it. Maybe I truly didn't need her anymore. Certainly a host of others did. Macfadden would be glad to have the chance. The rest of them too. But she wasn't gone quite yet. As long as the whistling kept on. Only God knew when it would end.

My brain began to blur. A fog descended on the cabin. I staggered back inside. My thoughts wouldn't form up. They became steam off a simmering pot. All I could do was stare at the wall and listen to her whistling. I realized I didn't feel much of anything. I'd come because of my promise to Elliott, hadn't I? It felt ridiculous not to know for sure. There wasn't a flicker of anger left though. That much I knew.

The fog lifted and the last yank boy stood there. The one I'd shot in the face. Bandages wrapped most of his head and his left arm lay limp in a sling, but otherwise he didn't seem much worse the wear. His uniform looked freshly washed and ironed. His long hair neatly combed. I nodded to him. He nodded back but said nothing. He stared at me in silence for a while then climbed out the window and walked off down the hill. He left a chill in the room. I wrapped up in the quilt and I sipped the smooth bourbon until my glass was empty. I tried to put him out of my mind. I looked at the locket again. Maybe I could make it right. Maybe someday I'd find Mrs. Gould and give it back. But what could I tell her? What could I say that wouldn't make it even worse? Maybe it was better to leave her alone. Let her keep her memories, her dreams.

The breeze blew through the open window and the sycamores rustled and waved to me with the last bit of the day's wind. The sun dropped lower. The sky was an indigo blue, deeper than I'd ever seen. The leaves of the trees so green they looked freshly painted. I thought of what Uncle Paul used to say about the evening sun as if he could still see. We'd be sitting out on the back porch facing the cornfields and the green marshy point jutting out into the rippling blue of Wadamalaw sound, with me on the steps and him in his wicker rocking chair.

He'd wave his cane in a general westerly direction towards the open water and the setting sun, I remembered his exact words.

"See there. See that there. See them colors. Richer and deeper 'cause the sun's low in the sky." I waited and listened for Uncle Paul to say it himself, to speak clearly to me right in my ear, but there was just the breeze, the brook and the whistling. It wasn't hard to remember Uncle's words though. I'd heard them a thousand times. He'd say it very slowly and emphatically, "It's the refractability of the atmospheric prism." He'd pause and sigh with a big smile and then add, "The blues are bluer and the greens greener 'cause when the sun's low, some rays get through and some get swallowed up."

He'd rock for a while, smiling contentedly, staring unblinking at the sun with his white-scarred, opaque eyes, repeating it over and over with a rhythmic rocking of his chair.

"The blues are bluer and the greens are greener."

The memory warmed me more than the bourbon. I watched the shadows lengthen and consume the sycamore leaves as the indigo sky faded into darkness. Then I realized that even though I couldn't hear Uncle Paul anymore, I could see clearly for the first time what a blind man had seen all along.

PERRY TROUCHE graduated from the University of Virginia and The Medical University of South Carolina. He is a psychiatrist in private practice from Charleston, South Carolina, where he lives with his wife and family.

www.ingramcontent.com/pod-product-compliance
Lightning Source LLC
Chambersburg PA
CBHW032143020726
47496CB00003B/685